# FALLING
# OFF THE BELIEF

# DEE YODER

*Falling Off the Belief: A New Order Amish Novel*
© 2019 by Dee Yoder

Published by Stewart & Madison

Cover Design: Dee Yoder

Scripture quotations are taken from the King James Version of the Holy Bible.

ISBN 9781449950569

Printed in the United States of America

*For Verna, whose friendship and mentoring have been with me from the beginning.*

# CHAPTER ONE

E xcitement buzzed through Leah as she and Jacob rode through the rolling hills of Holmes County. The van driver, Ella, was former Amish, so she kept up a running commentary about the area, filling Leah in on details about Amish shops they passed and businesses owned by the Amish, as well as pointing out long lines of cars carrying tourists.

"Yep. This area is nothing like Ashfield County. These Amish rub shoulders with the English every day. They have no problem making business deals with former Amish. Back home, I have to hold my tongue. Otherwise, I might slip at a market stand and give my Amish background away with my accent." She glanced to Leah. "You know what that would mean, right?"

Jacob smiled as Leah nodded. She was nearly overcome with the hustle and bustle in Holmes County, Ohio. Could this area really be only an hour south of her hometown? It might as well be as far as the moon is from the earth.

"Yeah, for sure, I'd be left holding the bag—an empty bag, if you know what I mean." Ella was a friendly, smiling lady blessed with a great sense of humor, who had entertained both Leah and Jacob on

1

the journey down. "Your place is off to the left there, Jacob. We're headed to the right, where Leah's going to bunk in with her roomie."

Leah stretched her neck to see the area the driver indicated. The road plunged into a tree-covered tunnel; an inviting leafy respite from the sun. She longed to see it right away. Jacob's new farm would be her farm, too, once they married. In the meantime, she'd answered an ad in The Budget for a roommate. The single Amish lady offered a room and kitchen privileges cheap and was even willing to wait for the first month's rent, as long as Leah got a job right away.

The driver guided the van smoothly to the right and before long, eased the vehicle into a white graveled driveway. The cottage she'd be sharing was neat as a pin and painted a pleasant blue, edged with snow white trim.

"It looks great." Jacob nudged her and pointed to the barn behind the house. It appeared to be built for a Lilliputian horse. "Only a pony could live in there, though. Good thing you aren't moving in a Clydesdale." He laughed, the smile lines stretching out from his chocolate colored eyes.

Leah loved watching Jacob's face. His gentle demeanor was evident in his sweet smile and laughing eyes. His lashes swept down and up as he gazed at the passing scenery. She was eager to be with him, but the time which loomed ahead as she earned her keep and Jacob got the farm under control before they could marry, seemed an eternity. There were moments when she allowed herself to dream about living life with Jacob as Englishers. A piece of her heart held to the freedom she'd known when she'd left her Amish way of life a couple of years back. If she were honest, she'd admit that missing family and Jacob were the main reasons she returned to the Amish.

Leah pulled her focus back to the moment, away from those kinds of thoughts. She was starting over. Now. Today. In Holmes County. Time to live her Amish life for good. No going back.

Her new roomie was a woman in her middle years. She was friendly, but with the normal Amish tendency to hold back when first meeting someone new. Jacob broke the ice and reached out to shake the older woman's hand.

"*Wie bischt?* I'm Jacob and this is Leah."

Leah leaned forward to shake hands. "*Wie bischt?* Nice to meet you."

"*Ja*, nice to meet you, too. I'm Sarah. It's enjoyable to see you and put a face to the name. Your letters were nice, but it's always *gut* to meet in person. Come on inside and I'll show you to your room."

Jacob grabbed the only bag she had. In it were a few items of clothing she'd picked up in the two weeks she'd lived several miles down the road from her parents' home in Ashfield County.

The English family that had taken her in were friends with Jacob's parents and were sympathetic to her desire to leave her family home to move away to Holmes County.

Leah hadn't shared much with them, though the husband and wife were kind enough not to press for details. They'd simply given her refuge during a trying time. She would always be thankful for their willingness to help her out. It was a safe place to be for a short time.

It hadn't taken long, though, for Leah's *daet* to figure out where she was. The next to last day she stayed there, he'd come with the bishop to try to take her home.

"You're my *dochtar* and you will do as I say!" His beard shook with the fury and frustration he'd unleashed.

*Daet's* strident voice rang in her memory, but more than that, the terrible way her *daet* and the bishop had treated her hosts brought a rush of heat to her cheeks, even now. She shook her head, trying not to think about those dark days. She glanced to Jacob in time to catch his eye. His puckered brow clued her in that she had missed something in the conversation with her hostess.

"I'm sorry. I was thinking of something else. What was it you asked?"

"Oh, I know how that is. I get quite *ferhudled* myself these days." Sarah chuckled. "I was just asking if you think this room will do? I have another spare room, but I think it's *bisli glay.*

3

Leah let her gaze sweep the room. It was painted pale blue and had touches of red on the embroidered pillowcases, curtain hems, and woven rugs. So pretty!

"It's beautiful! I've never had a room so colorful and lovely before." Leah turned to Jacob, her eyes shining. "Isn't it wonderful? It's homey and warm. I'll love being here."

As they passed back through the hallway, Sarah opened the door to the room next to Leah's. "This is the little room I was talking about. You can have this one, if you'd rather."

Leah peaked in. It was also a sweet room, but it had a smaller window and less charm. More plain. Plain wasn't what Leah longed for. "This is nice, too, but I prefer the first room. I feel at home there already."

"Fine. I'm happy you're pleased with your room. Come along and let's have a chat over fresh iced mint tea. How does that sound to you?"

"Wonderful!" Leah and Jacob followed Sarah to a kitchen so neat and tidy, Leah wondered if any cooking or baking was ever done in the room. Just then Sarah placed a plate of yummy smelling brownies on the table. Well, that answered that question.

During their snack, the ladies chatted about their backgrounds. Leah was pleased to find out Sarah's *maem* was from the Ashfield area, too. Jacob told them about his cousins, who lived near the farm Sarah grew up on in the late 1960's.

"I'm sure you know why our people moved to Ashfield from Holmes County, don't you?"

"Why, no. I don't think I've heard that story." Leah reached for a second brownie as Jacob turned a bright smile her way.

"Hungry, Leah?" he teased.

"I'm sorry if I seem to be a glutton! These brownies are delicious and, yes, Jacob, I did skip my breakfast this morning, so I am hungry."

They laughed as Sarah brought the ice-cold pitcher of tea to the table and refilled their glasses. "I'm glad there are folks here with me to help me eat them. Otherwise, I'd be the biggest glutton of all time and polish these off in two days."

Jacob downed his second helping of tea, wiped his mouth with a napkin and leaned back, sated and refreshed. "Please go on with your story about why the Amish from Holmes County moved to Ashfield County. I'm sorry I interrupted."

"No problem, Jacob. Getting back to it, I remember my parents talking with their bishop at the time about how slipshod some of the Holmes County Amish were getting with the rules. Modern ways were creeping in and some churches were even laying aside shunning. But the final straw was a new group that broke away and decided to call themselves the New Order."

She paused to wink. "Not that I think the New Order these days is wrong, I'm a member of a wonderful New Order church, and I love it. But back then, folks were anxious to keep to the forefathers' plans as much as possible. So one day I came home from school and just like that, *Maem* and *Daet* had things packed up and we moved in a weekend."

"Wow! That must have been a little tough for you. Moving so quickly." Jacob's sweet face showed concern. "How did you adjust to that?"

"Oh, not too well, at first. We'd left behind all the friends I knew and family, too. It was lonely there for a while. After school was organized, I quickly made new friends, but it was still hard to say goodbye to the old life. And it was a much lower church—that is, the bishop and deacons kept to a stricter *Ordnung*."

She laughed, clapping her hands together. "Why am I telling you that? That's where you're from, so of course, you know all about the Old Order church up there."

"Yes, we do." Leah and Jacob exchanged solemn glances.

"Though it was my home for all my life," Leah began, "I have to be honest and say I don't think I ever really fit in. I always wanted more, you see."

Sarah nodded and wiping the table with a dish towel, grew wistful.

"Leah, I sure do understand about that. Yes, it was hard to have things taken away. To have to give up some of my dreams and learn new ways. I think that's why I was delighted to meet my Andy. He was much less strict and had a happy demeanor most of his days."

She scurried to the sink, rinsing the tea glasses and placing the brownies in a covered jar.

"I thought—" Leah stopped.

Sarah sat down. "Yes, I am single still. Andy Miller was my intended. But sadly, he was killed in a buggy and car crash just weeks before we read the banns in church."

She traced a floral pattern on the oil cloth and sighed. "But that was a long time ago. You young people have much more timely things to take care of."

She stood and led them into the living area. "Leah, I'm so happy to have you here! Is there anything I can help you with as you unpack?"

"I think I can handle it. I'm afraid I left home so quickly, I didn't have time to pack much. Just what's in my suitcase there."

Jacob picked up the case and carried it down the hallway to her new bedroom.

Sarah smiled. "I expect there's a story behind that rushed packing. But we'll have many days to share our stories with one another. Right now, I think I'll head out back to take laundry off the clothesline. You and Jacob take your time with goodbyes." She waved to Jacob as he reentered the room.

He came to Leah and gently hugged her. "You're here at last. I've missed you!"

Leah snuggled close to him. "Me, too. I'm feeling a little lost, but there's no place else in the whole world I'd rather be right now. I'm so glad to be here in Holmes County."

"With me?"

Leah smiled up at Jacob, absorbing the quiet love in his expressions. "Yes. With you."

6

# CHAPTER TWO

Leah woke bright and early to the sounds of birds chirping right outside her window. She lifted the curtain and smiled at the colors of spring. Things were going to be much better down here; she just knew it.

She hopped out of bed and hurried to dress. Her Ashfield church clothing was a darker hue than the dresses she'd seen in Holmes County, but the three outfits and one Sunday dress would have to do until she earned enough money for yard goods to make new dresses.

She frowned as she pinned her hair up under her *kapp*. Where could she get a job? Jacob told her he'd made inquiries about serving work in the numerous restaurants surrounding the tourist areas, but nothing firm had opened up yet. One good thing about the region was there were many drivers willing to take the Amish workers from place to place for a fee. Transportation back home was always a problem, but it did tend to keep the *jungen* on the farm until marriage.

Leah and Sarah sat down to share their very first breakfast together. Soon they found themselves laughing at one another's tales of life on the farm.

"You know, Leah, my days on route 603 back in Ashfield County did have its idyllic times. My *maem* was a sweet, kind lady, and my *daet* wasn't too stern, either. I was the youngest so sometimes, I have to admit, I was a bit spoiled."

"How many siblings do you have?"

"I had an older sister, but sadly, she passed away at age five from a disease she had from birth. I was only three, but I remember that day so well. *Maem* was shocked to find her not breathing after she'd put her down for a nap. I can still hear *Maem's* low wailing as it dawned on her that something was wrong with Mary. Oh, my."

Leah couldn't help but fight tears as she watched Sarah's lined face crumble at the memory.

"I'm so sorry to hear that, Sarah."

"Well, I guess I should know by now that I'm not going to get past the sorrow of that day, but there were happy times, too. I also have three older brothers. John, Ivan, and Paul."

"Which one is the oldest?"

Sarah set her lips in a line and swallowed. "Um, that would be Paul." She stood unexpectedly and started clearing the table.

Leah took the hint and helped clear the dishes and put the butter and milk away. It was a pleasure to make use of the modern looking propane powered refrigerator. It was one of those little blessings that Leah was going to enjoy in this new life of hers.

Though she sensed her new housemate was unsettled, and she knew it had something to do with Sarah's brother Paul, Leah didn't feel comfortable pushing for more chat. They had many days ahead in which to share so if Sarah never told her the whole story, Leah was all right with that. Heaven knew she had her own stories she didn't really want to tell.

"Leah, how about we walk to my neighbors down the lane? She's a new mom and I think she told me she might need a *mawt* to help out for a few weeks."

"Really? That's wonderful! I was just thinking this morning that I sure do need to find a job right away. I'm really grateful you thought of her."

They gathered their bonnets and tied their shoes on nice and tight against the dusty road they'd be traveling. Sarah grunted as she straightened.

"These old knees, whoo! Well, I hope Henry has eased off his purse strings enough to agree to a mother's helper. He wouldn't let Clara have one last time, but she struggled with this newest birth and she's worn out."

The countryside was wearing its best soft spring hues and the pale sun radiated just enough warmth to keep them comfortable as they ambled along the road. The farmland quiet was only broken by the swish of their dresses, interrupted once in a while by a screeching hawk or trilling wren. Leah breathed deep of the zesty air, her shoulders relaxing into the safety of starting fresh.

"They live up this way." Sarah pointed to a long roughly kept lane. "Henry's not one to work too hard, I hate to say, so don't be surprised at the unkempt manner of his farm. His boys aren't old enough yet to really help him out, either, so sometimes, well ..." Sarah trailed off.

Leah eyed her landlady, waiting for her to continue, but again, Sarah seemed to lose the desire to share more, so Leah didn't ask. *Lord, please don't let this situation be more than I can handle.*

As they approached the farmhouse, she examined the lay of the land. Chickens roamed the yard, scratching away any vestige of grass, leaving dusty mini whirls behind their tail feathers as they plumbed the earth for worms.

A languid hound dog pushed himself up off a worn out porch and loped toward them. His grin and lazy manner showed he was no threat to anyone. He nosed Leah's hand and sniffed at their shoes and then happily followed them as they wound past the cluttered yard and stepped onto sagging porch floorboards.

All the paint was scuffed off the silvered wood and not one flower grew anywhere in sight. It was a dispirited home. Even the shutters at the lone window overlooking the porch seemed to be tired of trying to hang on, tilting precariously by one screw at the corners.

Sarah rapped sharply on the peeling door and then turned the knob, poking her head in. "Clara? It's Sarah here. Are you up to a visit?"

Leah heard a weak female voice respond, but she couldn't make out the words. It sure was a quiet house for a family with five children. She had expected a gaggle of giggling youngsters to meet them coming up the road, but so far, she'd spotted no little ones at all.

Sarah pushed the door wider and motioned for Leah to follow her inside. "Clara? *Wie bischt?*"

Leah examined the dim room they'd entered. Everywhere she looked, she saw chaos.

It certainly appeared as if children lived in the house from the state of the mess. A few toys lay where they'd been tossed, newspaper and mail were piled in a corner, crushed crackers were confetti on the sofa, and a sour smell, as if from a mildewed mop, caused her nose to wrinkle. Her hands were itching to get to work.

She glanced to Sarah whose furrowed brow brought worry to the surface. "I hope she's all right."

Just as Sarah started toward a closed door to the right of the kitchen, it creaked open and a slight, bewildered looking young woman shuffled out. In her arms she cradled a bundle that mewed like a weak kitten in its blanket.

"Oh, my! I'm sorry I didn't have the gumption to redd up the place. We're—well, we're all taking a nap, you see."

Sarah walked to the new mother and gently took the baby from her arms. "It's fine, Clara. I brought Leah here to be a mother's helper for you. I think you could use a little rest, don't you?"

Leah reached across to shake the pale woman's hand. The feel of Clara's fingers against Leah's was like holding a bird's scrawny foot.

Leah was startled by the weightlessness of her hand. She drew back and tried to smile away her instant concern for Clara's health.

"I hope I can be of help to you, Clara, if you still want a *mawt*, that is."

Clara gestured to the cluttered sofa and the loaded-with-laundry rocking chair. "Please sit. Oh, wait—let me just get this laundry off here." She hurried to the chair and gathered as much of the clothing as she could hold in her arms.

Already Leah could see Clara's body trembling with fatigue. Her heart went out to this fraught frail mother.

"Let Leah take that laundry – it's clean, *ja*? She can fold it for you while we chat."

"Yes, please, let me take it. I can sit right here beside Sarah and the baby and get right to work."

Sarah made room on the sofa for Leah and then turned back to Clara. "You look mighty peaked. Have you eaten much today? And where are the *kinna*? Were you able to get them all to nap at once?"

Clara wobbled to the rocking chair and let herself down easy. A sigh escaped as she folded her thin hands together in her lap.

"Now wouldn't that be a miracle? No, the two oldest are in school. But I did get Daniel and William to settle down long enough to sleep. The little one there—"she pointed a shaking finger to the baby. "—she sleeps all the time. I have a terrible amount of work to do to get her to eat enough when she's awake."

"I've heard preemies need to sleep a lot." Sarah snuggled the tiny infant closer and cooed to her under her breath. "She sure is an angel."

Leah cleared her throat as she shook out a small pair of pants. From the somber colors represented in the clothing pile, she could tell the Coblentz family was part of a conservative Old Order church. "What ages are your children and what are their names?"

"My oldest boy is Reuben and he's nine year's old. Next is Saloma at age eight. Then there's Daniel, aged five, and William, aged three. That there's baby Ada, just two weeks old."

11

Her mother's pride in her children brought a rosy tinge to Clara's pallid cheeks and she smiled as she turned back to Leah. "They keep me hoppin', but I'd be lost without them."

Clara rested her head against the back of the chair, closed her eyes and pushed the rocker into a swooshing motion.

The clock pendulum swinging back and forth within its arc sounded loud in the suddenly quiet room. Leah continued to fold the wrinkled, but clean, laundry, trying hard to think of something to say to fill the silence.

But neither Clara nor Sarah seemed bothered by the stillness, so Leah forced herself to relax and get on with the folding. The neat piles grew as minutes ticked by. Leah lifted her eyes to Sarah and watched as she held the baby quietly to her shoulder. She swayed softly, back and forth, back and forth, while the little one slept.

Leah slowly allowed the peace to seep into her bones and just when she grew calm, a sharp thud sounded upstairs, followed by a cry and then the sound of little feet thumping their way down the steps.

Clara's eyes flew open. "Well, so much for that rest!" she laughed.

The afternoon passed quickly with the entrance of the two little tow-headed boys, so by the time Leah and Sarah had made lunch, washed the dishes and settled on a plan for Leah to return to begin her new job, it was nearing dinner time.

Leah offered to put on a pot of chili soup, while Sarah made up a quick cornbread. Everything was well handled by the time they called their good-byes to Clara.

As they walked back down the lane to the road, they met the husband of the Coblentz family, leading a tired cow back to the barn.

Henry was lean, like his wife, with a nervous tic which caused his left eye to twitch.

He had the look of a man well used to life beating him down. There was no light in his eyes and he gave only a slight nod to indicate he'd even seen them.

When Sarah informed him of Leah's impending employment as his wife's *mawt*, he merely increased the nod in acknowledgement.

12

With him were a boy and a girl, unusually quiet and shy for their ages. They, too, were slim, frail and pale. Leah made up her mind that if she could do nothing else, she would put some meat on all their bones and bring a smile to the children's faces.

That night, she lay in bed thinking of the family God was entrusting to her care. Instead of apprehension for the start of her new job, she was eager to get in that house and make a difference.

"Lord," she whispered, "You brought me here just in time, I'm thinking. Help me do my best for this family."

Then she turned over, snuggled into her blanket, and soundly slept her second night in Holmes County, Ohio.

# CHAPTER THREE

The first week of working with Clara and her children was a fairly peaceful one. The older children were at school and the younger children still held back in getting to know her, so they were also restrained in doing anything that could get them into trouble. But by the time Monday of the second week rolled around, school was out, and the three oldest, Reuben, Saloma, and Daniel, were letting themselves run a little wild.

In a way, even though it made more work for Leah, she was happy to see them cavorting, yelling, and chasing each other in and around the house. They were more like carefree children, instead of silent and frightened overly burdened miniature adults. The only exception was when their father was in the house or nearby. Henry became even more of an enigma to Leah.

She was thinking about him while eating lunch outside on the patio of her shared home. Jacob had managed to swing by, the first time she'd seen him in two days, and they were enjoying chatting about their jobs, their future plans and the way things were going for both of them together in Holmes County.

Leah picked up her sandwich and took a bite. She tilted her head, concentrating on how she wanted to describe Henry to Jacob.

"It's not that he's loud or mean or demanding. It's more about, I don't know, I guess the word cold would be closest to what I mean. And ... stoic. Like a robot. Like he has no feelings at all. When he sits at the table with the children and Clara, there's an air of foreboding, even though he hasn't spoken a word. The children settle into this stilted, quiet pose. They eat, they chew, they swallow—all in silence. Once in a while, I catch the older ones, especially Reuben and Saloma, eyeing him like they're waiting for the other shoe to drop."

She shook off the feeling of anxiety that had followed her home from the Coblentz's place that morning.

Jacob touched her hand. "You're not worried about being there, are you, Leah? I don't want you to stay, if you are."

His loving concern melted her heart. It was just like Jacob to think of her safety.

"No, I don't feel afraid, just wary. Anyway, the way Clara is healing and bouncing back to being a healthier *maem*, I don't expect I'll be there too much longer. The way she's blossomed in just a week and a half is amazing!"

Jacob smiled, gently stroking her fingers as he captured them and held her hand firmly in his.

"I have no doubts that your good cooking, hard work, and care of the children and new baby are powerful potions for her."

Leah's laugh echoed off the roof covering the patio. "I can always count on you to support me, Jacob. I'm happier than I've ever been here with you."

They stole a quick kiss from one another before Leah pointed to his lunch. "Get to eating! You only have a couple of hours before you have to head to work at the factory. I don't want you to starve all night."

Jacob saluted her. "Yes, boss."

He took a huge bite of the cool, creamy chicken salad sandwich Leah had made him. "This is so good."

Leah took a drink and asked him about his second shift work in the door factory. "Is it getting any better with that fellow you said seems to hunt for trouble?"

"You mean Bert Small?"

"Yes. Why do you think he's so ornery?"

Jacob shook his head, wiping his mouth with the paper napkin Leah handed him. "I have no idea. He seems to like picking on the Amish working the line with him. I think I'm just the newest Amish guy there, so now it's my turn."

"I wish you didn't have to put up with that, Jacob. You're already working hard with the farm trying to get the soil renewed and ready for planting." Her brows drew together as she squeezed his hand. "Let's talk about the farm. Do you think it'll be ready by the time we decide our wedding date?"

"If there's anything that's going to be ready, it's the farm. I'm determined to get your future home in shape so we don't have to wait another season to get married."

Leah's face warmed as Jacob's gaze held hers. She was excited to be getting married, but with everything they both had to do, joining the church and then counseling, preparing the house and farm, and saving money for everything they planned for the wedding, it seemed the actual day of marriage would be a long time off. "Let's pray that God will help speed things up a little bit. I'm hoping to earn enough to help put aside money for the wedding." She smiled at her future husband, the delight of that day warming her heart.

"Speaking of church, it's church week. Do you want me to pick you and Sarah up? I'm not close enough to walk to the Mast's place where church will be this week, but you are, if you and Sarah would rather get out for a walk in the sunshine Sunday morning."

Leah chewed on the thought. Though getting in a decent stroll was tempting, it was more tempting to spend as much time as possible with Jacob. Sarah being along with them would be good because her presence would stop the gossip mill from churning out silly tales, too.

"I think we'll be happy to ride with you, Jacob."

They grinned at each other.

"I was hoping you'd say that!"

❧ 🏠 ❧

Leah cleaned up the lunch dishes while Sarah washed the floors. They chatted about this and that before Leah suddenly remembered she was supposed to be at the Coblentz farm to help with a spring wipe down of windows.

"Oh, goodness! I forgot I've got to get to Henry's at two! The children are supposed to help me wash the windows and shades."

Sarah shooed her off, saying she'd finish the dishes herself later.

Leah threw on her bonnet and grabbed a black sweater to take along. The sun was shining bright, so she knew it would be warm, but by the time she got back, there might be more shadows along the road and it would be chillier in the spring early evening.

She enjoyed the brisk pace she set for herself and her heart cheered to see a welcoming committee of children waiting for her at the end of the Coblentz lane. She smiled and gave the little ones a hearty wave. They ran to her, laughing, their cheeks rosy and their smiles easy.

"Ah, I suppose this cheerful greeting is because you *kinna* are chomping at the bit to work?" she teased.

Reuben came alongside her, his shining eyes bright with anticipation. "Nah, we just like you being here. You make everything fun—even work!"

"That's a nice thing to say, Reuben. How about you, Saloma? Ready to get those muscles warmed up?"

Saloma, shy and fragile in limb, glanced up at Leah under her lashes. She was a beautiful girl and her quick mind set the wheels to turning in her head at every curious turn. She loved reading books, which invigorated Leah to find time to go to the library in Millersburg so she could get a card and check out books to bring with her for Saloma. She wouldn't mind coming to the house, even when

17

her job as a *mawt* was finished, just to give the children a little attention.

Daniel, not to be ignored, skipped close and took her hand. "Leah, *Maem* says we can ask you to bake some cookies after we finish the windows. Please, please, please?"

Daniel's little pleading face was screwed into a knot of yearning, his brows furrowed and his mouth rounded.

Reuben snorted. "We're not supposed to beg, and *Maem* said only if Leah has time, Daniel."

Saloma couldn't resist adding her mild plea to her younger brother's. Cookies were such a treat, the thought of them enticed her to speak up, too.

"It would be so *gut* to have fresh cookies, Leah. We can hurry and be finished in no time."

Leah couldn't help but fall for their plan. "I think cookies will be a perfect way to end the workday. Let's get to work!"

She laughed as the children broke into a run ahead of her, turning back every now and then to urge her forward.

*Yes, Gott. I'm just where I need to be.*

As the jovial group neared the house, Henry Coblentz strode from the barn. His shoulders were taut and he was frowning.

Immediately, the children stopped their sing-song laughter and slowed to a halt just under the red maple tree that sheltered the house from the sun. Their gaze was fixed on their *daet*. Leah, too, couldn't help but make eye contact with Henry. He stopped near her and pointed to the windows.

"Clara says you're going to do the windows."

A puff of air blew her way and she caught an unmistakable whiff of alcohol. Was that scent coming from Henry?

"*Ja*, I agreed to come back to wash the windows and wipe down the shades." She nodded to the children, who were standing still as deer. "Reuben, Saloma, and Daniel are going to help me."

Henry chewed a ragged length of his beard and dropped his head. His voice was low, but the tone was charged with quiet irritation.

18

"My boys don't do housework. You can have Saloma, but the boys are going out to the field with me."

Leah glanced toward Reuben, but he hid his eyes by lowering his hat brim. Poor Daniel, being only five, couldn't stand the notion that cookies may not make an appearance after all and opened his mouth in protest. "Aw, *Daet*—Leah's going to make cookies afterward!"

Henry never raised his voice, but he skewered Daniel with a sharp stare, daring his little boy to defy him.

The air sizzled with uncertainty. Saloma ducked her chin, rotated on the balls of her feet and ran toward the house.

Henry broke the hard gaze he held on Daniel and glanced to Leah. "As I said, the boys don't do housework."

His repeated assertion was final. Again, as he let go a sigh, Leah caught the sour smell of alcohol.

She nodded to Henry, gave Daniel a shaky smile and told him she would be sure to bake cookies another day. "I'd best get to the house with Saloma and start the washing."

Henry said nothing, but as he turned back to the barn, he stumbled over his own feet. He grabbed at Reuben just in time to keep himself from falling. Reuben raised a skinny arm to help his dad balance and pulled Daniel along with them toward the fields.

Leah shook her head, certain now what was behind the misery in this family.

*Lord, Now I know You have a reason for me to be here.*

# CHAPTER FOUR

Sunday came faster than Leah wanted it to. Her heart was still wounded by the treatment she'd suffered from her home church in Ashfield County. Being shunned and accused of mental illness, to the point the Bishop had her *daet* convinced he needed to sign Leah into an Amish run mental health center, and all because she claimed to have a personal relationship with Jesus, caused her to build a wall of wariness about any church.

Though Jacob had told her their new church was a *hoch* group, less strict in many ways than the church she'd left behind, a part of her doubted she'd be allowed the kind of freedom she'd experienced when she'd left the Amish and attended an English church.

Sarah seemed to sense her fears and started off their Sunday with a little sweet tea and spicy talk, as she put it. Namely, she filled Leah in on the families who made up the church community they would soon be joining. Her descriptions were humorous and before she knew it, Leah was relaxed and ready to meet the future with Jacob and their home church.

The family hosting Sunday church was Melvin Mast, his wife, Barbara, and a long line of children too numerous for Leah to catch all their names. Their home was on the dairy route for a major cheese house; consequently, their farm appeared to be very prosperous and well maintained.

Sarah's earlier description of Melvin was spot on when Leah was introduced to him. An apple-shaped man with reed-thin legs, rotund belly, and bulbous red nose, she could imagine him in a Santa Claus suit, except that his demeanor was anything but jolly. His wife Barbara was just the opposite. She was tall and lanky, with arms that appeared extraordinarily lengthy. Her horsey face held a smidgen of color in her cheeks to give her pallid skin a tinge of life.

Both were formal and taciturn. Both gave off a self-righteous air that squelched chit chat or friendly joking. Even the women with welcome greetings and open smiles reined in their effusive natures once they stepped over the threshold of the Mast machine shed.

The service proceeded much the way she'd been brought up, including multiple sermons, hymns from the *Ausbund,* and lessons from the Old and New Testaments presented by lay preachers and the bishop.

Bishop John Troyer was like no other Amish bishop she'd met in the past. His face shone with light and his eyes wore merry lines radiating out from their corners, as though laughing molded his visage from crown to chin. He was kind-spirited and soft spoken, with a hint of humor behind every admonition or homily. Leah promised herself she'd have to find out what was behind his joyful, sunny personality.

The two ministers, of which Melvin Mast was one, the other being a quiet, shy man named Jonas Stutzman, thankfully kept their sermons fairly short. Melvin preached about following the forefathers, a topic pontificated upon so often in all Amish churches, that she was sure every member across the land could stand up and preach the stuffing out of it.

She found humor, though, in Sarah's accurate portrayal of Melvin's rocking back and forth as he spoke. But when he also began waddling a bit side to side as he warmed up to his subject, Leah had all she could do not to giggle out loud. Rock, rock, waddle, waddle. Rock, rock, waddle, waddle.

A tiny snort betrayed her near impossible repression of laughter, which brought a few stares from the ladies sitting nearby. That was enough pressure to return Leah's stoic expression and dampen any remaining flame of humor.

In comparison to Preacher Melvin's active style of sermonizing, Preacher Jonas could have stood in for a light pole, in that he appeared to not move an inch as he advanced the service through a series of scriptures concerning the history of sinful mankind, from Old Testament to New Testament. He possessed a sibilant "s", which cut sharp amid the rest of his milquetoast presented words. Leah wondered if he might literally melt right into the doorjamb he so eagerly propped himself against. He clearly did not want to be a preacher, and as sweat rained his collar, Leah's sympathies for his forced-upon position grew.

Once Bishop Troyer took the floor, it was like the door opened and God the Father, God the Son, and God the Holy Spirit walked right in and sat down among them. His words were mesmerizing. Leah's soul blossomed as she drank in spiritual manna, straight, it seemed, from the hand of God.

After the service, Jacob eagerly sought her out.

"Well? What did you think?" He twisted his hat between his fingers, keen to hear her report of the Bishop.

She smiled. "Bishop Troyer is wonderful! He has something I don't believe I've ever seen in any other bishop."

Jacob nodded in agreement, leading Leah by the elbow to a group of women gathering for their turn to eat lunch. "I'm sure Sarah will introduce you around, but I'm glad you liked the church."

He gave her a wink and went to join the men lining up to get their food.

Sarah hurried to her new roommate and steered her to a young mother, barely in adulthood, Leah guessed, and introduced them to each other.

"Anna Hershberger, this is my new housemate, Leah Raber."

Anna's grin was infectious and amicable. A few strands of her silky blonde tresses slipped from the *kapp's* prison and coiled around her eyebrows. She lifted a delicate ivory hand in vain attempts to persuade the curls to behave and stay hidden.

"Hello, Leah. We've met Jacob before, of course. He's told us how happy he was going to be when you finally got the chance to come to Holmes County. I feel like I know you already."

"Glad to meet you, Anna." Leah peaked behind the young woman's dress to make eye contact with the tiniest golden angel of a child clinging to Anna's apron. "Is this your little girl?"

Anna nodded. "Yes, her name is Susan and today she appears to have lost her tongue to the cat. Can you say hello to Leah?," Anna prompted her fairy-like daughter.

The child met her gaze, stuck her finger in her mouth and mumbled "Hello."

Leah smiled. "Hi, Susan. Are you ready to have lunch?"

The little girl nodded and looked away, intent on halting the conversation.

"My husband is standing over there with Jacob—his name is Liam." Anna pointed across the way to a handsome young man. He was tall and appeared friendly.

The women formed themselves into a line to claim their turn to eat. Sarah stayed close to Leah and was faithful to break the ice for her among the church women as the queue wound its way to the door of the spotless machine shed where the food and tables awaited.

On the way home, Leah thanked Sarah for being a good friend to her. She appreciated every kind word each church member spoke.

Jacob's eyes met hers and the pride she saw in his expression warmed her heart. It felt lovely to know she was on the path to being accepted by this new community. She was grateful and blessed beyond measure.

From out of nowhere, Leah thought of a scripture she'd heard among the English Christians she'd stayed with for a time. And though she'd wondered if coming to Holmes County was the right thing to do, the verse resonated with her and brought her peace.

*For I know the thoughts that I think toward you, saith the Lord, thoughts of peace, and not of evil, to give you an expected end.*

Jacob was invited to stay for a dish of ice cream and while they sat on the patio, hearing the birds and seeing all the growing things come to life, Leah sighed.

Jacob turned to her. "Are you all right?"

"Oh, yes. I was just thinking about how *Gott* brought a verse to my mind on the way home about His plans for us. How He wants to give us peace and a good end. Well, sitting here with you two, seeing the beauty of the awakening earth, I can believe every word. I feel so alive and free! I'm glad I jumped the fence, as they say. The first time ended in tears, but I have a feeling this time will end in complete happiness."

Sarah grinned. "Leah, my dear housemate, I know so, too. Everything has fallen into place and I take great comfort in knowing *Gott's* leading is always best."

As the day waned, Sarah got up and gathered their dessert dishes. "You two stay as long as you'd like out here. When it gets near dusk, you may see the first fireflies of the season. Nothing cheers me up more than spying one of those little beacons of joy."

The squeal of the screen door and the slap of it hitting the frame brought back memories of Leah as a child, hearing her *Maem* call out to her "Make sure you close that screen door all the way. The last thing I need is a bunch of flies setting up shop in my kitchen!"

The recollection brought a tinge of sadness with it. What would her parents think of her now? Would they be able to see any of the blessings Leah knew were the workings of her benevolent and loving Father in Heaven? More likely they would focus on her disobedience to parents and to church by running away and beginning again in a *hoch* church. The thought tired her out.

"Now you seem sad." Jacob reached for her hand and gently stroked it. "What's wrong? Nothing I've done, I hope."

"No—not at all, Jacob. I was just thinking about my parents. Thinking about how they'd be concerned that I'm going to a higher church."

Jacob nodded. "Hmm. And if they get wind of anything going wrong, we know they'll be thinking we brought every bad thing that ever happens to us on ourselves. Right?"

"*Ja.* That's true. I sure do wish they knew how happy I am, though."

Jacob stretched. "Well, when our wedding day comes, they'll see for themselves how contented we are." He stood. "Now come give me a sweet kiss. It's time for me to head home. I don't want Bingo spooked by car lights. He's still young and sometimes hard to handle on the roads when it begins to get dark."

Leah stood, wrapped her arms around her beloved and rested her cheek on his chest. "I could stay here all day," she murmured.

"One day, you will."

# CHAPTER FIVE

L eah couldn't wait to hear Jacob's buggy with Bingo's sure-footed trot coming along the road. Today she and Jacob had free time to be together.

It was the third week since moving to Holmes County. And So far, her job with the Coblentz family and Jacob's two jobs had kept them hopping, with little time to spend together.

Leah had only been to the farm once and that was a short stop just so she could at least look over the house. But now they had most of the day free before Jacob would have to go into his second shift job at the door factory. Their first stop was going to be breakfast at the diner in downtown Berlin. Leah was anxious to stroll through the shops located there, and perhaps, if they were lucky, greet some of the church families that might be in town.

"You look sweet with that anticipation showing on your face." Sarah chuckled as she watched Leah pace from door to window and back again.

"Yes, I'm ready to get in that buggy and take off. It seems like a long time since we had almost a full day to be together. And Jacob's promised to take me to the farm before he brings me home. I'm excited to see the barn and sheds. I didn't have the chance to do that last time."

"I know you got to see the house. What did you think of it?"

"It's big! And the *daadihaus* is nice, too. It's strange to think Jacob and I might be living in that *haus* one day."

"Believe me, Leah, time passes far more quickly than you'll ever think possible. My mind still thinks I'm in my thirties, but my body corrects that notion with every moan and groan. Old age is just around the corner for me, now."

Leah smiled at Sarah. "No, it's not. You're still young at heart and young in spirit."

"Well, this young-at-heart old lady thinks it's time to go out and check the strawberry patch." As she rose from the breakfast table, Sarah stifled a groan. "See? My body rejects the word young, in every way."

The back screen door slammed shut as Leah's gaze followed her housemate down the steps, up the neatly graveled path and through the arbor into the strawberry patch. Early summer was gracing them with sun, rain, and warmer nights, so every growing thing was sprouting up tall and healthy. This was the kind of weather farmers the world 'round loved.

Leah watched Sarah as she moved through the patch, lifting leaves to search out fruit and dipping a finger every once in a while into the soil to check for moisture.

Already this sweet woman was dear to her heart, but she knew there was a sad side to Sarah, too. One night last week, soon after Leah came, they'd gotten onto the subject of shunning. For the most part, Leah understood that the New Order didn't shun too much, if at all. It depended on each church. For Leah, coming from a background of shunning, some of the fear from that experience lingered. She had moments of self-doubt about God and her relationship with Him, in spite of learning about His grace through Christ and the finished work of Jesus on the cross.

Sarah had shared that she was filled with apprehension when she thought of death, for the very reason Leah had revealed: could she ever be good enough to get into Heaven?

Leah's heart went out to Sarah. She was ready to give her scriptures that would bring peace to that matter for Sarah, but the older woman had abruptly dropped the topic and went on to speak of the garden. Though Leah was disappointed, she knew the Lord would bring about the right time and the right place for the discussion in the future.

Leah's thoughts were interrupted by the *clop clop clop* of Bingo's hooves against pavement. She ran to the back door. "Sarah, Jacob's here. I'll be going now."

Sarah stood, cupping her ear to catch Leah's words. "Have a nice time!" she replied as she waved.

Leah returned the wave and raced to the front door just as Jacob called to Bingo. "Whoa, Bingo! Good boy."

Before Jacob could get out of the buggy, Leah was out the door and climbing to the seat beside him.

"Well, that was quick! If you get ready that fast once we're married, I think we'll have a happy life. A man can spend a lot of years waiting on his missus." The sparkle and laugh lines in and around his eyes showed his teasing, good-humored nature.

Leah grinned. "I can't guarantee absolutely no waiting, but I can guarantee low maintenance."

Jacob chuckled. "That sounds fair. You've got a deal." He backed Bingo up and headed out the drive to the road.

Since traffic was still light at this hour of the morning, they had a brisk ride down to Berlin. Once they got to town, though, traffic picked up, especially downtown, where the tourists flocked and hotels lined the back streets. It was something Leah struggled with. Back home, danger came in the form of fast country highways with hidden curves and hills, not to mention the restriction of the church that buggies could only be lit with a lantern and made more visible with a gray triangle on the back. Some bishops also allowed the plastic white tubes placed on the buggy wheels that glowed at night. But for the most part, visibility on the roads was limited.

Here in Holmes County, though, traffic was much thicker, buggy lights were bright and many roads were wider to accommodate both buggy and automobile. Still, it was sometimes scary to have tourists and natives alike drive closely behind or zoom around the buggy on hilly, curving roads.

Bingo was not normally a nervous horse, thank goodness, but he didn't like it when cars rode his "bumper." He'd twist his head to try and see the object behind him or start to dance away from what he felt was something too close to the back of the buggy.

But the ride into town was uneventful this day so Leah was able to relax and enjoy the scenery as they passed by. She was in awe of the beautiful rolling hills that were the signature of Holmes County. With the fresh growing crops dotting every field, and the neatly kept farms, it truly was a masterpiece to behold.

"Jacob, tell me more about the men you work with at the door factory."

"Well, there are about twenty people working on the line I'm usually at. Two are women, though."

"Really? Isn't it heavy work?"

"Not too bad on our line. Everyone does a good job and they work really hard. My supervisor, though, is another story." Jacob's mouth tightened and his jaw worked as he spoke of the man.

"How can a supervisor not be a good worker? How did he get promoted if he didn't do his job properly?"

"Some folks say office politics, but I don't know. Maybe he had his days of working before he got promoted. Some people allow promotions to go to their heads. But on top of that attitude, he can be surly and quick tempered."

Leah's brows formed a V. "I dislike thinking of you working so hard, after taking on the farm all day, only to be hassled by a bad boss."

Jacob sighed. "He can be tough, but really, I enjoy most of my time there. I have some good co-workers and they're great company as the shift rolls on."

"What kinds of things does your boss say or do?"

Bingo made a sudden dart toward the ditch as a pick-up truck with modified duel mufflers roared around them. Jacob pulled the reins tight, calling out to Bingo in a soothing tone. "There, boy! Settle down, Bingo! Settle down, boy!"

Leah gripped the dash with both hands, her heart accelerating by the second. How quickly accidents could happen! Jacob managed to get Bingo back on the road and trotting at a normal pace, but Leah knew he'd be skittish after that close call.

Finally, they reached their destination, pulled into a space off the main road and got the horse calmed and chewing on a handful of oats. Leah caressed his silky mane, whispering soothing praise as he munched his reward.

The line for the restaurant was out the doors, but the sun was warm, the morning breeze was light, and Leah was happy to put aside the fright of traveling and just enjoy being with Jacob.

As they joined the column of guests, Jacob hesitated, just a bit. He lightly touched Leah's back, guiding her to a stop. She glanced at him, wondering why he was focused ahead. She followed his line of vision to a stocky man about two inches taller than Jacob.

His butch haircut, worn jeans, and rugged boots gave him the look of a farmer, but a spotless black vest and shiny chain dangling from his waist to his pocket belied that profession. He was tightly wound, his feet shifting from one foot to the next, like an animal ready to pounce. The friends he was waiting with were loud, letting out roars of laughter in bursts. Leah noticed those waiting in line seemed to be put off by the boisterous group.

"Leah," Jacob leaned in close, "that's my supervisor, Bert Small."

Leah focused on the man who was responsible for giving Jacob a hard time. His fists were pulled tight against his thighs and from time to time, he scanned the line, up and then down. The second time, he spied Jacob. His face grew darker and his eyebrows came down over his eyes like shutters. He lifted his chin as he spat Jacob's name into the air. "Yoder! What you doin' out here with normal people? Ain't you s'posed to be on the farm – bein' a good Amish boy?"

The man's odious friends chortled like a gaggle of geese. Leah's cheeks warmed, not in embarrassment, but in anger. Her lips pressed into a tight line.

Jacob nodded to the brute but remained outwardly calm. He pulled his hat closer to his eyes and regarded the sidewalk beneath their feet.

She felt his muscles tense. Leah resented this Englisher trying to ruin their limited time together. She met the rude fellow's stare, refusing to look away. The man's smile grew ever more insolent the longer their gazes held. He stepped out of line and sauntered back to stand in front of Jacob, never removing his eyes from Leah's face.

He lifted a ham fist and threw out a thumb toward Leah. "This here your girlfriend?"

Jacob raised his eyes to Bert's. "Yes." His tone even and sure, Jacob didn't elaborate.

Bert laughed. "How'd a skinny Amish guy like you get a woman like this?"

His breath, even so early in the morning, released a hint of strong liquor.

Leah's nose flattened against the odor. The man stepped back, allowing his eyes to roam over her figure from bottom to top.

"Mighty fine, I guess. For an Amish gal."

Jacob took a deep breath, and Leah again sensed him tense, his right hand pressed deeper against her back. His left hand balled into a fist. Leah wanted this Bert to disappear.

Jacob nodded to the man. "We've decided not to wait for breakfast. See you later, Bert."

He guided her out of line and back around the corner toward the parking area where Bingo waited.

Leah caught Bert's parting shot. "*Ja*, make sure you're ready to work, *buvli*." The man spit out the Amish words like poison from his mouth. The rowdy bullies' laughter drifted over the crowds. Leah was near tears.

"How can you stand working with that ... that ... thug!"

Jacob, his sweet nature quickly returning, smiled at Leah. "Oh, that's just his way. He must be feeling insecure to act like that. It's a front. If I do my work, he leaves me pretty much alone. It's not so bad. But I didn't like how he treated you. That got me riled up inside, for sure."

Leah stopped. "Now that he's ruined our morning, where can we get breakfast?"

Jacob continued toward Bingo. "I say let's go get eggs out of our own henhouse and have breakfast at our own table. What do you think?" He threw Leah a wink over his shoulder and her bad mood instantly lifted.

"There's one thing you're forgetting, Jacob Yoder."

He turned to face her, squinting against the bright sun. "What's that, Leah Raber?"

"We aren't married so there's no 'our' anything yet!"

He walked back to her, pulled her close, whispering "Hopefully, that will be remedied soon."

She shook her head, her soft smile showing him her heart. "Yes. Soon, I hope."

## CHAPTER SIX

I t was the last day of officially working as a *mawt* for Clara
Coblentz. Leah was happy to see how healthy the young mother
looked.

She had gained a little weight and her skin glowed, it's youth
revitalized with rest and good food. The baby girl had gained weight,
too, and was spending more hours of her day awake and gurgling. She
was cute as a button and had an even temperament.

Leah picked up the bucket of water from washing the floors and
dumped the soiled liquid over the back steps. Then she grabbed a
stubby broom, its corn bristles worn down, and used it to swish off
mud clods, bird waste, and dusty debris. Keeping the steps and
porches clean cut back on how much dirt got carried into the house.
Leah had also scrounged around in the attic until she found two rag
rugs that she washed and then placed at both front and back doors.
She'd managed to get the kids used to wiping their feet before coming
inside, but Henry never even looked down when he strode into the
house. Still, it was easier to clean up after one than many.

She had also spent time teaching Saloma how to cook easy dishes
like scrambled eggs, bacon, ham steaks, and side dishes from the
canned goods Clara had stored. When Saloma made lunch for the

first time, it was a star day for her and Clara. Anything the children could do to help their *maem* made the days easier for Clara to manage.

Saloma caught up with her as Leah made her way out to the henhouse to gather eggs.

"Leah, will you promise to visit us next week, even if you aren't our *mawt* anymore?"

The little girl's worried face tugged at Leah's heartstrings. She was such a kind little person with a sharp mind. For just an instant, Leah wondered how far Saloma could go in life if she was allowed to bloom in her Amish world. She knew the child's interest in science would be rewarded in the English schools, but becoming a wife and mother would be the most Saloma would realize as an Amish woman. And that was wonderful in itself, but how she wished education could be open for girls like Saloma, who would stay Amish, yet be allowed to pursue higher studies and careers that could aid the Amish, too.

She grabbed Saloma's frail hand and swung their hands back and forth. "Don't worry, I'll miss being here so much, I won't be able to stay away."

They hurried to collect eggs and then made their way back to the house. Suddenly, Leah spied a caterpillar cocoon hanging close to the ground. Inside, something wriggled and cavorted, trying to get out. She stopped, pointing to the cocoon. "Look! I think a butterfly is getting ready to emerge, Saloma! Let's sneak closer to watch."

As they crept near the cocoon, the wriggling intensified.

"Why do caterpillars do that, Leah? What makes them turn into butterflies?"

"You know what? That's a good question. I bet you'd like to read a science book about that. I'll be sure to check one out for you at the library next week and bring it out so we can both look into that topic. Would you like that?"

Saloma's eyes danced. "I would! I love to look at picture books about bugs, animals, grass and trees. I wish I knew more about them all."

Just then, a hole appeared in the cocoon. Soon, the emerging butterfly had poked through the silky covering and sat preening on the top of the nest. The sun warmed the wings and pretty soon, the insect was flexing them. In — closed tight. And out — spread wide.

Saloma barely breathed as she watched the process. After a couple of minutes, the butterfly stretched out its wings and launched into the air.

Saloma squealed, clapping her hands as she tracked the new butterfly's flight. Leah was captivated by Saloma's joy. She was just about to hug the child when Henry appeared. He had to have seen what they were watching.

"Saloma, stop wasting time! Your *maem* has more chores than she can handle. Get back to the house and find something useful to do."

Again, he didn't holler or scream, but his cold quiet words were filled with threat and power. He didn't turn to Leah at all. In fact, he didn't even acknowledge that she was there. His bullying wasn't like Bert Small's loud boasting and ranting. It was robotic and detached, but it was still bullying.

"Henry, Saloma and I were just watching a butterfly come out of its cocoon. I really think that's a good thing to do, too. We were headed back in to work, but a little stop along the way isn't so bad, now, is it?"

Henry ignored Leah. He kept his eyes fixed on his daughter. Slowly, the joy drained from Saloma's face.

Her frail shoulders sagged and her cheeks flamed as if caught doing something naughty. She broke eye contact with her *daet*, dropping her chin until Leah couldn't even see her eyes anymore. The young girl slowly turned and moved back toward the house.

A searing burn in her heart caused Leah to face Henry. "She wasn't doing anything wrong, Henry. She's a very smart little girl and has a sharp mind. She's just curious about the world, is all."

Henry sighed, that wisp of alcohol scenting the air, broke his gaze from Saloma and fixed it on the ground in front of him.

"My girl will be a wife and mother. She's wasting time doing anything else. Wife and mother. That's all." He spoke so quietly, she barely heard the words.

He did face her then and the baleful glare he gave her made Leah's knees tremble. His stare continued, until Leah couldn't take it anymore and moved off. As she neared the back steps, she paused, glancing over her shoulder to see that Henry was still scowling at her back. His dark demeanor spoke louder than any shouting Leah had ever heard. She shivered and hurried in to finish her work before it was time to head home.

On the walk back to her house, Leah prayed for Clara, the children, and Henry. The shuffle of her shoes on the dusty road kept a rhythm that she matched with her requests. She lifted her head as she whispered her prayers and saw that the sky was darker, with gathering clouds on the horizon foretelling a storm. Shadows formed along the hedges and under the canopy of trees lining the road as the storm grew in intensity. A heavy wind suddenly raised her skirt hem and tugged at her bonnet and the *kapp* beneath it.

Leah sucked in her breath, a swift unexpected fear crawling up her spine. She swiveled her eyes from side to side, sure that something was near. She stopped, rotating her feet to scan the road behind her.

There! In the ditch along the right side of the road, something skulked. A flash of movement, a glimmer of white teeth, and then, she lost sight of it.

For a few seconds more, she waited. The shadows increased as clouds rolled over, black and roiling in their clash of warm and cold air. Gusts of wind sent leaves, dust, and dirt swirling, blocking her vision. Yet, she could not stop staring into the hazy air. She felt she was being hunted.

Just as she turned back toward home, she caught a glimpse, out of the corner of her eye, of a man running. Behind her. Running and screaming at the top of his lungs.

She swung around in time to see Henry, arms stretched wide, eyes flashing anger, every bone in his body tuned in to her, running full tilt right at her! She tried to move out of his path, but she was too late. He hit her body with such a force, she spun completely around before slamming into the ground. She let out a cry of pain as her head bounced once, twice, off the pavement.

She instinctively covered her head and face, coiling into a ball trying to protect herself from whatever else Henry was going to do.

But he did nothing more. He stood up, straightening his shirt into place. He was breathing hard, but he visibly pulled himself together as she cowered. He now stood silently above her, watching with his normal mechanical expression.

She flinched as she tried to scoot away from him. The pain in her head exploded with each little movement and her stomach lurched with fear and sickness from the horrible pain. She outstretched a quivering arm, warding off anything else he might do.

"Henry—"

He turned on his heels, but when he'd walked a few feet away, he looked back at her as his lips formed a malevolent grin. He stood staring and smiling for a few more seconds, than as calmly as if he were out for a stroll, turned back toward his lane and disappeared into the shadows.

Leah dragged herself to her feet, gathered her wits and shot toward home. Though her head was killing her with each slam of her feet against the pavement, with her heart beating so hard she thought she might pass out, she increased her pace. She couldn't shake the feeling he might be chasing her and every fiber of her being was propelled violently toward safety.

She saw the lights of her cozy house in the distance and sobbed out a prayer that Sarah would be home when she got there.

"Thank you, *Gott!* Thank you, *Gott!*" she cried as she caught sight of Bingo in the driveway, serenely munching the grass near his feet as he waited for Jacob.

She stumbled through the door as Jacob opened it and launched herself into his arms. She sobbed loudly, shocked at her own voice— it sounded hysterical even to her ears.

"Leah! What is it? What's happened?" Jacob held her close, staring intensely as he tried to understand her wailing words.

Leah forced herself to stop howling long enough to gulp in air and take a deep, shuddering breath. Her hands were shaking so hard, she couldn't seem to control their movement. Suddenly, her knees buckled and she barely flung herself to the sofa before she collapsed.

Sarah was halted in the doorway between the kitchen and living room, her hand to her mouth. "Oh, Leah—tell us! Tell us what happened!"

Jacob rushed to the sofa and sat down, pulling Leah close to him, as he asked Sarah to get a washcloth. He had spied dark red blood leaking from the back of Leah's head and onto her snowy white *kapp*. "You're bleeding! Did you get hit by a car? Are you hurt any other place?"

Leah shook her head. "Noooo!" she cried as the tears began again. "It was Henry! He attacked me like a maniac as I was walking home!"

Sarah hurried into the room and handed the cloth to Jacob, her face a mixture of confusion and fear. "What! Henry attacked you?"

Jacob turned Leah around as he gently removed her *kapp* and lifted the cool damp cloth to the wound on the edge of Leah's hairline. "I don't understand! Why did Henry attack you?"

Leah shook her head and then groaned as the nauseating agony rolled through her head once again. "Oh, my—I'm feeling sick! I think—I think— I may have really hurt my head on the road."

Alarm grew on both Sarah and Jacob's faces as they tried to figure out what had happened to Leah. Jacob leaned her back softly, still holding the cloth to the wound, as he directed Sarah to use the black box phone their church allowed to call for medical aid.

Sarah dialed with shaking fingers and made the request for aid. Then she scurried to the door to watch for the rescue squad.

Leah fixed her gaze on Jacob. "He was terrifying, Jacob! I did nothing wrong. I was just coming home ..." she shuddered. "He—he stalked me like a cat would stalk a mouse. He was hiding in the ditches and weeds." She moaned and closed her eyes against the frightening memory of the flash of Henry's white teeth among the weeds.

"Oh, Father, thank you, Lord, for protecting me from worse harm!"

# CHAPTER SEVEN

Leah spent the rest of the day in the hospital. After a scan, the doctor determined that she had a small fracture of her skull, though it wasn't serious, and she was given instructions to care for herself and then sent home. Jacob and Sarah rode along home. Ella had been called to the hospital in Millersburg once Sarah knew her friend would be released soon.

Though it was good to see Ella once again, Leah's head was still pounding and the circumstances were less than happy.

Ella eyed Leah through the rear view mirror as she carefully maneuvered the van toward Leah's home. "I'm shocked you went through that with Henry. I truly am."

"It was a shock for me, too, Ella. I still don't know what set him off." Leah leaned her tired body against the seat and closed her eyes.

"Did the sheriff come to the hospital?"

Jacob glanced at Leah, his arm cradling her protectively. She felt his heart race at the mention of Henry's rage toward her. She still felt ill and couldn't help swallowing repeatedly to keep the bile down where it belonged.

He leaned close. "Are you feeling nauseated?"

She nodded a little, too afraid and sick to set the pain off in her injured head by motion. "Yes. I'm trying hard not to lose my lunch in Ella's nice, clean van."

Ella chuckled. "Well, I can't say I'd want that, but it wouldn't be the first time, and won't be the last. Anytime I haul Amish kids anywhere, especially the little ones, I have to expect somebody's going to be carsick. Some just can't get used to the speed of a vehicle."

"I know how they feel. Ohhh." She pressed an arm against her upset stomach. "But to answer your question, yes, the sheriff came and took a statement from me. I don't want to cause more trouble for Clara and the kids, heaven knows, but Henry needs help. I'm worried now that he's capable of hurting his wife or one of the children."

Sarah spoke up. "I think you may have found why the whole family clams up when he walks in the room, Leah. I pray he hasn't shown this kind of violence to his own family."

"The sheriff let me know they would go out to Henry's place tonight and see how everyone is. They may file against him in the morning." Leah grimaced. "I hate to think what this will do to Clara. I hate to be the cause of more trouble for her."

"No, don't you feel guilty. Henry brought this on his family, not you. The sheriff mentioned they'll try to get him evaluated at the mental health center, too. It was such an odd attack, he thinks something might be going on in Henry's brain."

Ella made eye contact with Jacob through the mirror. "I won't be surprised. He hasn't attacked anyone before, but a lot of folks think he acts weird."

Leah moaned and closed her eyes again. She thought of the odor of alcohol she'd smelled on Henry and wondered if that didn't also contribute to his reckless and frightening violence. Maybe this was a blessing in disguise. Maybe Henry did need mental health help, and now, since this incident, his need was brought out in the open. Still, the almost demonic frenzy of his assault played over and over in Leah's mind. She prayed *Gott* would ease her thinking and give her peace and sleep, once she got home.

41

By the time they reached the house, Leah was nearly in tears trying to hold back the nausea. She couldn't even speak for fear she'd lose whatever was in her stomach if she opened her mouth.

It was such a relief to have Jacob help her out of the car, Sarah hurry ahead to open the door, and Ella help support her with Jacob as they led her down the hall and to the bathroom.

She closed the door on her friends as she rushed to the commode. After emptying her stomach, some of the pain eased, too. But as she leaned over to grab a Kleenex she'd dropped on the floor, the pain came back in a pounding roar. "Oh, Lord! Help me make it to the door and to bed!"

Jacob, hearing her cry, opened the door and hurried to her side. He gently took her arm and led her slowly across the hall to her bedroom. As he helped ease her onto the soft mattress and gently pulled the covers to her chin, she nearly cried again. But this time, out of deep gratefulness for his sweet attitude and care.

Ella poked her head in the door, whispered a quick goodbye, followed by Sarah, who brought Jacob a glass of water and the pain pills the hospital had given Leah. She blew a kiss to Leah and headed to the living room.

"I hate to make you sit up again, Leah, but I think you should take one of these pills so you can get some rest. You need that more than anything."

He helped her sit up, supporting her back as she took the pill and washed it down with the water. Since it left a bitter taste on her tongue, she took another gulp. "Oh, that water *smachs gut*, Jacob. I needed that."

She lay back on her pillow and met his gaze. "I don't know what I'd do without you, Jacob." Her voice came out hoarse and wobbly.

He brought her hand to his lips. "You had me scared, for sure. I don't want you to worry about Henry tonight so I'm going to bunk in the barn. I don't want to leave you and Sarah here alone."

Leah's eyes widened. "Do you think he would come over here? Why don't they just arrest him?"

"Shhh. Everything's going to be fine. I'm pretty sure they'll keep an eye on him and will probably take him as soon as possible."

"Oh, I hope this pill conks me out quickly. I don't want to keep thinking about what he did." Tears shimmered in her eyes and her chin trembled. "It's a terrible feeling to be so afraid of another human being. I pray to *Gott* Henry has never done this to Clara or the children."

"I do, too. But right now, I want you to think about good things, Leah. I'm going to pray for you and then sit here in the rocking chair for a while. In that time, I want you to feel safe enough to be able to fall asleep. I won't leave for the barn until I know you're resting."

Leah's voice slurred as she asked "Who will lock the front door?"

"Sarah is still up and she'll be sure to lock the door. Now close your eyes and just relax." He bent low to plant a soft kiss on her lips. "Goodnight."

"Goodnigh—". And she slipped into sleep.

Filtered sun fell over her closed eyes as her dreams faded and she woke the next morning. She remembered right away what had happened, immediately scanning her bedroom for Jacob. And there he was, his chin propped on his fist, asleep in the rocking chair. She blinked. As she slowly raised her head off the pillow, she realized the pain was significantly less and had left her wounded area with a dull ache instead of the pounding, nauseating pain of last night.

She wondered how long he'd been in the chair. She dimly recalled him telling her he was sleeping in the barn overnight, so did he? Reluctant to wake him, she sank back into the bed and snuggled under her covers. It felt good to rest here, knowing Jacob was mere feet away. She dozed a while, and when she woke again, the room was empty.

This time, she tested her ability to sit up and then put her feet on the floor. So far, so good. Her head was sore, but there was no dizziness or nausea.

She wriggled into her slippers and stood, resting her hand against the wall as she steadied herself and headed toward the door. In the hallway, she smelled toast and heard the low murmur of voices in the kitchen. How sweet it was to know she was not alone. How sweet to know two dear people were waiting for her—caring for her—and praying for her.

"I'm so blessed!" she whispered. She peaked around the doorframe, letting a smile grow as she watched Sarah and Jacob conversing at the table. It warmed her soul to see them there.

Jacob saw her first since he was facing the door. "Leah! Are you all right?"

He moved swiftly to her side and led her to a chair at the table across from him. "Here, sit down."

She eased onto the chair and looked to Sarah. "That toast smells like Heaven on earth. I'm actually starving this morning."

Sarah jumped up and hurried to the stove. "I saved a couple of pieces for you and kept them warm. Would you like butter, church spread, or jam on your toast?"

Leah considered. "Do you happen to have salted butter out?"

"Sure! How about coffee?"

"I don't think so—my tummy's still a bit wobbly. But maybe some hot tea with honey?"

"Coming right up!"

Leah chuckled. "You know what? I'm as hungry as a wolf. How does the body recover so quickly? I feel myself salivating just thinking of hot tea and toast."

Jacob smiled, relief written on his face. He stretched the tension from his shoulders as he shook his head. "I don't know, but I'm sure glad you feel much better this morning."

Sarah brought the tea and toast, along with the honey jar, and placed them in front of Leah.

"Yum! Thank you, Sarah!" She proceeded to slather the warm toast with the salted butter and waved a stream of honey into the steaming cup of tea. After a first satisfying crunch into the bread, she focused her eyes on Jacob. "So did you really sleep in the barn last night?"

His brows flexed into a V. "Of course I did. Where do you think I slept?"

She giggled. "Well, I woke up an hour or so ago and you were still in the rocking chair."

Sarah snorted. "He woke me up at the crack of dawn. Made me let him in, so he could sneak into your room. I bet he got all of three hours of sleep in that barn."

Jacob's sheepish smile confirmed Sarah's story. "The barn felt too far away from the house, is all."

Leah laughed and reached across the table to pat his folded hands. "It's okay. That makes me love you all the more."

After breakfast, the sheriff stopped by to let them know Henry was arrested for assault last night. "He'll be in jail a day or two, or until he posts bail. It's a first offense, simple assault charge, so he won't be held in custody until he goes to court."

Leah frowned. "It was frightening, what he did to me, but I feel so bad that Clara will have to suffer, too, because of this charge."

Jacob spoke up. "What about a hearing to see if he has mental health issues?"

The sheriff shifted on his feet. "I think the assistant prosecutor is looking into that. They may make that part of his deal to get out. He'll most likely be required to be evaluated."

Leah nodded, her large brown eyes wide with concern. "Do you think I should just drop the charges, if he gets an evaluation, I mean?"

Sheriff Thomas shrugged. "I think he needs that charge hanging over his head—it will make him think twice before he does that again, I hope. By the way how are you feeling?"

"I'm much better today. I'll be fine. I'm worried about Henry's family, though." She chewed her lip.

"Children's services is supposed to stop by today to check on the family."

Leah gasped. "Oh, no! Will this get Clara in trouble?"

"Not likely. Unless they find something to worry about, it's just part of the process when children are involved. They'll want to be sure his family is safe from harm before he'll go home."

Leah sighed. "It's so sad that Henry seems to have something going on with him, but I hope this will lead to his getting help."

After the sheriff left, Jacob sat with Leah a while before he had to go home to get ready to go to work. It was hard to see him leave, but Leah knew things would be okay as long as Henry was still at the jail.

# CHAPTER EIGHT

A few days after the attack, Leah was left with a bump on the back of her head, a slight headache, and a heart that was filled with confusion and sadness. Henry Coblentz's lawyer asked for a mental health evaluation, which meant he was staying at the hospital for a time until the assessment was completed.

Clara was home with the children. When Leah stopped by to see how she was doing, Clara was reserved and hesitant to ask her in. Leah expressed her sadness about Henry being away, but when Clara didn't respond, she dropped the subject. The children held back when their *maem* was in the room, but when Clara went to the kitchen for sweet mint tea, they ran to Leah. The two older ones skirted the issue with their *daet*, but showed their concern by looking at her wound and asking how she was feeling.

"I'm doing well. Hardly any pain to speak of. How are all of you doing?"

Reuben bent down and picked up a few toys, his avoidance letting her know he wasn't going to talk about what happened. Saloma turned sad eyes to Leah, tears glimmering on her bottom lashes. She tapped Leah's arm softly and whispered, "I'm glad you're okay."

47

Daniel, with his typical five year old curiosity asked where she'd been.

"Uh, well, my head was hurt so I had to go to the hospital."

His blue eyes rounded. "Where *daet* is?"

"In a different part of the hospital, but I was only there one evening."

"Did *daet* get hurt, too?"

Leah paused, touched by his innocent questions.

"Daniel, you have to get a nap," Clara said as she came back into the room. "Scoot on up to your bed."

"*Maem*, do you have cookies on that plate?" Daniel stood on tiptoes to spy out what his *maem* was bringing from the kitchen. "I love cookies, right?" He nodded his own head to indicate the truth of that statement.

Clara's face relaxed and a small smile tugged at her lips. "Okay. One cookie—just one."

She handed the treats to the other children and shooed them off to the upstairs. She offered Leah the refreshments, set down the tray and took a seat in the rocking chair.

Silence was deep as they chewed the cookies, drank sips of tea, and tried to ignore the elephant in the room. The swing of the pendulum clock kept time as the minutes ticked past.

Leah ate the last bite of her cookie. She dusted the crumbs from her fingers, took a big sip of the tea, and cleared her throat.

"I guess we'd better talk about what happened, Clara. All right?"

Clara closed her eyes and nodded. Her voice was barely audible when she finally spoke. "Yes. But I don't have anything to say about why Henry—why he did what he did."

"I don't expect you to know, Clara. I just wanted to tell you that I'm sorry it happened—it has nothing to do with you and the children. And, well, I'm praying *Gott* works it all to your good, in the end."

"*Danke.*" Clara turned her eyes to the window, seemingly entranced by what she saw out there.

Leah sighed inwardly. This was going to be difficult, but she really didn't hold Clara responsible for anything Henry did. It seemed, though, that her friend might be holding Leah accountable for some of the trouble. If only for the children's sakes, Leah wanted more than anything to maintain a friendly relationship with Clara. And, even if Clara wouldn't admit it, Leah was sure the young *maem* needed her friendship as much as Leah did. She tried again.

"I was thinking about coming to see the children once in a while. Do you think that'd be okay?"

Clara started the chair to rocking, one foot, and then the other, lifting and pushing. Finally she met Leah's gaze.

"I guess so, but when Henry's here, you'd best not come or stay if you walk over and find he's home."

"Of course. Whatever's best for you and the children."

Clara smirked. "But not what's good for Henry, eh?"

Leah took a deep breath and let it out slowly. She had to remember that Clara was suffering for her husband's behavior. She could only hope that her friend would be less resentful, once everything settled down.

"I'd best get going. Thank you for the tea and cookies. And please let the children know I'll try to stop by to see them from time to time."

She wanted to hug Clara, but knew that wouldn't be a good idea at the present time. Instead she gave Clara her warmest smile, waved, and headed out the door.

Later that day, Jacob showed up unexpectedly. She was always delighted when she saw him, but to have a happy surprise? It was wonderful!

"Jacob! I'm so glad to see you. Come on in."

He wiped his boots, gave her a quick kiss on the cheek and placed his hat on the rack by the door. "I'm glad you're glad," he teased.

She laughed. His humor and kindness were just the remedy she needed to chase away the doldrums that grew after she'd left the Coblentz home.

"You don't know how much I needed to hear your laughter." She closed the door and led him to the kitchen. "Look who's here, Sarah."

"Hi, Jacob. Care for a cup of coffee and cookies?"

"Coffee and cookies. The *real* reason I keep coming here." He smiled at Leah, pulled out a chair from the table and settled into a seat.

Leah laughed. "Now the truth comes out."

Sarah brought the snack and coffee to the kitchen table.

Leah sat across from Jacob while he told of the work he'd done that day on the farm. "I got some of the field plowed where I'm going to plant timothy for a late summer crop. The corn is coming along well and we've had just enough sun and rain to get the soy beans sprouting up, too."

Sarah smiled. "Sounds like the animals will be well-fed this winter. Will the corn be knee-high by the fourth of July?"

Jacob tapped the table top in luck. "I hope so! I wondered, Sarah, if you'd like to go over with me and Leah this afternoon to see our future home."

"I'd love to, but I don't want to interfere with your time together. I know you get very little of it."

Leah clapped her hands. "That'll be fun! And you won't interfere—not you, Sarah. Never."

The older lady smiled and jumped up. "Let me get myself together and we'll be off."

Leah reached across the table and grabbed Jacob's hand. "You're sweet to ask her. I can't wait for her to see the house, and I'd really like the extra company today, too. Sarah's so much fun to be with and she's very encouraging. I've been blessed to live here with her."

Jacob squeezed her hand. "I know you planned to see Clara today. How did that go?"

"It went well with the children, but Clara was a little distant with me. I think she's afraid I'm going to blame her for what Henry did. And she's also feeling some guilt, in turn. But what I'm most concerned about is what will happen to them once Henry's out of the hospital."

Jacob nodded. "Me, too. I'm hoping they'll have a report finished soon that will keep him confined, somewhere, until he can get treatment. I'm convinced he has mental health issues."

"Me, too."

Sarah bustled into the room just then. Jacob and Leah stood as she hurried to get her bonnet and sweater on. Leah followed behind her.

As she glanced out the door, bright sunshine and blue skies met her scrutiny. A glorious early summer day—just what she needed to lift the burden of all that had happened in the past week.

Bingo saw them coming and started pawing and stomping the drive. He was anxious to be moving along, just as much as they were. Leah ran to him and smoothed his sweet brown coat.

"You good boy, you! So patient. When we get to the farm, I'm going to hunt you up an apple. Or a carrot. Or whatever Jacob has there that's a yummy treat for you."

Jacob climbed into the buggy and helped Leah and Sarah climb up, too. "Bingo gets a lot of snacks, but I guess I can let you spoil him one more time today."

He snapped the reins above Bingo's shoulders and they were off along the drive, Jacob allowing the horse a little haste in his pace while they were safe in the driveway.

Once they got to the end of the lane, he slowed the horse to a stop. Automatically, all passengers turned their heads together, first one way, and then the other, as they watched for signs of vehicles on the road.

It was a calm day on the highway so Jacob turned Bingo to the left and they were off to see the farm. The clopping of the horses' hooves created a brisk rhythm against the paved motorway. Leah and Sarah kept up a chatter about the neighbor's gardens, and who was growing celery in anticipation of a fall wedding, and who was seeing whom at the singings. Leah was thoroughly enjoying the beautiful day and her time with her two best friends.

The sun was glaring in their eyes as they headed west, so much so that Jacob kept his hand raised to his brows to shade his vision.

Before they knew what had happened, Leah heard the blast of a car's horn, the screech of tires, then the force of a mighty crash.

The next thing she knew, the buggy was going over on its side, Sarah was tilting wildly with it, Bingo was squealing, and Jacob was flying past her like gravity no longer existed.

Leah felt her stomach hit the paved road so hard, the breath was knocked out of her lungs. She struggled to sit up, but she couldn't think straight for the urgency to take a breath.

It was like her body had hit a wall and absolutely no air was being brought into her throat. She fought the space around her, clawing and willing some little bit of oxygen to give her breath. Time stood still as she suffered through the deprivation of air that sustains life. The last sound her ears carried to her brain was of Jacob shrieking her name.

## CHAPTER NINE

Her little brother Benny soared through the air on his tree swing, his feet pumping against space as he surged for more height. "Leah, look! I'm flying! I think if I pump harder, I'll be able to touch the clouds!"

Leah doubled over as she laughed at his antics. He sure had a lot of energy! She was so happy to be with him again. It had been a long time. Hadn't it? Why had it taken her so long to see him?

She glanced back toward the house and waved as her mom carried the laundry to the clothesline. "*Maem*! Hello! I'm so glad to see you!"

*Maem* waved back and set the laundry basket down on the sidewalk. She shaded her eyes against the sun and her smile faded.

"Leah? Leah! Where are you?"

Leah turned back toward her brother just in time to see the ropes break and the swing go soaring through the air, tossing Benny into a loop that ended with a loud crack as he hit the ground.

"Bennnnnny!" Leah screamed his name, but she wasn't able to run. Her legs were tangled in the weeds and something kept her from getting loose. "Bennnnny! She screamed again, so loudly and so forcefully, her throat shut tight, and she was no longer capable of making a sound.

Tears poured down her cheeks and onto her neck. She ached all over—her heart, her head, her arms and legs—everything throbbed from the effort it took to try to move.

"Leah!" *Maem* cried. "Leah!"

Leah turned back to where *Maem* had been standing. *Maem* was running to her, but the closer she came, the less sound Leah heard. By the time *Maem* was standing beside her, she was whispering.

"Leah …"

Leah strained to hear *Maem*'s voice but the harder she tried, the fuzzier everything became. She saw Benny's crumpled body on the ground and shut her eyes tight. "Oh, Benny!" she sobbed. He throat ached from the wracking cries for sweet Benny.

When she dared to open her eyes again, *Maem*'s face was nearly touching her nose. She was stroking Leah's face, whispering her name. Leah shook her head, moaning from the ache that covered her body. She felt like her heart was breaking in two, the sadness for her little brother was so deep. "Leah … Leah" *Maem* said over and over again.

Leah was surprised to find her eyes were shut, when she didn't even know she'd closed them.

Finally, with great effort, she pulled them open once again. Dim lights danced in a whirling haze behind *Maem*'s face. She was no longer outside the house—no longer by Benny's swing. Her blurry gaze darted around, realizing Benny wasn't to be found. She was actually inside a room.

She refocused on *Maem*'s face. "*Maem*? Where's Benny? Is he—alive, *Maem*?"

*Maem* drew back, gesturing behind her to someone else who was in the shadows of the room. "She's awake! Jacob, she's awake!"

A stirring in the area behind *Maem* drew Leah's attention. Someone moved forward, took her mother's place and drew closer and closer to Leah. Her vision cleared and she saw Jacob. She burst into tears at the solace to have him near her when her heart was breaking over Benny. "Jacob! Oh, my sweet little Benny!"

Her arms tried to reach for him, but they were tangled. She was confused. Weeds? This high? Inside the house?

She tried to pull the weeds loose, but they were too tight for her shake them away.

Jacob grabbed for both of her hands and held them tight. He kissed her fingers while trying to calm her.

"Leah, you're going to be okay. Hush now. Just rest, okay? Don't bother the lines, Leah. Just let me hold your hands."

She squinted, trying to bring Jacob's face into sharp focus. She stopped struggling. She sighed deep, but the breath going out caused a stinging pain to radiate in her side. Her eyes widened as the pain grew with her ever clearing vision and mind.

"Oh! It hurts! What's hurting me, Jacob?"

He held her hand with his left, and reached forward to caress her face with his right hand.

"Shh, Leah. Your side is hurting because we were in an accident. Do you remember the accident?"

Leah shook her head, confusion and pain causing her heart to gallop again. The sound of its pounding grew louder and louder in her ears. A shrill beeper came to life somewhere in the room, and Leah lurched to sit up. An alarm! What was going on?

As the chaos grew in her brain, she felt herself getting hot—too warm! She struggled to throw off the covers as she realized she was in a bed. It wasn't weeds or grass holding her down, it was blankets. She was lying in a bed, in a semi-dark room. Where?

*Maem's* voice cut through the muddle of noise. "Leah! No—sit still!"

She saw her then, coming quickly to the bedside, her face tense with fear. "Leah! *Schtobb!* Calm down."

Leah stopped trying to move. She willed her heart to slow its frenetic beating. She lowered her head to the pillow, keeping her eyes on Jacob. "Wha—what's happened to me?"

Jacob smoothed her hair and turned to her *Maem*. "You'd better tell the nurse that she's awake. They may have to give her something for the pain."

Leah's *maem* hurried from the room. Jacob leaned closer to her.

"We had an accident two days ago. Remember that we were heading to our farm with Sarah? Sarah and I were thrown into the ditch where the ditch was soft. We got bumps and bruises, but you fell onto the road. You re-injured your head—from when Henry had hurt you. You also got three broken ribs. But you're going to be all right. And, Leah, I need to tell you that your parents—"

Jacob was interrupted by a nurse, who swiftly came to her side, checking the lines of an IV that was attached to Leah's arm. *Maem* was right behind her.

"Hello, Leah. You've been having a nice, long nap, haven't you?"

The nurse's voice was soothing, causing Leah's anxiety to dissipate.

"My name is Sharon. I'm the nurse on night duty. We've been taking good care of you while you've been sleeping."

She turned to *Maem*. "Ms. Raber, why don't you take a break while I give Leah a quick check? I'll get her freshened up and call you as soon as I'm done."

She turned to Jacob. "Take a minute or two with her, Jacob, and then go along for a break, too. Okay?"

Jacob nodded and came back to stand by her bedside. Leah raised her hand to wave to *Maem*.

"I'll see you soon, Leah," *Maem* responded.

After the nurse hurried off to get supplies, Jacob drew near and softly kissed her cheek. "I was so worried about you."

But Leah was still thinking of what Jacob had tried to tell her before the nurse came in. "What's going on with my parents, Jacob?" She heard her voice's stiff tone and tried to smile. But honestly, the pain and the confusion were making it difficult to think clearly.

He cleared his throat. "They think you should be taken back to Ashfield for rehab. You might need that with the repeated head injury."

Leah tried to sit up but decided it was best not to move. "What? They can't do that, can they? Against my wishes?"

"I don't think so now, but if you hadn't wakened by tomorrow morning, they were making arrangements for that to happen."

"But didn't you tell them I wouldn't want that?" Her tone was strident. She again made an effort to compose herself.

He nodded. "Yes, I did, but I'm not your next of kin—your parents are, so they have, or had, the right to have you moved. But I don't think they can do that now that you're awake."

Leah sighed and felt her chin trembling. What now? It seemed one thing after another was threatening her new life in Holmes County. "Oh, Jacob, I can't go back with them."

He smoothed her hair. "Again, I don't think that's an issue any more. But you should be prepared that they might try to talk you into going home with them. Especially since your *daet* and the bishop—"

"The bishop? Has he been here?" Leah felt tears welling and tried hard to hold them back. "No! I don't want that man in my room!"

As she spilled out the statement, the nurse came in, pausing in the doorway as she tried to decipher the meaning of Leah's raised voice and declaration. "Is everything all right?"

Jacob nodded. "Yes, but I just told her that her parents and the bishop want her to go back with them."

The nurse shrugged, and came quickly to Leah's side.

"Oh, that's nothing to be concerned about, Leah. You're awake and aware, and you have full rights to state what you want."

She prepared to change the IV bags.

"Don't worry about that. And, Jacob, why don't you have a break now? I'll get Leah fixed up in a second or two, and then you can come back in. But I think we'd better wind up the visits tonight in a few minutes, okay? It's past midnight. Leah needs to sleep in order to heal.

This has been a good night—to see her wide awake, but she'll still be dog-tired, I'm sure."

The nurse's matter-of-fact tone brought normalcy to the situation. Leah was relieved. She didn't really want Jacob to leave her at all, though. And she really wanted to say good-bye to *Maem*. She decided she'd think about the rest of everything else tomorrow.

After a few minutes of the nurse bustling back and forth with dressings, Band-Aids, and ointments, she used a warm washcloth to wipe Leah's face, arms, and legs. She patted her dry with a soft towel and then stepped back to look Leah over.

"You feel better, honey?"

Leah nodded, a smile spreading over her face. The nurse's kind care made her feel safe, clean, and warm. She was surprised to find herself relaxed enough to finally sleep.

"Jacob?" Leah mumbled.

"Sure—just let me pop out to get your mom and Jacob. A few minutes only, though."

Jacob and *Maem* were led back into the room, with the nurse gently reminding them the visit had to be short.

"*Maem*, thank you for coming and staying up here while I was, um, sleeping. I'm sure I'm going to be all right now."

She smiled and when *Maem* came closer, Leah reached for her hand.

"I sure do miss you. But I know I'm going to be okay here in Millersburg, and when I get released, I have Sarah at home to look after me." She turned to Jacob. "That is, when Jacob can't be with me."

She turned back to *Maem*. "I'll stay in touch, though, and hope you and *Daet* will come to visit me at home when I get out of here."

Leah felt her *maem* stiffen. She loosed her hand from Leah's. "I see. Well, *Daet* will be back in the morning. You can let him know your plans then."

Leah felt tears coming to the surface again. When she saw *Maem's* disappointed look, she was heartbroken.

"*Maem*, I'm sorry, I really am, but I want to be with Jacob in Holmes County. I don't want to hurt you and *Daet*, but I've made a home here now. I enjoy our new church and the people very much. I'm doing well—"

*Maem* interrupted. "If you call having a man attack you and an accident that could have killed you doing well, then I hope nothing else '*gut*' happens to you! You're in disobedience to your parents, Leah. That's not something you should be proud about." *Maem* turned on her heels and stalked out.

Jacob followed her with his eyes. He shook his head. "I don't understand your parents, I'm afraid, Leah. Mine have been very supportive."

He moved over to stand near her bed. "I'm going to go now, too. I think you should forget about all that and just try to sleep. I promise to be right here when you wake up in the morning."

"But Jacob, how are you getting off work?"

He laughed. "You should know Bert Small is glad to have me off the line. The boss was okay with me being here—especially while you were in a coma. I'll call him tomorrow to update him on your condition. I think he'll be okay with me staying through tomorrow. We'll know more of what the *doktahs* think about your condition and go from there."

He bent low and softly kissed her. "You have no idea how happy a man I am tonight. Seeing you awake, I now know you're going to be better. Now rest. Don't fret about anything. I love you, Leah."

"I love you, too. Goodnight."

It was only after Leah had settled in, the nurse had checked on her, the night light was turned on, and Leah was drifting off to sleep, that it suddenly came to her about where Jacob was sleeping. Was he going home? How? Did he have a driver? Who? Was he staying in the hospital?

Before she could decide how to find out the answers to her questions, a dizzying wave of sleep overcame her and she closed her eyes. She'd have to figure that all out tomorrow, too.

# CHAPTER TEN

L eah woke to find her *daet* sitting in the corner of her hospital room. It surprised her that he'd not woken her. When he noticed her eyes were open, he stood, hesitating a little as she continued to watch, but not speak to him. Finally he came to her bedside.

"So, you mean to defy your parents even after *Gott* has sent you a sure message that you're on the wrong path?"

His beard quivered as he spoke, and Leah, who hadn't seen *Daet* in some weeks, was fascinated with her lack of fear of him. How did that happen?

After all she'd endured during her last months at home, she'd expected to dread seeing him while she was convalescing—sure that his powerful voice and unrelenting demand that she obey him would be difficult to defy in her weakened state.

"*Daet*, I'm sorry you've come here hoping I would change my mind. I'm sorry you feel disrespected and angry with me." She spoke quietly, yet firmly. "I want nothing more than to have a renewed relationship with you and *Maem*. But leaving my new life in Holmes County isn't in the best interest of both Jacob and me."

He shook his head. "You're a rebellious child. If you think I'm going to be fooled by your big talk and sure manner, you're sadly mistaken. You were born in the Old Order church and *Gott's* will is for you to stay there." His eyes held genuine sadness. For a moment, Leah struggled not to give in.

She sighed, breaking eye contact with him. "I know you fear for my soul, *Daet*, and that fear causes you to try to force me home, but I don't believe that way anymore. I don't believe *Gott* has plans for my life that will hurt me." She turned back to *Daet* and attempted to take his trembling hand in hers. He pulled away and walked to the door.

"I won't have any part in supporting your rebellion. If you refuse to heed my warnings, I have no choice but to turn you over to Satan." He met her gaze and held it a second longer.

"*Daet—*"

Before she finished her sentence, he was gone. Was this the end of their relationship forever?

◈

Leah settled in at home a few days later. She was still sore when she tried to take a deep breath because of the broken ribs, but the therapist at the hospital warned her not to breathe in shallow gasps to avoid pain. It was necessary to continue to take deep breaths so her lungs wouldn't be susceptible to pneumonia. Still, it was difficult to ignore the sharp ache when she followed through on the therapy.

The latest scans on her head showed a small fracture, which had caused a bleed that put pressure on her brain. That's why she'd been in a coma, but it was healing and she would be fine. Nothing special to do for that injury except let it heal.

"Let me help you into bed," Sarah insisted. Leah allowed her housemate to aid her, for now, but she knew soon she'd need to push herself to get out of bed and get back to living. Jacob had returned to work on second shift, Bingo was recovering at home, as well, and most of life for everyone was resuming.

61

The driver who hit them was cited for the collision, but the woman driving was blinded by the late afternoon sun, so essentially, the accident was just that: an accident.

The middle-aged lady had visited Leah while she was still in the hospital. Her anxious face told Leah all she needed to know. She was terribly sorry and worried about them. Her insurance would cover the accident, so Jacob had filled out the proper forms.

In the meantime, one of the church members was helping out with a buggy for Jacob to use, once Bingo was well enough. Thankfully, since the crashed buggy broke free from the horse, his injuries were minimal.

Leah sighed—even though she was injured, it could have been so much worse. The slow speed the driver was going minimized the effects of the crash.

"Tell me again, Sarah, what the sheriff said about Henry."

Sarah tucked the sheet blanket under Leah's feet and pulled the rocking chair close. She lowered herself in it with a grunt and then started the rocking motion with her feet. "He said Henry was in jail a week. They filed a charge against him, but I don't know what it was. He's out now, waiting for a trial or he has to go before the judge or something like that."

Leah frowned. "He's back with his family?"

Sarah nodded. "Yes, I think the bishop went to court with him— not sure about that, though. Or maybe he plans to go with him."

"I hope he's learned his lesson. I hope his family won't have to be hurt before something's done with him. He was either drunk, or something went wrong in his mind, the way he acted that night."

"Uh-huh. I'm praying he's got it out of his system now, at least."

Leah wasn't so sure, but she didn't say anything else about it. When the church stepped in, local authorities sometimes backed away. If Henry was secretly drinking, and that caused him to get violent, would he be able to control his temper around his wife and children?

Staring out the window, Leah watched a robin guard her nest. A squirrel came too close. The angered robin chirruped, dive-bombing the animal until he scampered away.

"Scripture says the Lord has His eye even on the sparrow, Leah, so I trust He's watching out for Clara and the *kinna*, too."

Leah tilted her head, thinking about that. She knew the Bible said it, but there were times when she wondered if He missed some things. Martha being abused ... Henry drinking ... Clara so frail and the children so timid around their father ... well, she wasn't *Gott*, so how could she possibly figure out humankind and all the troubles and trials in this world, let alone the ways of *Gott*.

Long about *suppah* time, Leah threw off the lightweight blanket and tentatively swung her legs over the side of the bed. Time to get up. She just couldn't lie there another minute.

She stood, fighting the urge to suck in and hold her breath. Every movement caused her ribcage to follow and those three broken right ribs protested mightily.

She stood slowly, pulled her right arm close to her body, and eased her way to the door. Once in the hallway, Sarah heard her shuffling along and rushed to her side.

"Hey, you were supposed to call me so I could help you get up."

Leah chuckled. "I know, but I was suddenly tired of being an invalid. I just had to do it myself."

Sarah gripped her around the waist. "Where're we headed? Living room or kitchen?"

"Bathroom, first! I've been putting off going in there and my kidneys hate me right now."

When Leah was ready to move on to the kitchen, Sarah was waiting, right outside the bathroom door. She took hold of Leah's left side and proceeded to guide her down the hall. "I wasn't going to take any chances you'd try to do this again without an escort, so I waited."

"Oh, boy! I'm glad I didn't know that—you might have inhibited me in there."

"Ha! I can bet you're wrong about that, since your bladder was fully in control."

They laughed, causing Leah to wince with the pain.

"Ouch! How rude can three ribs be? Can't even have a laugh without them carrying on."

Once Leah was settled at the kitchen table, she noticed milk, cream, and sugar on the counter. The ice cream churn was nearby, too. "Oooo! Ice cream for dessert tonight?"

Sarah smiled and indicated the pantry where the cocoa was stored. "I was thinking chocolate—how does that sound?"

"Yum! Put lots of cocoa in there—I'm in the mood for dark chocolaty goodness."

Sarah crossed to the pantry and pulled out the cocoa. "I was also thinking about those cherries we have in the freezer. How about adding some of those to the mix?"

"Chocolate and cherries! I'm being spoiled rotten."

Sarah rushed around, getting the cherries, chopping them and making the ice cream mixture just right. Then she added ice and salt to the churn and carried it to the table.

"I'll churn while you read, okay?" She pointed to a new Guideposts Magazine.

Leah smiled. "Sounds perfect."

She read and Sarah churned for several minutes before Sarah checked the ice cream and pronounced it ready. After scooping three scoops into Leah's bowl, she did the same with hers and then put both bowls on a tray. "It's so nice outside tonight, why don't we sit out on the patio and enjoy the dusk?"

"I'm all for that."

Sarah scurried to the screen door, calling to Leah "Don't you move—I'll be right back!"

After they got settled in their chairs, Leah took as big a breath as she could force herself to take and sighed. "Oh, it smells and feels so good out here. And this ice cream is heavenly."

Sarah smiled. "I'm happy to have you back home. I really missed you while you were in the hospital."

"I missed you, too. This house has really become my home, Sarah, and you're responsible for making it feel that way."

"Now, let's not get mushy." But her friend blinked away a tear.

Leah let her eyes drink in the wonderful colors spread all over the yard. Along the edges of the veggie patch, marigolds threw out warning scents of spice and pepper to insects with plans to invade the garden. Here and there, peonies bloomed, releasing their own woodsy floral aromas. A patch of irises was just beginning to bloom and their heady sweet fragrance drifted by when the wind puffed through the trees. Everything was new, extra green, and fresh.

She loved June gardens because of the perfection shown by each blade of grass, tree leaf, and flower petal. The sun and rain were perfect this time of year, nudging the growing things to show off the beauty and flawlessness of the Creator's hand.

"Art, music, and beauty are proof to me that there is a God," she murmured.

"I hadn't thought of that before, but you're right. Why else have art, beauty, and music for any other reason except a Creator wanted it for us to enjoy?"

"Yes. And this garden, oh, it's filled with His touch!"

"Leah, you're an old soul and I appreciate you."

Leah glanced to her roommate, and smiling, raised her bowl of ice cream. "I appreciate you too, Sarah. Here's to us!"

# CHAPTER ELEVEN

L eah was really missing Jacob. Since she'd been home from the hospital, they'd only seen each other the day of her homecoming. And that day was cut short when he had to rush off to work.

Once he got off work at eleven in the evenings, he headed straight to bed. Then bright and early, hit the fields and the farm.

The planting season was finished, but he had so much more work to handle with the barn, the sheds, and the chicken coop, that he continued to work right up until he had to hurry in, shower, get dressed, and catch the van ride in to the factory.

She moaned and wrapped her arm around her sore rib cage as she reached across the table and marked another X on the calendar.

"Look at that! Five days since I last saw Jacob. I hope, with this being Saturday, he can come over after he gets the farm chores done."

"That second shift job sure cuts into his day." Sarah sipped her coffee.

"It does, but with the farm and all, he has to work that shift. It's not a popular shift for most people, but it works out fine for farmers." She gently stretched as a yawn escaped. "He sent word last night by one of his co-workers who passes by our house that he'd try to come over sometime today."

Sarah shook her head. "Why in the world doesn't he call? That phone over there isn't just for decoration."

A grin creased Leah's face. "He's still got the *Ordnung* from our old church stuck in his head."

Sarah snorted. "Well, he uses that broken-down phone shanty at the end of his neighbor's lane to call in to work, so why not just break down and put in a black box phone?"

"For some reason, calling from outside seems holier to him." They both broke into laughter.

"Oh, dear! The things we Amish do sometimes." Sarah got up and stacked the dishes in the sink. "Ella's coming by this morning to take me to town for groceries. Do you need to add anything to the list?"

Leah thought a minute or two. "How about some crackers—I'm thinking of trying out a new recipe for chicken taco soup."

"Okay—sounds *gut.* Oops! There she is! Hear that horn? I'd better get hopping."

"Are you going alone or with a gaggle of women?"

Sarah paused, pretending to be offended. "Gaggle? Me? Part of a gaggle? Why, of course, I'm going with a gaggle of women! That's the whole fun of it."

She winked and took off, calling back to Leah, "Don't do too much while I'm gone, you hear? See you later."

Leah waved to Sarah, cautiously stood, walked carefully to the sink, and ran water for the dishes. She'd improved a lot in the days since leaving the hospital. In fact, feeling better had given her a case of cabin fever. The sun was shining in their little corner of the world and Holmes County was experiencing early summer. She didn't want to miss any more of it.

She contemplated taking a short walk along the road, but changed her mind thinking she might miss Jacob when he came. But she could ramble about in the front and back yards—maybe feed the birds, perhaps even hang out a few clothes if she didn't load the basket too full.

Once she redded up the kitchen, she made her way to her bedroom, straightened her bed, and put on her shoes. Since Sarah had already washed her clothes, Leah grabbed a basket in the hallway and headed to the back porch, where the wringer washer sat with the rinsed clothes to be hung out, waiting in the rinse tubs. Leah pulled a few damp dresses into the basket and made her way to the clothesline.

She loved hanging out clothes. The sounds of the birds and scent of flowers cheered her. Her dresses always smelled so fresh, too, when she brought them into the house. As she pegged each garment carefully, she listened for Jacob and Bingo to pull into the drive. It was still a bit early, but her heart kept hoping he'd missed her as much she'd missed him, so he'd hurry over as soon as possible.

Time passed into an hour as she returned to the porch a few times to refill her basket, and still Jacob hadn't come.

She glanced to the window of the kitchen where she could see the clock. It was only ten-thirty. Highly unlikely Jacob would get here before noon. Maybe she could kill time by making the chicken taco soup for lunch. But would Sarah be back in time with crackers? Leah smiled to herself as she pegged her socks. Once those ladies were let loose to shop, it usually turned into an all-day event—better not count on having those crackers for lunch.

She nodded her head—ham and cheese sandwiches. That sounded good—and with fresh strawberries they'd picked this past week, it would be a perfect summertime meal.

Just as Leah headed into the house to slice the bread and cheese, she heard the crunch of the gravel driveway. Jacob!

As she rounded the house, she realized she'd heard no horse hooves striking the road ahead of the sound of the stones. She stopped, just shy of the house corner and peeked around it. An unfamiliar car, blue with white stripes along the side, sat in the drive. Inside she could barely make out a male driver. But who was it?

The man seemed to look right at her, but he made no move to get out of the car. She hesitated, but then made her way down the drive. As she neared the auto, the driver's door swung open and out stepped

Bert Small. She was astonished he'd come to her house. What could he want with her?

She stepped back, putting herself closer to the front door of the house. "Hello. Are you looking for Jacob?" She overlapped her arms protectively around her healing ribcage.

The man swaggered forward and then leaned his body against the front fender. He folded his arms and crossed his booted feet as casually as if he'd been to her house a thousand times.

"Nope. Not looking for Jacob."

He spit tobacco onto the white stones. Leah looked away as the brown dribble settled into the cracks.

So awful! Why did some men do that?

She backed further away, half-turning her body toward the door. "Well, I don't think you have any business with me, but Jacob is expected any minute now."

He lifted his head and chortled. "I think I'm making you a little nervous, ain't I?"

She frowned.

"Nope—didn't come to see Jacob, but I do have business with *you.*"

Leah shook her head. Her brows knit together, trying to think of any reason at all that he'd say something like that.

Before she could speak, he pointed to her, his finger jabbing the air. "You need to tell that boyfriend of yours to keep his nose out of my business. *That's* my business with you, lady!"

Her eyes narrowed. "I'm sorry, but I don't tell Jacob what to do with his work life."

He lifted his weight off the car, clomping closer.

"Seems like you have the same problem he does, woman. Trouble knowing who's the boss! I own that boy from two to eleven five days a week. I do what I want, and when I say 'jump', I expect that Amish boy to ask 'how high'! He's just like all of you. You Amish do whatever you want. Nobody takes them down a peg, but this here

69

man will do it! You hear me? I don't put up with no disrespect from you buggy people!"

He pulled his arm back, his ham hand fisted, and raised it in a threat. His face grew redder by the minute as he waited for her response.

Leah swallowed as fear took hold of her. He was menacing. After what she'd been through with Henry, her stomach recoiled at the thought of more violence.

She tried to keep her knees from wobbling and her hands from shaking, but the powerful urge to run inside and lock the door was hard to resist.

She eased back further, shaking her head. "You don't need to get upset. I'll give him your m-m-message."

She hated hearing herself stutter, but there was no way now to stop the feeling of absolute terror that was unwinding in her body. She shook from head to toe.

She stumbled backward over the first step leading to the stoop and caught herself before she fell. But she twisted at the waist, which sent an overwhelming shot of pain through her body from her newly mended ribs. Tears sprang to her eyes as she bent over.

She looked up from under her *kapp* when she heard Bingo's hooves ringing against the pavement. In a flash, Jacob called her name and the buggy raced into the drive.

Jacob was by her side in an instant. "Leah! Are you okay?"

He slipped his arms around her and helped her to sit down on the stoop.

"I hurt my ribs, I think," she moaned.

Jacob continued to hold her tight, but whipped his body around to face Bert.

"What do you think you're doing here! Get out of here right now before I call the sheriff!"

His voice was taut with anger. Leah glanced at his face, never having heard that tone from Jacob before. He was seething!

Bert Small took a step back before his bravado kicked in again.

"You don't tell me what to do! Nowhere! No time!"

He doubled his fists, coming toward the both of them.

Bert grabbed Jacob by the shoulder, attempting to make him face him, but Jacob jerked away, pulling back toward Leah.

Bert tried and failed to land a hit on Jacob's jaw, but his swing was filled with swagger instead of aim, so he went sailing into a tumble on the grass when he missed.

He jumped up, wiping a bloody nose he'd given himself when he hit the ground and cursed at the top of his lungs.

Leah, terrified, tried to intervene by standing between the two men. Bert's face was filled with rage. He pulled back a fist, taking careful aim at Leah.

Leah screamed in panic.

"No! No! Noooo! Stay away—stay away from me!"

She was sobbing, shuddering and couldn't stop screaming at the top of her lungs, ignoring the pain that radiated from her side with each shriek.

Jacob gripped her shoulders, concern widening his eyes.

The unexpected reaction from Leah halted Bert in his tracks. He frowned, unfisted his hands and turned on his heals as he ran for his car.

He jumped in the driver's seat, yelling out the window as he ground the gears into reverse,

"You've got a crazy lady on your hands, Amish boy!"

His tires threw white stones into the air as he squealed away from the house.

"Leah! Shhh, he's gone now. He's gone." Jacob hugged her close, careful of the ribs that had recently healed.

Leah shuddered and coughed, struggling to gain control of herself. She grabbed at Jacob's shirt as she pressed her face deep into his chest.

"Jacob, I was so afraid!"

Her sobs shook her body, wrenching her inside and out. Finally, Leah took a deep gulp of air, pulled herself out of Jacob's arms and stumbled into the house.

Jacob followed, quietly pulling the screen door shut behind them. She sank into the plush rocker in the corner and held her arms tight around her sore ribs.

"Leah? Are you hurt—did he try to hurt you?" Jacob's gentle voice was the sweetest sound she'd ever heard.

She sniffed, reached for a Kleenex and wiped her nose. After a few hiccups, she straightened as much as possible. Shaking her head tenderly, she tried to find a smile. "You—you are the best man in the whole wide world, Jacob Yoder!"

He sighed. "I'm so relieved to hear you're okay."

He crossed the room and pulled a chair close to her as he reached for her hands, warming them soothingly between his calloused palms. "I'm so sorry! I have no idea why that man came here."

"He—he—told me to tell you that he's in charge of you," she replied between sniffles. "He said he owns you from two to eleven, five days a week."

"What? Why, that's just crazy. Why would he think something like that?" Jacob frowned, his brows puckered as he shook his head.

Leah inhaled before speaking. "He said you should stay out of his business, too."

"I don't know what he's talking about. I just—I just go to work. I try to do my job. I don't interfere with him at all."

Leah pulled her hands free and circled them around his shoulders. "I know you, Jacob. You're a peacemaker not a troublemaker. This man is a hot head and a bully. That's the only thing I can come up with to explain his outburst."

Jacob pulled her gently to her feet. "I can't understand Bert Small, but I'm not going to let him spoil our time together. First, I want you to check your wounds. Are they worse?"

She felt her tender side, inching her fingers softly through the valley of her ribs. She winced when she hit rib number three, but it wasn't any worse than before, she didn't think. "I think I'm okay."

She walked stiffly toward the kitchen. "I'm so thirsty, though. I need a drink of cold water. And you're right—I'm not going to let Bert Small ruin this day, either."

Jacob, anticipating her next move, swiftly reached the counter ahead of her and pulled open the cabinet door. He chose two glasses and turned on the kitchen tap. After filling her glass with water, he handed it to her and filled his.

He led her to the table and helped her ease into a chair.

Leah flinched as her body folded, but once she was settled, she tried to pin her hair and straighten her *kapp*.

"I feel like a total mess."

The water tasted good. She was attempting to slow her breathing and heart rate. Her hands were still trembling and knees were like Jell-O, so she took another gulp and let the cool water dribble down her throat. Two more sips and she was feeling in better control of her body.

Jacob's eyes softened, a loving smile creasing his face. "No—you're not a mess. Not at all. I'm glad you're feeling better and I'm happy with you, however you look." He touched her cheek. "I hate that this man scared you so much. It made my stomach churn to see the fear he stirred up."

Leah dropped her eyes, feeling a rush of emotion and warmth flood her cheeks. "I went berserk! What got into me, I'll never know."

"Aw, Leah—you've been through the mill these last few weeks. Don't apologize for something any normal human being would feel."

She cleared her throat. "Okay. But that shrieking banshee that escaped from my body scared even me."

Jacob stroked her cheek. "Listen, what's done is done. Let's start this day over."

She met his gaze with a twinkle in her eyes. "Are you hungry? I am. Let's get something to eat."

# CHAPTER TWELVE

Jacob had Bingo back in the traces, but Leah couldn't help wondering if the horse was stable enough to drive in traffic now. She wouldn't blame him one bit if her were even more gun shy with cars and trucks around him than before. She was certainly more wary.

As they drove toward the farm, *Gott* graced them with a clear road, warm breeze, and blue skies. The lane leading back to the farm was lined with tall, shag-barked hickory trees. To Leah, entering the green tunnel formed by them was magical.

The air grew cooler in the shade and the draping trees framed the white two-story farm house at the end of the drive. Every time she saw the *haus*, her heart sped up. Her future was in that place. Her future with Jacob and their *kinna*.

Jacob dropped her off at the front porch while he drove the buggy back to the barnyard. He wanted to give Bingo a break from the gear since they planned to stay for a while. She watched as he tenderly untethered the horse from the lines and leads before guiding Bingo inside for a drink and some oats.

She turned then, drinking in the peace and simple beauty of the front porch, knowing this was soon to be her home, too.

Leah's dress and apron swished against her knees as she scampered up the steps to the front door. As she pushed it open, the squeal of the hinges on the screen door was a familiar and comforting sound.

Inside, the living room spread out from east to west in a large square. The kitchen was given its space tucked behind two oak pillars. There were no walls between the two rooms so it would be easier to clear out the furniture and create space for benches for church and other large gatherings.

Jacob had moved in a settee, the only upholstered seat in the room, two rockers, and a footstool in front of a wood burner. The floors were golden oak, with a small round blue braided rug in front of each rocking chair, and a matching oval-shaped rug in front of the settee.

Oil lamps were perched on simple circular oak tables beside each rocker, and a plain propane powered floor lamp provided reading light at the settee. Gas lines ran along the ceilings with modest brass lamps connected a few inches below. At the windows, hung neatly pressed blue curtains.

On the walls were spaced a few plaques with verses or Amish proverbs.

Jacob had bought the lot of the furnishings at an auction. While she was grateful they had this much to begin their married life, a part of her longed to add her own touches to the stark décor.

For the kitchen, Jacob had plans to replace the old wood cook stove with a propane powered stove and oven combination. He told her he'd saved almost enough to order the stove soon. He'd already found a propane powered refrigerator at a house sale.

Leah took off her bonnet and laid it neatly on the square oak breakfast table that sat in the corner by the window. She adjusted her *kapp* back into place and pushed a few escaped tendrils behind the snow white covering.

She was glad to have such a modern kitchen and even more happy to have some shelves and actual cupboards, too. Jacob planned to build a pull-out pantry into one of the tall floor-to-ceiling units.

Nothing would be fancy, but it would be convenient and easy to keep clean.

Today she planned to go through the house with Jacob, making a list of items that each room needed, plus noting where repairs would have to be made. Though the house was older, it had been kept in fairly good condition by an Amish family who had lived on the farm through three generations. Once the grandparents had died, the family decided they wanted to move to Kansas in order to be closer to the wife's family.

Jacob was blessed to be able to get a loan for the house. He had a plan to pay the money back as quickly as possible. He needed his factory job in order to do that. Leah whispered a prayer that God could keep Bert Small from ruining Jacob's chances to continue at the factory.

Leah peeked into the fridge to see what she could find for their *suppah* that evening. Trail bologna, Swiss cheese, apples, butter, and milk were the sparse foods chilling on the shelves inside. On the windowsill sat three plump tomatoes, their red skins enticing her to pick them up. They felt heavy and smelled spicy and ripe.

So it would be fried bologna, wedges of cheese, fried apples, and fresh sliced tomatoes.

Cold milk would be a nice change from water and she'd be sure to use the few plates and glassware that sat on the shelves. The last few times she'd been here, she'd used paper plates and disposable cups and silverware since Jacob hadn't bought glassware or pottery plates yet.

Leah puttered about the house, cautiously and slowly sweeping floors and cleaning windows, wiping up the bathtub and bathroom fixtures; generally getting a feel for how it would be when she and Jacob were finally married.

She stopped a few times to rest and give her muscles a chance to unwind. Her ribs were still tender, but they didn't hurt nearly as much when she bent or stooped. That was encouraging.

Jacob told her later that he'd been busy with the two milk cows in the barn. One had been ornery and kicked all the straw from her stall.

Then he needed to feed the chickens and mend a hole in the chicken run.

As they sat down to *suppah* about six that evening, Leah was deeply content. It had been a quiet day. One in which they'd not had the opportunity to spend much time together, after all. But she was happy and felt a good kind of tired.

"This is great, Leah. How'd you manage to pull together a meal out of what was in that fridge?"

She smiled. "Well, it was all that was in there so I had no choice. Time for you to hit the grocery soon, I'm thinking."

Jacob winked. "I was hoping someone would do that for me this week. I hear Ella loves to take ladies shopping."

"Ha! I try to stay out of gaggles of women, you know." She forked the sweet tomatoes into her mouth and chewed. They tasted like pure summer.

Jacob put down his fork and grinned. "Really, though, if I gave you the money, could you write a list and have Ella take you? Are you up for that?"

She nodded. "Sure. Are you stretched for time this week?"

He swallowed. "Yes, I'm taking some extra overtime. It's one of the few times my co-worker decided to by-pass overtime, so when it was offered to me, I snapped it up." He took a long drink of the icy milk.

"You mean, Bert actually offered you overtime? That shocks me."

Jacob put down his fork and pushed his empty plate away. He patted his stomach. "Boy, that sure hit the spot! I haven't been this full since the last time you made *suppah*."

He reached across the table and patted her hand. "Thank you. But back to Bert. No, he was off a couple of days last week, so he didn't get the chance to overlook my request. The assistant gave it to me."

Leah finished eating and stood to carry their plates to the sink. She turned on the water and proceeded to wash. Jacob picked up the glasses and added them to the hot dishwater. Leah paused, turning a surprised look to Jacob. "Bert missed a couple of days of work last week? Why?"

Jacob nodded. "He wasn't there, is all I know. I wasn't going to ask a question, that's for sure."

Jacob pulled out a clean dish towel and helped her dry the *suppah* dishes. He stacked the plates and glasses carefully back in place. Once everything was spic and span, they wandered out to the porch, settling on the top step, side by side. The warmth from Jacob being so near gave Leah a safe, loved feeling. She leaned her head against his shoulder and rested there.

Jacob put an arm around her, gently remembering not to press her too close to protect her sore ribs.

"This is nice, Jacob. And just think—it won't be long before we'll be doing this as an old married couple."

He chuckled. "I know. But first, we have to get married." He dropped his arm and tenderly turned her to face him. "I was thinking we should do that as soon as possible in September."

She nodded. "I'm all for that. We need to see the bishop and join the church ... and what will we do about preparing for the wedding? Will your family help? I'm not sure mine will. Plus, I don't know many folks in this community yet."

He pulled her close once again.

"Yes, we'll have to figure all that out soon. Summer will pass quickly. But for now, let's enjoy our time together a few more minutes before we start back to your place. I don't want Bingo to be spooked by anything on the road so, even though I don't want the day to end, we'll have to go before it gets dark."

They sat close, listening to the birds, the frogs, and the insects. Summer was marching into its element with increased heat, higher humidity, colorful flowers, and intense fragrances. The farm was coming back to life in full measure, too, and for Leah, her new life in this place was growing ever more real. She could envision a future with Jacob, and endure the sorrows they'd be handed, if they were together. And with *Gott* by their sides, she knew everything would work out. Somehow.

# CHAPTER THIRTEEN

June passed into July and summer was rolling quickly by. July fourth celebrations kept Leah, Sarah, and Jacob busy. But the decision to marry at the end of September pushed Leah and Jacob's schedules to the maximum.

The couple had been taking membership sessions with Bishop Miller since the end of May, which meant they would become church members at the end of August. That would give them four weeks to finish their wedding plans.

"It shouldn't be too hard to get it all together," Leah explained. "We don't really have anyone but church friends to invite. Jacob's family will come and my friend Martha from Ashfield County will come. I plan to send an invitation to my family, but I don't think they will come at all."

"Hmm," Sarah was adding folks' names to a list. "I think we should be prepared to serve about two-hundred people then."

"Two-hundred? That many?"

"Well, with all the families in the church, Jacob's family—I'm guessing about thirty or so—maybe more if he has cousins, etc. to invite—and your friend, who will probably want to bring someone along with her, I'm pretty sure we'll be close to that number."

"Yes, I guess it's better to have too much food than too little."

"Right." Sarah pulled out a bakery book with photos of cakes in it. "Do you know what colors and what kind of cake you'd like?"

"I haven't thought about it much. I think Jacob likes chocolate. Maybe we can have a lavender and white color scheme. What do you think?"

"That's a pretty color. Do you know where you plan to have the *hochzich*?" Sarah made some notes as Leah spoke.

"Bishop Miller said there's a hall we can rent that a few brides have used. Since we're not really a typical Amish couple, we have to be prepared for some in the church who will object and not attend."

Sarah nodded. "I can guess who those families will be. They aren't fond of Bishop Miller—they think he's too high church."

Leah grimaced. "I feel bad for Jacob. It's not his fault we had to leave Ashfield and it's not his fault that my family isn't going to co-operate. Or that some will be judging us even here."

"Well, we'll do our best to give you both a wonderful wedding. And don't fret over Jacob. He's getting *you*, and for him, nothing else could matter."

❧ 🏠 ❦

At church that week, Leah discovered what some families thought they should do instead of having a traditional wedding, once it had leaked that Jacob and Leah were planning to marry.

She was outside with a sweet young lady, Anna Hershberger, just four years into marriage and another *bobli* on the way to join their angelic little girl. They were chatting about her garden, when Leah overheard three women talking nearby.

She recognized they were *schvetzing* about her and Jacob when she overheard Barbara Mast, the wife of preacher Melvin Mast, telling Elizabeth Miller and Hannah Yoder that "it was a shame the new couple was allowed to marry as members in good standing when they had no family in the area."

81

"After all," Barbara had added, "who can the bishop talk to in the church in order to know what kind of good Christians they are?"

"Yes, I wish they could just get married by a justice of the peace," intoned Hannah Yoder. "That's what English people do." She snorted.

Elizabeth covered her mouth with one hand as she offered her opinion about that idea. "Oh, we don't know if they've had reason to be ashamed of their behavior. Isn't that usually what the English do when they have no choice--for those who have been, well, too intimate? I mean, they *will* be church members, after all."

Barbara Mast glanced her way and moved her group of friends toward the back porch when she realized Leah was standing close.

Leah's emotions were raw as she thought about over-hearing the talk. It reminded her of what had happened in Ashfield at her brother's wedding when gossip was going around about Leah and her friend Martha—her friend's rebellion and Leah's questioning had made the church members quite upset.

Leah's faced grew warm and she was sure her embarrassment was noticed when Anna patted her on the arm after the older women had moved.

She leaned closer to Leah and whispered, "You and Jacob are welcome to use our place for the wedding. Liam put in a nice concrete floor just for these types of occasions."

"That would be so kind of you, Anna. I'll certainly talk it over with Jacob. We've been trying our best to figure out where to host our wedding. Jacob's farm is really not ready yet."

"I'm sure we can work it all out. Don't you fret. By the way, I'll be canning cherries this week, and I'd love to have your company and your help, if you'd like to come over."

Leah was thrilled to find the possibility of making a new friend in the church and was even happier to learn the Hershberger place was a couple of miles down the road from her and Sarah's house.

After Leah mentioned the invitation to Sarah, she said she knew where it was and she could hitch up the horse, Daisy, to the buggy and drop her off. Sarah rarely used the horse and buggy these days, but she kept both just in case. Sarah usually hired a driver because she wasn't comfortable riding alone as she got older.

After Leah confirmed with Anna the day and time by phone, Anna was delighted to include Sarah in the invitation, too.

The day for the gathering came. Both ladies were excited to be helping out Anna.

As they approached the lane where the Hershberger farm was, Sarah slowed Daisy so they could survey the house's beautiful property from the road. Anna certainly had a green thumb, that was evident.

Her garden was pristine and she had planted marigolds in a neat square all around the plot. By her front porch were colorful ornamental cabbages, interspersed with lovely spiked coral bells. Visitors were welcomed by the sparkling white house with hanging baskets of fragrant wave petunias, bright red hummingbird feeders, and a miniature windmill whose whirring blades verified a cooling breeze.

"Oh, how beautiful this place is!" Leah exclaimed.

"It is—Anna had a Ladies Day here a few weeks after she and Liam got married a few summer's back. She's a charming hostess."

Daisy made the corner to the lane with a smooth gait, her small hooves ringing on the chalky concrete drive. Before they could halt the horse, Anna came out on the porch, drying her hands on a kitchen towel.

"*Wie bisht!* I'm so happy to see you both." Her friendly smile lit up her face.

Anna's handsome young husband greeted them with a handshake after he helped them from the buggy.

"Hello—I'm Liam. I'm heading out to the field, but let me take care of your horse first. I have a paddock right there where she can get out of the sun and have some grass, too, while you visit."

Sarah returned Liam's firm shake with one of her own. "*Danke*, Liam. Daisy will enjoy that."

Anna led her guests through the immaculate beige and white living room to the kitchen. It was long and shining clean, accented with apple themed cushion pads and decor. She had modern propane powered appliances and she'd set up the oak table with a cherry pitter attached to one end, under which gleamed a huge stainless steel bowl to catch the pitted cherries. On the floor by the sink sat a basket filled with red ripe, juicy cherries.

"I have a pot of coffee ready and a plate of Danish if you'd like to have a little something to tide you over until lunch break."

"Oh, that would be nice, Anna."

Leah and Sarah removed their bonnets, handing the hats to Anna who placed the black caps on a wrought iron set of hooks by the back door. Then she invited her helpers to have a seat at the table, where she'd set sweet delicate plates with cups and saucers which were hand painted with matching purple violets and butterflies trim.

She poured them each coffee and placed a fresh from the oven plate of apricot Danish on the table.

"Such a wonderful looking treat. It makes my mouth water," Leah declared. "Smells delicious."

The women nibbled the pastry and shared recipes, laughed about kitchen disasters, and told of home remedies they'd tried over the years. And then they set to the task of washing, draining, and pitting the cherries.

As they worked together, they chatted about Leah's wedding ideas, sharing interesting tidbits from weddings they'd attended in the past.

The day passed swiftly. At noon they'd taken a break to have delicate chicken salad sandwiches, fruit salad, and mint tea. Then it was back to a fun day of work and chat.

Once the last of the cherries were processed, Leah and Sarah helped clean up the kitchen before joining Liam in the barnyard. He called Daisy to the gate and got the rig ready for the road. Anna waved them off, standing on her porch until her friends were out of sight.

When they got home, Leah and Sarah took a much needed rest.

"What a wonderful couple, Sarah." Leah fanned herself with a newspaper she picked up off the lampstand. "So kind. And Anna sure can bake and cook."

"Oh my, yes. I don't think I'll need to eat much of a *suppah* tonight. We can wash these cherries Anna gave us and pop some popcorn later."

"That sounds good to me." Leah yawned. "I'm a bit sleepy now, too. I don't dare lie down, though. I might end up napping all evening."

Both women rocked gently in their chairs for a minute or two, drinking in the peace and quiet. Sarah yawned, too.

"*Ja*, a nap would be tempting." She spied the mail in a pile on the table. She'd gotten it out of the mail box just before they left for Anna's house. "Oh, I'd better sort through that pile."

She retrieved the stack and handed a letter to Leah. "From Ashfield, Leah."

"Really? Hmm ... I don't recognize the address." She loosened the flap of the envelope and pulled out a short letter. "It's from my friend, Martha! She wants to come and visit with me soon. Goodness! I haven't heard from her in a while."

Sarah put down her mail and resumed her comfy seat. "Is she the one you said went back to the Amish—she has the little boy?"

Leah nodded. "Poor Martha. She sure has had a difficult life. Her boyfriend abandoned her and their baby not long after she left our church."

Sarah leaned her head to the back of the rocker and pushed her toes against the floor to put the chair in motion. "That's sad to hear."

"*Ja*, she had a chaotic home life growing up. Really mixed her up."

"I feel for her."

Leah glanced to her housemate's corner. "She was abused."

Sarah stopped rocking. "Was she?"

Leah nodded. "I never felt the church there treated her fairly. Her step-*daet* and her brothers were abusive to her verbally and physically."

Sarah sighed, long and slowly. "It *ferhudles* me why some of our churches turn a blind eye to that mischief."

Leah shook her head. "She was sexually abused, too."

Sarah shut her eyes. "I was, too," she quietly replied.

Leah stopped rocking, her heart breaking for Sarah. "Oh, I'm so sorry." Tears sprang to her eyes to learn this unhappy news. Sarah was too tender hearted to be treated that way.

"Well, it was a while ago now, but that was the main reason I was so devastated when my sweetheart was killed. I just couldn't wait to be out of the house and away from Paul."

"Did your fiancé know about the abuse?"

Sarah picked at her fingernails. "I think he did, though I never came right out and told him. He seemed to pick up on it when Paul—my brother—was in the room. You know, abusers tend to be mean to their victims, even when they aren't currently abusing them. It keeps the victims off kilter and in fear of reporting them, so hearing the way I was talked to in my house showed him something wrong was going on."

"I hate that you were abused like that, Sarah! Oh, why does this world have to be so cruel!"

"Yes, well, it was a long time ago, but still, my mind and my heart were forever changed."

The two friends continued their rocking, sharing a silence that was filled with a kind of sadness for abused people the world over. Leah didn't press Sarah any more that night, but she now knew how to pray for her sweet friend.

## CHAPTER FOURTEEN

E arly one morning a few days later, Leah was very surprised to discover Jacob guiding Bingo off the road and into their driveway. It was barely seven! She hurried to the door, sure that this unexpected arrival meant something had happened. She leaned out the door as he got down from the buggy. "Jacob—what's wrong?"

His usual easy manner greeted her, but she sensed something more was under the surface. "I have something I need to use your phone for, if that's okay."

"Of course!" She held the door open for him as he came inside.

He removed his hat, twirling it around and around. "Actually, I have to call the sheriff."

Leah's mouth fell open. "What? Why?"

"I think someone's been breaking into my place. The barn and shed first, over the weekend, and when I got home from work last night, the front door of the house was open."

Leah's eyes rounded in alarm. "Jacob! You didn't tell me!"

He shuffled his feet. "I wasn't really sure about the barn and shed. I mean, things were shifted, so I thought maybe I'd done that myself and just didn't remember doing it. But when I saw the front door, standing wide open, I knew I wouldn't do that. It's part of my routine to lock that door before I go out the back door to work. Every night I do that. I wouldn't forget."

"My, goodness, Jacob! Was anything stolen?"

He shook his head. "Not much to steal, but there was some, um, stuff written on the living room and kitchen walls. It was—not nice, I'll put it that way."

Leah's heart sped up and she placed her hand over her chest, surprised by something like this happening to good-natured Jacob.

"Do you know who could have done it?"

He met her gaze. Suddenly, one name immediately came forward.

She whispered "Was it Bert?"

"That's the same person I thought of, but I don't know for sure. What I do know is he was off work last night and off on Friday night."

"And I saw you on Sunday morning and Sunday afternoon and you didn't say one word to me about the barn or shed, Jacob Yoder."

She had been suspicious that Bert had kept up his vendetta against Jacob, yet he hadn't told her anything after the time Bert confronted them in the front yard. When she'd asked, he'd shrugged and said "Oh, he's Bert being Bert."

Jacob walked to the phone and picked it up. "Like I said, I wasn't sure if I had moved that stuff. And besides, I didn't want to worry you. You've had too much on your plate as it is."

He opened the phone book and got the non-emergency number of the sheriff, punching in the numbers as he scanned it. While he waited for a response, he turned to her. "I can't really say it was Bert though, Leah. I didn't see him do anything."

She snorted, hands on her hips. She had no doubt it was Bert. But what was he playing at? It didn't make sense for him to put himself in trouble with the law just because he didn't like Jacob or Amish people in general.

She sighed as she sat on the settee. Being Amish had its good points, but one thing that bothered Leah was the seemingly two-sided ways English folks saw her people. They either adored them to the point of adulation or hated them fanatically. She spread her hands on her knees. Why couldn't they be seen as just people—like everyone else?

"Hello. This is Jacob Yoder. I need to report a break-in at my farm."

Leah went to the kitchen while Jacob gave details. She opened the fridge and got out juice, eggs, bacon, and butter.

Might as well make them all a good breakfast. She and Sarah were planning to weed the garden this morning and Leah needed to go over her membership lesson before Sunday. But getting to the bottom of this problem came first.

Sarah came down the hall, surprised to hear Jacob's voice in the living room. "What happened? I heard Jacob telling about a break-in."

"Yes, last night at the farm. He's calling the sheriff."

She cracked open the eggs and gently placed them in the pan, got the bacon going, and poured juice into three glasses. "And, it seems whoever did that was also at the farm Saturday night, in the barn and shed."

Sarah stopped in her tracks. "What! Who would do that? Oh. Wait a minute."

Leah turned, pointing the spatula at her friend. "Yeah. *Him.*"

"Really?"

Sarah pulled out a chair at the table and sat down, stifling a huge yawn. "Excuse me—I read too long last night. That's too bad, if it was him. But what do you suppose he was doing?"

Leah placed the glasses on the table, got out the plates and silverware, and set a place for the three of them. She turned back to the stove to tend the cooking food. "Jacob said there were not-so-nice words written on the living room and kitchen walls."

Sarah's eyebrows went up. "What words?"

"He didn't tell me. I have a feeling I don't want to know."

Her housemate cut a generous slice of bread, slathered it with church spread, and took a bite. "That's kind of creepy, eh?" she mumbled.

Leah nodded. "More than kinda creepy."

She heard Jacob hang up the phone and waited for him to come into the kitchen. She pointed him to a seat at the table and placed cups of coffee at each setting. Sarah reached for the sugar as Leah set the creamer on the table.

"What did they say, Jacob?" Leah served the eggs and bacon on a platter and sat down. She sliced bread for Jacob and herself.

Jacob glanced at the breakfast spread before him and smiled. "Wow—I didn't think I'd get a breakfast feast just by using your phone. Thanks!"

Sarah laughed. "Dig in"

Leah, focused on the phone call, urged Jacob again to tell her what was said by the officer.

Jacob took a huge bite of eggs and gulped a swallow of coffee before answering. "They're sending a deputy out to take a look and file a report."

Leah turned to Sarah. "Is it okay if I skip the weeding so I can go with Jacob back to the farm?"

Sarah waved her fork at Leah. "Sure. We wouldn't have gotten the whole patch done, anyway, before I have to go to my doctor's appointment."

"What time's Ella picking you up?"

Sarah glanced at the clock hanging on the wall over the stove. "About ten-thirty."

"Okay. Jacob, what time will the deputy get to the farm?" Leah ate the last of her eggs and bread before washing it down with the tangy juice.

"We should get going. They said about an hour or so."

By the time the two of them stacked their dishes, drank the last of the coffee, and got on the road with Bingo, it was going on a good forty-five minutes since Jacob had called.

"I hope we don't have a lot of traffic this morning." Jacob clicked Bingo into a fast trot.

The farm lay about five miles northwest of Leah and Sarah's place. It was situated off a main road, too, which meant more cars and trucks sped past them than Leah was comfortable with. But they reached their destination safe and sound, something which Leah breathed a prayer of gratitude to God for.

She and Bingo seemed to carry the memory of the accident with them. The horse tended to be even more skittish when vehicles approached him from behind and she could barely contain her gasps anytime she thought a car was too close.

They pulled into the lane leading back to the farm. Jacob led Bingo to the barnyard and stopped the buggy. He helped Leah down and went around to provide Bingo with water and feed before heading with Leah to the house.

"I'm going to leave Bingo hitched since I have to go to work today and need to take you back home before then."

"No telling how long the deputy will be, too," Leah agreed.

Before Jacob opened the door, he paused, facing her with somber eyes. "What's on the walls isn't *gut* to read. So I'm warning you it might be upsetting."

The heavy front door opened with a whoosh, and immediately, Leah could see the graffiti covering the wall in front of them. It was scrawled in bright red paint, barely legible print.

She haltingly read it aloud, substituting the word "blank" for the swear words.

"You dirty blank blank Amish boy! I will bea—no—that says burn. I will burn you out!"

Leah turned frightened eyes to Jacob. "Fire? He's threatening to set fire to the house?"

Jacob nodded. "Seems that way."

She hurried to the kitchen and read a similar profanity-laced threat there.

"Jacob! This is worse than I thought." She whirled to him. "Should you stay here? What if he comes when you're sleeping? When you're not at work? That awful Bert Small!"

He pulled her to him. "Leah, we don't know if it really is Bert who did this. We have to see what the deputy says before we get all worked up."

She wiped tears that had suddenly flooded her eyes and spilled to her cheeks. "But, he's already threatened both of us. You know that! You have to report that today, too."

He patted her shoulder, easing away as he heard the sheriff's car pulling up outside. The deputy who arrived made his way to the porch as Jacob opened the door to meet him. "Hello."

The officer reached out a hand. "Hello. I'm Derek White."

"Pleased to meet you," replied Jacob. "This is Leah Raber."

Leah and the officer exchanged greetings. The deputy asked Jacob to explain what had happened.

As they walked back into the house, the deputy reached for his cell phone and snapped photos of the walls and also made note of what the scribbles said.

After a few minutes looking through the entire downstairs, upstairs, and basement, the men went outside to the barn and shed.

Leah waited on the porch, her arms crossed against the distress the threats were causing.

A shrill screech swung her gaze skyward, where a lone hawk soared on a high wind, its wings stretched to catch the energy propelling it upward.

What must it be like to be that free? Everything in nature looked calm and peaceful from afar, but she knew closer inspection revealed the struggle to exist that each living being suffered. She sighed, her heart and soul weighed down with the constant skirmishes human kind and animal kind wrestled with each day.

Her attention was caught by the voices coming her way.

As the men stopped below her, the deputy asked "Do you have any idea who could be behind this?"

Jacob hesitated, lifting his gaze to meet Leah's. He shoved the toe of his work shoe in the dirt, hesitating in his reply.

Leah was just about to declare Bert's name when he spoke.

"Yes. There's a co-worker at the factory that threatened Leah and me a few weeks ago. His name's Bert Small." Jacob dropped his eyes, reluctant to throw Bert's name into such a dirty deed. "He's also my supervisor on the line."

The deputy paused notetaking. "What did he do last time, and does he do anything to you at work?"

"He drove to Leah's house and was yelling at her—swearing and telling her to pass the message along to me."

The deputy looked to Leah. "Can you recall what he said to you? Was he threatening to make physical contact?"

Leah nodded. "Yes, he balled up his fists when I asked him to leave. He wasn't happy with me. But Jacob pulled into the drive just as Bert came across the grass toward me."

Deputy White returned his focus to Jacob. "Sir, did this co-worker make physical contact with you or Leah?"

Jacob told the officer the details of the encounter with Bert. When he revealed the things Bert said and did at work, Leah's heart sank to learn Jacob had been enduring an increasing amount of hostility, including shoving matches with Bert at work. He had not told her any of it.

She shook her head, fighting anger and tears as she listened.

The deputy was professional and detail oriented, but he offered them both advice to call the sheriff's office, as soon as possible, if they saw Bert Small near or if he made more threats.

"I'll let you know if anything else is needed from you. Have a good day."

As they watched the police officer's car roll out of the lane and pull onto the main road, Leah wrapped her arms around Jacob.

"I hope they do something about Bert. I'm worried he won't stop unless they make him."

"I hope so, too. But I also hope filing this report doesn't make his behavior worse. And I don't want to lose my job—I really need it."

Leah stepped back so she could look Jacob in the eye. "Is that why you didn't tell me about what he was doing to you at work? You were afraid I'd say something to pressure you into reporting him?"

"Maybe. But more than that, I just didn't want you to be worried. I know he can be aggressive, but I still feel I can work with him." Jacob's brows creased. "I really want us to get married soon, Leah, and it takes money to do that."

He pulled her close again. "I'm tired of all we've had to endure to get to this place in time. We're ready to be man and wife, and I don't want anything else to get in the way."

She pressed her ear against his chest, picking up the beating of his heart. The sound was calming and reassuring.

"Me, too, Jacob. It's been a long, long road."

# CHAPTER FIFTEEN

After a restless night, Leah woke Sunday morning to bright sunshine pouring into her room. She sat up, dislodging the membership articles pamphlet she'd been reading.

Jacob and she had met with the bishop and ministers Friday night for the *unterricht*, or teaching meeting. The ministry team took turns reading the eighteen Dordrecht Confession of Faith articles and then asked if Jacob or Leah had any questions. Did they still want to join the church? After assuring the bishop and preachers that they wanted to continue, a little more discussion followed. Then everything was confirmed for this very day.

She stretched her aching muscles and slowly edged to the side of her bed. She and Sarah had spent yesterday morning finishing the weeding of the truck patch. Jacob had picked her up so they could re-paint the walls of the living room and kitchen at the farm.

Both chores gave immediate satisfaction that something had been accomplished, the garden by sporting neat, weed-free rows, and the farm house by displaying fresh, sparkling clean white walls. But the side effect of the physical exertion left her muscles tender and throbbing.

As she crept gingerly to the bathroom, she reminded herself that regular physical exercise and work would keep her body supple and her muscles from aching.

"*Ach*, I have to remember that so I don't feel decrepit the next day after hard work."

She washed her face, brushed her teeth, and pulled her hair back to pin it. Today she and Jacob would be baptized and join the church and she was excited. This was the last step they needed to fulfill before being able to marry.

She hummed as she hurried through breakfast, Sarah watching her with a bemused look on her face.

"This is the day, eh, Leah?"

Leah nodded, munching her last bite and swallowing a sip of coffee. "*Ja.* I'm happy as a clam!"

"I'm sure Bishop Troyer is happy, too. He's one of the kindest people I've ever known. A true man of God."

Leah slowed her eating, pausing to consider Sarah's statement. "I think he is, too. He certainly has something extra—that's for sure."

Sarah carried her dishes to the sink and then unexpectedly approached to give Leah a hug.

"I'm glad you're going to be a member of my church, Leah. You and Jacob will be wonderful church family."

Jacob picked them up and the drive to church, which was being held at preacher Jonas Stutzman's house, was perfect.

Bingo was lively and brave, the temperature was warm, but not too hot, and the late summer morning gave off just a hint of autumn.

Jacob was smiling, his usual calm, collected manner rattled a little by the approaching service, but he seemed excited, too.

Just before he halted the buggy at the side of the Stutzman house, Leah reached for his hand and gave it a squeeze. He turned to face her, his eyes tender as they shared the unspoken anticipation of what this service would mean to their future.

Around eight-thirty, preachers Melvin Mast and Jonas Stutzman, and deacon Andy Troyer, the nephew of bishop Troyer, followed the elderly bishop into the freshly cleaned barn. Outside, the men lined up, the oldest married man first, who led the rest of the married men into the shop. The boys, twelve and under, went with their fathers. After a few minutes, the oldest of the single men lined up and filed into the building.

Like the ages of the men set the order for entering the building, the women then followed the same order with their daughters and babies. The men sat on one side of the barn while the women sat on the other side.

Leah tried to fall into line where she guessed she fit in age. The procession into the building was solemn and sober. There were a few whispers among the teen girls, but their mothers gave them quick enough frowns to halt that behavior. Several women had nodded a greeting to Leah, while the women she'd overheard gossiping about her ignored her.

As she filed in and took her seat, beads of moisture formed at the base of her neck. The longer she sat waiting, the more nervous she grew. Several minutes of silence passed as each member's grave demeanor was held in place. Leah waited uncomfortably, deciding finally that the only thing to do was pray.

She bowed her head, catching a glimpse of her shoes. They were dusty and worn. Leah slid them back under the bench as far as she could. The row of shoes she glimpsed to her right and left varied, but most looked more comfortable than her sturdy black, thick-soled shoes.

She glanced along the line of seated women. Never before had it struck her how precisely identical the women looked in their black and white Sunday outfits.

Not a single stray hair poked from beneath the *kapps*. Not a flaw or *fronzel* marred the white aprons and black skirts. The women's faces were scrubbed clean—she didn't see one bead of sweat on a single brow, even though they had just hustled and bustled, gathering their children together for the march into the building.

She dropped her gaze. Even now, she often still felt like an outsider. She raised her eyes and searched for Sarah, a couple of rows behind her. Sarah caught her eye and gave her an encouraging smile.

Leah glanced to the men's side of the room and spotted Jacob looking back at her. His face was taut with nervousness, but his mouth upturned, just a little as he, too, gave her a nod of reassurance. She smiled back and sat up straighter.

She noticed a few young mothers sitting in a small area divided from the rest of the church. Their infants and toddlers would be given cookies and pretzels to help them pass the time.

She remembered how, as a young teen, it was sheer torture when she observed the young ones eating their treats while her stomach rumbled and growled all the way through the service. She also remembered how, when she was younger, she and her friends would make dolls from their handkerchiefs to pass the time during the long sermons and hymn singing.

Finally, at nine sharp, Deacon Troyer passed out hymnbooks to each man and woman, and the congregation waited for the lead singer to start the songs.

Leah was thankful that in the New Order church the singing was a bit livelier in pace and enthusiasm. But the hymns were still long. While they sang, the deacon and ministers followed the Bishop to another room. There they remained until nearly an hour had passed in singing.

The preachers returned. The first preacher led everyone in prayer, with the congregation kneeling at their place by the benches. After they rose and took their seats again, the deacon read the Scriptures.

The service followed the basic form, except the preachers sermons were about the church patriarchs and the New Testament verses that speak of baptism.

Preacher Mast gave his sermon. He used the sing-song style that tended to put Leah to sleep, so she sat as ramrod straight as possible, trying hard not to blink or let her eyes droop.

His sermon went on for nearly half an hour. Since he spoke his memorized homily in German, the least understood language among the Amish, it was sometimes hard to follow his thoughts. She made a concerted effort to focus on the words, trying to piece out enough German to grasp his narrative.

As soon as he finished talking, Preacher Stutzman stood to deliver his sermon for the morning. He read the scriptures in his timid, unsure manner. After his sermon, he led the congregation in prayer from the German prayer book. The congregation knelt again while following the lead of the second preacher.

Bishop Troyer then stood, and in his engaging and affable way, he told the story of Philip from the book of Acts. He motioned the couple forward and asked them to kneel. Once they complied, he began the baptismal questions.

To each question, Leah and Jacob replied yes.

Then the last question came: "Do you also promise before God and His church that you will support these teachings and regulations with the Lord's help, faithfully attend the services of the church, and help counsel and work in it, and to not forsake it, whether it leads you to life or death?"

Leah struggled with the doubt that she could, indeed, support the church and not forsake it. She remembered the months away from the Amish church, in which she'd given her heart fully to Jesus. A secret part of her still believed the grace of Christ was sufficient for living life as a Christian.

Was she lying when she finally whispered yes?

While she pondered these thoughts, Bishop Troyer asked the congregation to stand and asked Jacob and Leah to kneel again.

Deacon Andy Troyer came forward with a pitcher of water. The bishop cupped his hands on Leah's head and the Deacon poured water into them.

Once, twice, three times, while Bishop Troyer pronounced the baptism. "Upon your Faith which you have confessed before God and many witnesses, you are baptized in the name of the Father, the Son, and the Holy Ghost."

The kindly bishop's wife offered her handshake and a kiss of peace to Leah. And the rite was given to Jacob, with the bishop offering his handshake and kiss of peace to him.

It was finally time to sing the closing song. And just like that, they were now part of the membership.

Leah followed the women out of the building to the kitchen in the back of the house, where they put finishing touches on the lunch, while the men set up tables and chairs in the barn for the church meal.

Once they accomplished that chore, the men went to the barn or stood around in groups to talk.

Sarah came quickly to Leah's side and gave her a handshake and kiss. "You're one of us now! I'm happy to call you my sister in Christ."

The afternoon drew on. More than once, Leah was interrupted in her chat with one member, to be greeted and welcomed by another member. She was starting to believe that this church truly did want her in it. Perhaps she was finally accepted.

Jacob found her and indicated it was time to leave. Sarah joined her as Leah waited by the front porch for Jacob to get the buggy and Bingo hitched for the ride home. It had been an exhausting day.

"Sarah, I'm so glad this day has come! Now we have only a few weeks to wait—"

"And prepare for your wedding!" Sarah interjected.

Leah laughed. "Yes, prepare for my wedding! How happy I am to finally say that."

Sarah pulled her into a little jig of joy just as Jacob brought the buggy to a halt.

"Come on up here, you two. Let's get going before you get us into trouble right away," he teased.

Leah followed Sarah into the buggy, smiling at Jacob's cheerful tone. As they headed to the road, they drew up beside a group of women in the front yard. Leah caught a glimpse of Barbara Mast's face, staring at them as they drove past. Her expression wasn't one of gladness for them and Leah's confidence level plummeted.

*Will we struggle here, too? Will Jacob and I ever truly fit in?*

# CHAPTER SIXTEEN

L eah threw herself into her work and her church. She baked pies
and cakes. She frosted piles of cookies for bake sales and looked
forward to the day when she and Jacob would have a home to offer to
the church for services.

Jacob likewise continued to excel at his job and made a name for
himself with his good friendly manner, except for Bert Small, who had
managed to calm himself during work time.

Leah wondered if being contacted by the sheriff's department had
scared him enough to keep him in line. A part of her worried that
Bert's new attitude was the calm before the storm, but Jacob was
convinced his vendetta was done.

Not everything was perfect, though. There were still women who
held themselves back from Leah's friendship at church, even when
others were coming forward to become new friends.

Anna continued to be a valued friend in the church. Leah had
warmed to Anna's infectious view of life and they were beginning to
form a friendship as couples. Their time together was uplifting, filled
with laughter and the promise of a life-long bond.

It felt good to be able to hurry to her friend's side at services as the
women lined up to enter church. It was wonderful to catch Anna's eye

during the service and hide a smile as the spunky young woman waggled her eyebrows at Leah—just to make her giggle. There was a comradery growing each time they saw each other that filled Leah's heart.

Sometimes the couples met together from time to time after church or in town where a true relationship developed from their honest discussions. Leah discovered a yearning in this couple to know more of Christ and His ways.

One day, after Leah had spent the day with Sarah looking through a book of wedding ideas, she walked to the mail box and brought the mail back to the house. As she sorted the pile, she noticed a letter, written in a hand she recognized. Her fingers shook as she ripped open the envelope; her breath caught as she read *Daet*'s words.

Dear Leah,

I write to tell you your sister Ada is in the hospital. She is recovering from an accident at the neighbor's farm. It looks like she will be in recovery a long time. *Maem* said I should let you know. As always, we hope this letter reminds you of your family and that you are not forgotten. We are still waiting for you to decide to come back to church and be a part of us again. I'm sure your new ways seem better, but never forget the path to heaven is a narrow one. Compromising to the world's ways is not better if it leads you to destruction. Let go of comfort and come back to where we have answers for life's troubles once and for all.

Your *Daet*

Leah dropped to the sofa, the letter clutched in her hand. Ada. Injured! *Lord, don't let anything happen to my sister!*

She rushed to put on her bonnet and sweater. She had to let Jacob know and she needed to reach him quickly. She glanced to the clock over the stove. One-thirty. Jacob would be leaving for work at two-fifteen. She rushed to the phone, hoping she could reach Jacob's neighbors so they could get the message to him to call her. She wanted to go home—to see Ada.

After she reached the neighbors, as she waited for his call, she thought of the rest of *Daet*'s letter.

It discouraged her to think she would never be back in his good graces, even though she was living the Amish life. But in his mind, the *hoch* church of New Order Amish meant something of the old ways had been dropped. That equaled compromise with the world and compromise was not a word *Daet* could ever accept. Neither could his bishop.

She savored that thought: *His* bishop.

Leah glanced around her at the autumn leaves beginning to fall and breathed in the spicy air. No longer was Henry Miller *her* bishop. No longer did she have to take his council.

Her steps lightened, as she walked to the kitchen for a drink of water.

Once she spoke with Jacob, she hoped she would be on her way to Ashfield soon. She paused. It wouldn't hurt to go ahead and see if Ella could take her to the hospital in Ashfield, while she waited.

The road back to Ashfield became a blur to Leah's weary vision as she stretched her legs in the front seat of Ella's car. She was a little disappointed Jacob couldn't take time from work to make the trip with her, but she was equally grateful Ella had free time to drive her.

Leah raised her arms above her head in a long stretch, trying to ease the tight muscles that were beginning to bring on a headache. She squirmed into a more comfortable position, lowering her arms and pressing her back firmly into the soft cushion.

Silence settled between Ella and Leah as they neared the hospital in Ashfield. Leah had decided not to go to the house first. She didn't want to take a chance that someone might warn her family about her visit with Ada. Though she hoped they would not try to intervene, it wouldn't surprise her if the bishop would put roadblocks in her path to keep her from seeing her sister.

Leah glanced to the west, noticing how the sun, a miniature fiery red marble, sat just above the horizon, lower in the sky much earlier than a few weeks ago. Summer was fading. They'd gotten on the road later than she'd hoped, so daylight was beginning to diminish.

She sighed as they pulled into the parking lot of the hospital. As Leah and Ella walked toward the automatic doors of the hospital, she observed a barely visible star slide earthward, vanishing into its mysterious bed, leaving nothing behind to show it had flamed and lived with intense light before its abrupt fall.

Night would be here soon and with it would come the questions about what Leah would find inside this building. She whispered a prayer for Ada, for herself, and for her family as the elevator lifted her and Ella upward.

Ella indicated she would wait down the hallway from Ada's room as they scanned the information signs attached to the corners of the hospital corridors.

She found her way to Ada's door. Leah's hands shook as she pushed it open. Who else was on the other side of this entry? Would Leah be welcomed or asked to leave?

Leah had not been told what Ada's injuries were, but when she saw her sister's quiet form, covered from shoulders to feet in a sheet and white blanket, only a light above the bed casting a gleam over Ada's face, Leah paused. She moved her gaze from her sister's head to her feet. There was a cast on the right leg, from knee to foot.

She glanced around. No one else was in the room. Leah let out her breath in relief. So far, it appeared to her untrained eyes that Ada was not in serious condition. There were no bandages on her head or upper body—only the cast, as far as she could tell.

She approached the bed softly. She didn't want to disturb her sister if she was sleeping, but she did desire a closer look at Ada. Leah stood by the bed, praying silently.

The sweet face of her younger sister filled her with love and a deep sadness that religion alone had the power to separate them.

*Why, God? Why should our faith be the knife that wounds us?*

She whispered her prayers of healing over Ada. Just as she turned to go, her sister's eyes opened.

"Leah?" Ada's gaze was startled, as if she were viewing a ghost, or perhaps something a part of her imagination.

Leah reached out and grabbed Ada's hand. "Yes. It's me. I had to come and see you."

"How did you know?"

"*Daet* sent me a letter. I got it today. When did you get hurt? What happened?"

Ada scrunched her brows in concentration. "I think it was a couple of days ago? I'm not sure now—all the meds I've taken make me fuzzy-headed. But I had to have surgery, so that was yesterday ... yes. I think I broke my leg and ankle the day before yesterday. I was helping the neighbors in their barn loft—getting it swept out before church next week and I missed a step on the ladder. I fell several feet, but it was landing with a twist that broke the bones."

"Oh, Ada! *Daet* said you have a long recovery ahead."

Ada frowned. "Yes, I think the doctor said I might have to get some kind of rehabilitation somewhere."

"Will the bishop allow that?"

Ada shrugged. "Right now, I don't know what I'm going to be doing. Are you going home tonight? How'd you get here?"

Leah glanced over her shoulder. "I came with a friend. I'm not sure if I'll go out to the house or just head back to Holmes County. What do you think? Will *Maem* allow me to stay?"

Ada snorted. "Better be more concerned about *Daet* letting you stay. *Maem's* changed a little since she saw you in Holmes County."

Leah held her sister's gaze, surprised after the last conversation she'd had with *Maem*. "Did she?"

Her sister nodded. "Yep. She was upset with *Daet* and the things he said to you when they saw you in the hospital. And she said it hurts, having to ignore one of her children."

Leah thought about that and felt tears well in her eyes. If only they could mend fences and begin again.

She reached for Ada's hand and held it. Finally, Leah drew away. "If you think it will cause trouble for *Maem* and even make her sad, then I should go on back to Holmes County tonight."

Ada shifted her weight and carefully rearranged the covers over her broken leg.

"Leah, are you okay there? Is the New Order, well, different? Really different, I mean?"

Leah nodded. "It's funny. It's different, but the same. You know?"

"Still Amish." Ada giggled.

"Yes. Still Amish." She smiled as she shared a laugh with her sister.

It felt good to see her—to be with Ada again. They chatted for a few more minutes as Ada filled her in on things that were going on in Ashfield County—mostly about who was seeing who. Before she knew it, a knock sounded at the door.

"Leah? The nurse told me it's past visiting time."

Leah motioned Ella into the room and introduced her to Ada. After a few exchanges of pleasantries, she told Leah she'd wait outside for her while she said goodbye to Ada.

"Is that your new roommate?"

Leah laughed. "No, Sarah stayed home. But did you know Jacob and I were finally able to join the church and are getting married at the end of September?"

Ada clapped. "Oh, I'm so glad! I hope I can find a way to come to your *hochzich*, no matter what I have to do to get there."

Leah nodded. "I hope so, too. It wouldn't be the same without you. I'd better get going. If I write to you, will you get the letter?"

Ada nodded. "Yes—if *Daet* doesn't get to the letters first. I think *Maem* won't mind if she sees you writing me. And if I go to rehab, I'll try to call you. Is there a number?"

"Yes—here's Sarah's number."

Ada's eyes rounded. "You mean, you're allowed to have a phone in the house?"

Leah laughed. "Yes! It's a black box phone—you know: the kind that works with a modem through the Internet."

"Computers? I'm shocked!"

"No, no computers and we can't get on the Internet to look anything up." Leah winked. "That's what the library's for."

They shared a laugh as Leah turned to leave. "Love you, Ada," she paused to say before walking to the door.

Ada nodded. "Me, too."

Ada waved as Leah hurried away, but she glanced back to see her sister, sitting quietly and looking totally lost in that big modern bed in the big modern hospital room.

Leah swallowed down tears, her heart constricting. *Poor Ada! I wish I could stay all night with her.*

She forced a smile and flashed the thumbs up sign to Ada.

"Take care of yourself," Leah whispered.

# CHAPTER SEVENTEEN

L eah hadn't been to the Coblentz place for a few weeks. After Henry had been released from jail, her presence would have been very hard on Clara and the children. But she wanted to know how they were doing, so she decided to take a walk down the road, in case any of the *kinna* were close enough for her to see them playing in the fields.

Autumn was giving a preview of spicy colors among the trees lining the way, but it was still summer's stage, even if the characters in the seasonal play were showing signs of wear.

Scraggly Queen Anne's lace swayed on weak-kneed stems, while the last garden flowers were too drained by summer's heat to flaunt passionate hues. Their washed-out colors and shabby petals were a portent of their coming demise.

The call of robins had all but disappeared as those red-breasted fowl had packed their bags when Leah wasn't looking and struck out for warmer regions.

Mini dust whirlwinds swirled up from her feet as she scuffed her way toward the Coblentz farm. She raised a hand to shade her eyes as she scanned the field closest to the road.

There! She caught a glimpse of a towhead among the near-ready corn field.

She paused, waiting for another glimpse. Sure enough, laughter rang out and two sets of heads disturbed the crop. Saloma and Daniel ran between the stalks, calling to each other as they took turns hiding.

She hesitated to shout to them for fear Henry would hear and come to investigate.

Suddenly, Saloma spied her, grabbed Daniel by the arm and pointed to Leah. Both children raced toward her, their smiles wide and friendly. Daniel's bowl-cut flopped up and down as he ran, while Saloma held a hand to her head to keep her *kapp* in place.

They were out of breath by the time they got to her. She was pleasantly surprised when they threw their small arms around her waist in a snug embrace.

Saloma was the first to speak. "Leah! We've missed you so much!"

"Me, too! Me, too!"

Leah smiled and reached down to hold both of the children close. "Oh, I've missed you, too! How are you?"

Saloma stood back and fixed her gaze on Leah. "We're okay."

But her face, just seconds before beaming and shiny with excitement, lost the huge smile and twinkling eyes. She'd grown somber at Leah's question.

Leah stretched out a hand and softly touched the little girl's cheek. "Is your *maem* happy to have your *daet* back home?"

Daniel shook his head, flinging his hair back and forth across his cheeks. "No! And I'm not happy to have him back, either!" He flushed, lowering his eyes to the ground in shame.

Saloma lobbed a warning look to her little brother. "Daniel—that's not what *maem* would want you to say."

He moved away from Leah, kicking at pebbles and scowling at his sister's reprimand. "Well, I know *Maem* doesn't want him home and I'm not lying," he muttered.

Leah ignored the outburst and reached out to smooth his messy hair. "I'm glad to see you two, that's for sure."

"Are you coming in for a visit with *Maem*," Saloma carefully enquired.

"I'm sorry, Saloma, but I don't have much time today for visiting, but please let your *maem* know I said hello."

Out of the corner of her eye, Leah caught a movement. Startled, she turned her eyes to the field. There Henry stood, dead still, scrutinizing her and the children.

She cleared her throat. "I guess it's time for me to get back home, children. Please know I'm praying for all of you. Be sure to say hi from me to Reuben, too."

By this time, Daniel and Saloma noticed their *daet* eyeing them, too. They retreated, slipping into the rows of corn like little ghosts.

She spun on her heels and headed back the way she came, feeling Henry's stare go right through her. *Oh, Gott, please protect those children and Clara! Bring restoration and health to Henry so he's no longer a threat to his family.*

The prickling at the nape of her neck didn't ease until she was out of sight of the Coblentz farm.

Her fear of Henry hadn't lessened, but lately, she hadn't been thinking of him every day, either. She hoped seeing him and the wary faces of his children, didn't make the nightmares recur.

She met the mail truck as she approached the driveway and stepped into the grass, waiting for the mail carrier to roll to a stop beside her.

"Hello. Nice day, isn't it?" The lady who delivered the mail was pleasantly friendly. She often went out of her way to satisfy her customers.

"Yes, it is. I love that this good weather is holding out so far."

Leah took the stack of mail she was handed and waved as the mail carrier went on with her route.

She walked slowly toward the house, contemplating the job that might come next. Earning money would be an important contribution to hers and Jacob's future. She only had a little savings left from the job with the Coblentz family and from a few house cleaning duties she'd picked up here and there in the community. And there were still finishing touches to purchase for the wedding. She'd applied to a couple of restaurants, but had not been asked to come in for an interview yet.

Since Sarah had gone into town to meet with some of her church friends, Leah had the house to herself. She grabbed a glass from the cupboard and poured herself a drink of cold mint tea, sat down at the kitchen table and sorted through the mail. A handwritten letter from Ashfield County caught her attention.

Leah examined the letter in her hand. Another letter from Martha! She tore open the seal and eagerly read. Her lips moved as she silently mouthed the words Martha had written.

Dear Leah,

I know you're surprised to hear from me again. And you'll be even more surprised to hear that I've stayed at home. I think you know that my English so-called boyfriend took off. It was okay because I found out he was already with a new girl. I sure can pick the rotten ones.

My little boy is doing good, though he doesn't think of me as his *maem* sometimes. That makes me feel bad, but it's not his fault. I'm the one that left. *Maem* makes me take care of him. I don't mind that, but she throws it in my face every day that I was, and still am, a terrible mom. (I already know that.) She's not treating me very well and neither is her husband (I don't even want to call him my step-*daet*.)

The really bad news, though, is that my brother Abner will be taking over the farm soon. That snake is over here all the time, when he isn't busy beating his poor wife, that is.

He has the nerve to come up to me and whisper nasty things about my little sister. It makes my heart about leap out of my chest. I don't know what I'd do if he ever touches her the way he touched me. But, I just don't have any fight left in me, I guess, because I can't think how I'm going to change anything. I'm as stuck as his wife is.

Well, so much for my cheery news. I hope you are doing good. I'm not even going to bore you with the gossip about you and Jacob Yoder.

The church people talk about him when his family is not around (they know they'd get an earful if they did it in front of his *daet* or *maem!*), but I hope you two are doing okay.

I saw your *maem* and told her I was writing you a letter. She said to tell you hello from her. So, hello from your *maem*. Ha ha ha.

Write me back as soon as you can. I hear, through the Amish grapevine, that you and Jacob are finally getting married! About time, I say. I hope I can come to your *hochzich*.

Your long lost friend, Martha

Leah folded the letter and placed it back in the envelope. She blinked back tears as she thought of the despair she sensed in Martha's letter.

Abner—back on the farm! That had to be bad for her. Leah's stomach lurched when she thought of what he'd done to his stepsister. She prayed right then and there that, somehow, *Gott* would keep that from happening to Martha's little sister, too.

Abner was a mean man and it seemed he was continuing on that path with his wife, even after the church had made him stay home for weeks as punishment for what he'd done to his sister.

She whispered a prayer for Martha, her little sister, and Martha's son. She glanced out the window to the road. They lived less than an hour apart, but it might as well be worlds apart in how they lived as Amish.

She thought of her *maem* taking the opportunity to send her a greeting and tried not to allow tears to slip down her cheeks. How she missed her family! How she longed for reconciliation.

When Sarah got home a few minutes later, she sat down at the table with Leah. In the silence after their initial greetings, Leah was embarrassed to admit she was struggling. Sarah didn't push her, but stood and made a pot of coffee and sat down again. "Okay, so what's up?"

113

Leah met her friend's direct gaze with a watery smile. "I'm sorry I'm so glum, Sarah. I got a letter from an old friend back home. It made me a little homesick and a little worried, I guess."

"From Martha?"

She nodded. How much had she already shared with Sarah about Martha's troubles? She tried to recall a time when they discussed her wayward friend.

Sarah, guessing her discomfort, supplied the answer. "We talked about her once when we talked about abuse."

"Oh. I'd forgotten about that."

Sarah stirred her coffee. Her smile was genuine and friendly. Open. Warm. Her roommate had become a true friend.

"Leah, you know we might be able to help Martha. I've heard of a couple of places that could support her as she tries to get back on her feet. Maybe she could get some counseling for the abuse. She could begin a new life, if she would give it a try."

Leah paused, surprised that she had not thought of that herself. "Hmm ... that's a great idea."

Her housemate nodded. "There are shelters that take in women who have kids, too."

Leah rested her hand on the edge of the table. "That would be wonderful! Let's look into what we can find out about those places, and then I'll write Martha, as soon as I can."

Sarah paused. "Or maybe we could take a trip to Ashfield, so we can talk with her about it in person. Sometime after your wedding, of course. We're all way too busy to do that now."

Leah considered the notion. Meeting with Martha would be the best way to talk with her. Maybe they could get a feel for how things were working out for her at home.

"Okay. Let me get with Jacob to see what he thinks. It would be good to see his family while we're up there, too, if you wouldn't mind coming along, that is."

Sarah stood, heading down the hall to her bedroom. "I'd love to do that with you and Jacob. That would be fun."

"Yes. I'd love to see Ashfield again, too."

Leah sorted through the rest of the mail, mostly catalogs about wedding stuff. It hit her suddenly that her marriage to Jacob was less than two weeks away!

"Oh, boy. What am I doing sitting here? I have to get on the ball and get busy."

# CHAPTER EIGHTEEN

C hurch service the next few weeks after joining was interesting. She couldn't help but reflect how different it felt to be a member. Though she had not changed a thing about herself, the other church attenders appeared friendlier. There were still those who held back, but taking the step to join church looked as if she was finally accepted within the community.

She stole a glance at Jacob seated with the men and perceived a settled expression in his smile, too. It seemed that everything was falling into place. She had wholly walked into the Amish way of life and she felt glad. She couldn't help but smile in return as her heart warmed to see Jacob's happiness.

As she wiggled into a more comfortable position on the hard bench, a soft whisper spoke to her.

*Are you for Me and I'm for you?*

Where had that thought come from? What did it mean?

She shook her head, trying to quell the sudden unfathomable longing that grew when the whispering Voice repeated the query.

Her brows knitted together as she squirmed against the uncomfortable question, but over and over throughout the service, she heard it reiterated.

116

*Are you for Me and I'm for you?*

She recognized the Voice. Hard as she tried, she could not quench the searing searchlight God was applying to her soul.

She moistened her lips, her gaze swinging from row to row to sweep the faces of her brothers and sisters in the Amish faith. Their expressions reflected serene acceptance, though some, admittedly, appeared bored or sleepy. She sat straighter, pulling her shoulders tight and stiff against the truth growing in her heart.

*Are you for Me and I'm for you?*

Why here? Why now?

Leah stifled the urge to get up and leave the assembly. She was both drawn to, and repelled by, the pressing question and she wanted to run.

*Why are you calling me again, Lord? I've given everything to my Amish faith now. I've settled it, once and for all. Vater Gott, why are You asking me that question?*

Leah dipped her head, her gaze scanning the floor, her mind frantically trying to shut out the resolute intensity of the inquiry being repeated in her heart.

But she recognized His dedication to her and was overwhelmed with shame that she was not readily offering an unqualified *yes* to God's persistent question.

Was she His? Had she, instead, given over her heart to her church? Was God asking for more? Or less?

He appeared to want nothing more from her than her devotion to Him, not to the church.

Tears stung her eyes as a Scripture captured her thoughts: Surely goodness and mercy shall follow me all the days of my life.

*Goodness and mercy. Is that who You are, God? Are You pursuing me? Following me? You who are good and merciful? Is it You who is calling me to a holy, set-apart life?*

She examined her skirt. It was just right. It was lengthy and dark, covering her lower legs as the *Ordnung* required. It was pressed and wrinkle-free. It was somber. Modest. And—what?

Holy?

Her gaze traveled to her neighbor's *kapp*. Its tilt upon the head was just right. Flawless.

Holy?

All the bowed heads were the same. All the colors. The humbled postures.

Holy?

Sacred holy lives. Made holy and sacred by—whom? The people? Their acts? Their obedience? To what? The *Ordnung*?

Were they prideful in their humbleness? In their sacred strivings?

She recalled a conversation she'd overheard at the market one day. An Amish gentleman was disagreeing with his brother, who had left the Amish and was living English. The Amish man had pointed out to his brother how the English women dressed immodestly. How the Amish women always had modesty in mind.

His brother, in turn, pointed out that English Christian women relied on the Holy Spirit to encourage modest dress. He told his Amish brother the Amish were prideful in their obedience to the *Ordnung*.

At that, the Amish man had huffed "We are *not* prideful! Just look at how plain we dress!"

At the time, the Amish man's obvious pride had amused her, but now she wondered if the former Amish man had been right. Were her Plain people relying on their obedience to the *Ordnung*—taking pride in how far they would go to look *gut*? To look holy? To look right?

She shook away the thought that, she too, had replaced her sacrifice to God with sacrifice to the Amish church. Sacrifice to the *Ordnung*.

*Am I really for God? Or am I for the Amish church? Lord, I want to be right with You. I want to be holy by You and not by my own strivings.*

Leah leaned over, her hands covering her face as the desire to please her Lord pressed in, pressed in more, causing her to almost weep with the need to please Him. And Him only.

Silently, she prayed. She implored God to guide her and Jacob. Her prayers poured out of her heart. Her desire to be on fire, to be used for His kingdom, in His way, in His time, and for His purpose, flowed from her soul.

She breathed in His will for her life with Jacob. She knew the Holy Spirit was permeating her heart with His comfort and peace. His brand was placed upon her being.

Time stood still as she allowed God's love, grace, and divine plan to be infused into her life. She sat up, but kept her head bowed, her eyes closed as she meditated on the Lord and what He wanted her to do with her life.

Then she became aware of silence. Slowly, she raised her head and looked around, blinking against the light that streamed through the window in front of her. Most of the women were scuffling toward the exit. Just outside the doorway, stood Jacob, his arms crossed. Waiting for her.

Panicked, she stood, the blood rushing to her face as she stumbled to gather herself. What had happened? How had she missed the service, the prayers at the end? How had she missed the leave-taking as folks visited on their way out the door?

Her cheeks flamed when she realized that all had seen her—sitting, praying, her head bowed and eyes closed.

There was no preparation underway for the meal, even though the men were already outside. The benches were still in place. No tables were arranged around her.

Her gaze flew to the window. People were gathering in groups, chatting and amiable.

She fumbled her way to Jacob. Shame washed over Leah. She had made a fool of herself among her new church people.

"Jacob, I—I'm sorry! So sorry!"

Her eyes met his and she saw admiration. Love. Even a hint of amusement. "Leah, you never cease to amaze me."

She released a deep sigh. "Oh my. I never cease to amaze myself at how embarrassing I can make my own life."

119

He shook his head and nodded toward the outside. "They don't think that. They knew you were communing with God."

Tears sprang and welled over. Gratitude to her church family. They understood. They did not reject her.

The bishop entered the door from the yard. His gentle face was relaxed and a genial smile lit his eyes.

"It's *gut, ja*? We're ready for lunch?"

Laughter spilled out of her relieved soul. "Yes! And I'm so sorry I delayed things a little."

He came to her, placed a trembling old hand on hers and shook his head. "*Gott* decides these things. No need to apologize when He talks to one of His servants."

He winked. "But that's not to say our human hunger pangs will be put off forever." He chuckled. "Time to get the food ready."

As the church people filed in and set about their ordinary Sunday tasks, she hesitated, holding back from entering in readily because her embarrassment of daydreaming was still uppermost in her mind.

A couple of the ladies hurried over and covered her awkwardness with clucking orders and good-natured guidance as to what went where. She gave up her pride and entered in to the fellowship. Her heart-filled gratitude grew.

In the following days, Leah was kept busy preparing for the wedding. She had hired a driver to take her to do some shopping and he had also stopped to pick up an older Old Order Amish mother with two daughters. They were also going to the same fabric shop for wedding materials and supplies.

After greeting one another, Leah settled back to relax and enjoy the sunny autumn day.

The driver they had hired was born Amish but had left the church long ago. Retired from trucking, he filled his days with "hauling" Amish, as it was known, instead of cargo. It was a win-win for all of them. He still went by his Amish name, Red John, and it helped that he spoke Pennsylvania-Dutch.

Her mind reflected on how her people's language had changed over the years.

They came to America from German regions to seek asylum from persecution. They settled in Pennsylvania. Their German dialect gradually added more and more English words. Though it had never been taught as a written language, and every group of Amish had added specialty words or dialects to their language over the years, most Amish still used the common language of "Dutch"—as they shortened it to— to communicate with one another.

She leaned her head against the van window and smiled as she suddenly recalled how *Maem* had chastised her children when they spoke Dutch while English visitors were at the house. "It's not polite to speak a language our guests do not understand. In this house, we speak English when English are present."

There was so much about *Maem* that Leah loved. Tears threatened as her heart longed for home and her family. When she had left the Amish for life among the Englishers a couple of years ago, she had been unofficially shunned. Now, even though she was Amish again, the way her bishop from her old church handled his people was to press them to continue the unofficial shunning of Leah. And even Jacob.

But Jacob's family didn't adhere as strictly to his orders as Leah's dad seemed to do. Jacob heard from his family regularly. They seemed accepting of his New Order Amish church. He was sure his family would come to their New Order wedding.

Leah, on the other hand, was sure her family would not come, even though she and Jacob would be marrying as Amish.

She watched the rolling landscape rush by as the van was skillfully guided down narrow lanes and along country roads.

She finished her shopping as quickly as she could, anxious to be back home where she could look through the things she'd bought and sort them according to her plans.

After she was home later that evening, Sarah sat across from her in the living room and asked how the plans were coming along for the wedding. The wedding stuff was splayed over the tables and some were still in bags in a corner.

Leah had come home, pulled out her wedding dress and was finishing up the sleeves, pumping the manual sewing machine as they chatted.

"I'm meeting myself coming and going these days. Getting things ready for the wedding, not to mention being the *mawt* for the new Amish family, Jake and Lizzie Swartzentruber, down the road past the Coblentz place. It's going to be a short job, but I welcome the money. I'm out like a light as soon as my head hits the pillow."

"How are things going at the Jakes'?"

Leah took a moment to stop, remove her dress and cut the threads neatly from the seams she'd just sewed before guiding the other sleeve under the needle and pressure foot.

"Pretty good. I won't be there after this week, though. Their little baby boy, Mose, is cute as a button."

"That pay will help, I'm sure. Did you decide which cake to order?"

Leah nodded, smiling as she told Sarah about the wedding cake. It wasn't as fancy as many, but it would be elegant and tasty.

"Did Jacob get to taste the flavors?"

Leah laughed. "No, he's interested in the marriage, but not so much the details leading up to the marriage. I did show him some of those cakes we saw from the bakery, but he just told me to choose the one I liked best."

Sarah leaned back and sighed. "I suppose he's working hard trying to get the house in order, plus still working at the factory." She stopped rocking. "And how is everything at work for him? Is that Bert Small keeping himself under control?"

Leah shrugged. "You know Jacob; he's not going to tell me if anything else has happened. I sure hope Bert's controlling himself. I still worry he'll come back to the farm one day and really do damage."

Leah flicked a *fronzel* off her wedding dress. "I wonder where I picked up that huge dust bunny?"

"Speaking of dresses, do you need help putting the hem in?"

Leah snipped the last sleeve free from the threads, stood to shake out the lovely blue outfit and nodded. "*Ja*, sure. That would be a big help."

As Leah stood on a low footstool, Sarah, pins sticking from a pin cushion cuff around her wrist, slowly secured the hem in place.

"Oh, I meant to ask if you're interested in coming to the Ladies Day at Alma Miller's next Tuesday. She said they're starting a new quilt for the auction coming up at Christmas."

"Yes, I think so. It depends on what time they plan to start."

"I'm guessing about nine, but you can come on over after you finish at Jakes'."

"I'll try to."

Sarah stood, groaning as she unfolded her legs. "I sure know my age when I try to stand up from kneeling. There—that looks good. You just need to sew it down and you're finished." She smiled as Leah slipped the dress over her head.

"I love this color. It's going to be beautiful with the lavender."

"I think so, too." Sarah yawned. "Well, I'm heading to bed. Don't stay up too late."

"I won't. It won't take me long to get this hem in place."

Leah swept the dress under the needle one last time and pumped the pedal. The machine whirred as the fabric slipped under the needle and threads.

"It won't be long now and this wedding will be all ready and I'm more than ready for that day to come," she mumbled as she sewed.

As Leah slid into bed after pressing the dress and hanging it in the closet, she lay listening to the sounds of the evening outside her window. The wind whispered, blowing the curtains gently under the bottom edge of the window she had raised an inch or two to let in the clean crisp air.

Leah stared out at the moon. It's time to shine, to show off and be the host for many autumn soirees, was upon it. It glowed, orange and round, in its glory.

She rested her hands under her head and lay back to enjoy the striking radiance. Wisps of clouds veiled the pale moon's face. Its shimmering blue light bathed the hills and woods and streams in calm tones of midnight, ivory and pearl, shifting and using slight-of-hand magic with the dark tree trunks and shivering dying leaves.

Could she feel anything but peace when viewing the great light? After the hot summer, the tranquil orb was a refreshing image to behold.

She smiled into its gentle glow, raising her toes to let them reflect gray silly shadows against the wall. Her *maem* had shown Leah and her siblings a series of ghostly silhouettes she could create with her hands. Leah tried to remember how she'd positioned her fingers for the shadow puppet show. She giggled as odd shapes played on the flat surface next to her bed.

"Leeeaaaaaah!"

The cry came from outside, somewhere in the back garden. It hissed through the night air, almost feral in tone, resembling an animal caught in a trap or in the talons of an unrelenting night hunter. The sound sent her reeling in shock.

She pushed her body against the headboard, her neck tingling and the skin on her arms prickling in fear. She was trembling from head to toe, but she managed to jump out of bed, scurrying to the door and slamming it open. She ran to Sarah's room and entered without knocking.

"Sarah! Hurry! Someone—something—in the backyard! It was calling my name!"

Sarah sat up, startled wide awake by Leah's outburst. "What's the matter, Leah? *Was in die welt?*" She scrambled out of bed, hurrying to follow Leah back to her bedroom.

The two grabbed each other's hands as they pushed the door back and eased into the room. Leah tried to hone in on the night sounds outside her window, but the roaring fear inside her own ears made her nearly deaf.

She crept slowly to the bed, her housemate right beside her, and leaned over her warm covers.

She could not hear anything. Not a sound. Not even the chirruping of the frogs on the pond. Not even the murmur of the wind through the pines. All was dead still.

Had she imagined the cry? The night sounds? Had she been halfway between slumber and wakefulness? A dream?

Sarah lifted her free hand, her finger pointing to the window. "Leah," she whispered, "Look."

Leah turned to follow Sarah's pointing finger.

What she saw sent waves of new distress rolling through her body: The window screen was slashed, from one side to the other.

# CHAPTER NINETEEN

Jacob sat in the living room, shaking his head and asking Leah, again, if she was okay.

"I'm okay, Jacob. Really. Last night, when we saw the screen, it gave me a jolt, and I had a lot of trouble sleeping, for sure. But when the sun came up this morning, it was hard to believe there was any mischief done at all—like it was a dream—the whisper, the screen being cut—I'm feeling more annoyed than scared, in the light of day."

Sarah jumped into the conversation. "Well, I'm more than annoyed. I'm ready to hunt this Bert Small down and give him a piece of my mind!" She rocked faster as she spoke.

Leah smiled. "I know it's not funny, Sarah, but I can't help imagining Bert being told off by you. I think he might faint just from the sheer shock of seeing a little Amish woman shaking her fist in his face."

Jacob stood and began pacing from one corner of the room to the other. "I just can't figure out why Bert would go this far. Really, I've done nothing to get in his face, or be rude—except when he came at you, Leah." He rubbed his face with his hands. "I'm *ferhudled*. What do you think about calling the sheriff?"

Leah frowned, wishing she'd actually seen Bert last night. Then she'd not even hesitate to let the sheriff's office know he was at it again. She turned to Jacob. "There is a possibility he isn't even the culprit. He didn't do anything violent this time, just mischievous, like a little boy, really. I don't think we need to alert authorities, do you?"

"No—I agree. He's acting like a *jungen*, not a grown man."

"I have a feeling, Jacob, that he has a problem with Amish in general. I think he's taking his anger out on you and I'm just part of your life so I'm being included." Leah shrugged. "I've seen this before—some folks love Amish people and some despise us."

"He needs to learn how to behave himself, I'm thinking," Sarah sputtered.

Jacob's brows drew together. "I'd really like to hang out here all the time, because I am worried he might go too far one night and one of you may be hurt. But I have a shift tonight and I still have some things to do at the farm." He glanced toward Leah, his voice softening. "We'll be married by this time next week."

Leah held his gaze, the wonder of that fast-approaching day causing her heart to speed up. "I know, Jacob. Can you believe it? And I have a lot of things to do, too."

She squared her shoulders. "Fussing over Bert Small and his silly tricks isn't on that list, though, so it's time to get busy and let him stew in his juices. If he thinks he's going to scare me—" she pointed to Sarah, "I mean us, he's got another think coming!"

Sarah stood, too, and walked to the phone. "I have to get someone over here to repair that screen, but what time did you hire Ella to take us into Millersburg?"

"She's going to be here about nine o'clock."

Worry lines pulled at Jacob's face. "Sarah, I can fix the screen tomorrow, if you're okay to wait. Are you going to be all right, I mean, after the wedding, living here by yourself?"

Sarah paused, the phone in one hand as she waved the other in the air. "Yes, I'm grateful you offered to repair it. I'll take you up on that tomorrow. And, for goodness' sake, that little guy doesn't make me fret about being here alone after Leah moves out. I've been here on my own for years."

Leah nodded. "I'm sure you'll be fine here, Sarah, but I have an idea about who might be able to move in when I move out."

The two housemates locked eyes and spoke a name, at the same time, "Martha!"

Jacob burst out laughing. "You two share one brain, evidently."

Leah giggled and the humor felt good—like a balm to calm her soul.

"Yep—we do think alike. But really, Martha needs a new start and I can't think of a better place for her to start over than right here with Sarah." Leah gave her housemate a warm smile. "No one could help her heal better than you, Sarah."

"Now don't get me to crying. But I do think that poor girl needs some guidance and some love, and with *Gott* helping, she can get on her feet pretty fast, I'm thinking."

"I agree. After all, you've done wonders with this wayward girl, Sarah," Jacob teased, pointing to Leah.

Leah tossed a sofa pillow at him. "Now don't *you* get started. Didn't you say you have a lot to do before work today? Time to move, Jacob Yoder!"

He came to her, pulled her close and gave her a sound kiss, right in front of Sarah.

Leah's cheeks flamed, but she was reminded why Jacob Yoder was the man for her. "Silly guy," she whispered gently, "don't make Sarah have to get between us."

He gave her a wide grin, plopped his hat on his head and waved goodbye to them as he went out the door.

"Talk to you later, okay? After all, I need to give you my new phone number," he called as he hurried to the buggy.

The two women shared another look, spluttering, "Phone number?"

Sarah laughed. "Jacob Yoder has gotten himself a black box phone at last."

Leah shook her head. "He's gone *hoch gmay*."

# CHAPTER TWENTY

The day had come at last. Leah hopped out of bed early on the morning of September twenty-seventh.

She peeked out the window. A fine fall day. No hint of rain with lots of warm sunshine, which was a good thing because they had to use Liam and Anna Hershberger's barn for the wedding dinner and the service. Having no family in the area meant no place to host their wedding, other than with friends.

Jacob and Leah had spoken with the bishop and two preachers about the service. At first, Leah was anxious the preachers would nix the idea of the *hochzich* being at Liam's place. After all, Leah wasn't well-acquainted with the congregation yet and those two preachers, especially Melvin Mast, thought Bishop John Troyer was too soft on his church already.

To be fair, preacher Jonas went along with whatever Melvin wanted since it was in his nature not to buck a stronger voice. They weren't as open to the idea of the wedding being at the Hershberger's place as Bishop Troyer had been, but some gentle coaxing from the kind bishop had eased their minds.

Not having a separate venue for the service and the wedding meant more to do for all of them, but things worked out. With careful planning they were able to divide the old barn into two sections. One side was lined with church benches. That area was kept simple and tasteful in decoration—just a few natural elements, which included mums and a few corn wreaths, to celebrate the service.

They had asked the preachers to prepare sermons which talked of forgiveness, marriage, and the gift of Jesus to a relationship. Bishop Troyer would follow up with the wedding vows and then would come the singing of the wedding hymn, the *Hochzeit Lied*.

Leah looked forward to celebrating with Jacob's family, too. To her surprise, they had sent word they were planning to attend.

She wished, with all of her heart, that her own family would be there. But with the bad feelings between Leah and her *daet*, not to mention with the bishop back home, there was no chance she would see them on this important day.

If her sister Ada had been married, Leah was certain she would have come, but living at home, there was no chance she'd be allowed to attend. Her *maem*, too, would have come, Leah was pretty sure of that, but again, *Daet* would be in control of his wife and there was no way he would allow her to come to the wedding of their disobedient *dochder*.

Before she took another step to dress, Leah stopped beside her bedside. She spoke a heartfelt prayer aloud as she knelt.

"Lord, you know how much this day means to me and Jacob. Please bless us with Your love and care and bless those who come to celebrate and witness this day before You. Bless my parents and my family and all those in my old community. Lord, may they think of me, just once, with fond memories on this day. And thank You for the presence of Jacob's family. What a gift to us! But thank You most of all for Your gift of salvation through Your son, Jesus. In Christ's name I pray, Amen."

After she carefully slipped into her beautiful blue dress, gauzy white apron, and snowy white *kapp*, the rest of the morning flew past.

Sarah bustled about, fussing with Leah's hair, putting pins in just so and generally taking the place of a *maem* on her daughter's wedding day.

At first, Leah held back, feeling a little bit sad and wistful that her mom wasn't part of this day. But the love that shone through Sarah's eyes allowed Leah to let go of the sadness and embrace her friend's attentions as the gift it was.

Ella's van crunched the gravel outside in the driveway, followed by a short beep of the horn. Soon enough, Leah and Sarah were hurrying out, Leah on her way to her wedding day. At last.

When they pulled up to Liam and Anna's place, Leah was amazed to see so many buggies in the lane! She watched as, one by one, church folk arrived, ready to step in and become Jacob and Leah's support. Her eyes misted, feelings of gratitude rolling over her soul.

The farm looked gorgeous. Anna had added even more autumnal décor, apparently, in the form of asters and boughs of sweet scented lavender after Leah, Jacob, and Sarah had left last night.

"I'm blessed," Leah whispered.

Sarah reached over and squeezed Leah's hand. "You're loved, too, and your friends and church want to show it."

Ella pulled close so it would be a short walk for Leah through the barnyard, then she found a place to park, and caught up to her friends as they walked to the house.

Soon, Jacob rolled into the barnyard with Bingo—each of them looking their best. Bingo had gotten a good rubdown and wash, and even the buggy was spotless.

Finally, the time had come. Everyone was assembled in the barn. Wedding guests had filed in and Leah enjoyed peeping out the window of Anna and Liam's house to catch a glimpse of all the guests as they walked back to the barn.

The lane leading to the venue was decorated with white, gold, and lavender mums and cheery pumpkins were dotted between them. The pastel chiffon bows, tied to baskets and trees, swayed in the gentle breeze.

The few English guests, co-workers of Jacob, were dressed in their finest clothing. The Amish women and girls were garbed in pristine pastel-colored dresses in hues of blue, pink, yellow, and green with lovely white and black *kapps* perched on their heads. The men wore their best broadcloth suits.

Jacob looked more mature, more settled, in his black suit and tie. Leah had proudly regarded him as he made his way, surrounded by a sea of young men, the preachers, and the bishop, to the barn.

Just as Leah ducked back behind the curtains, she caught a glimpse of an Amish woman, carrying a very cute little boy, hurrying up the sidewalk to the house. Leah blinked. It was Martha!

She rushed to the kitchen door and flung it open. Before her friend knew what was happening, Leah was out of the house and hugging her in a tight embrace.

The little *buve*, crushed between them, squirmed to get loose. Finally, Martha broke the hold Leah had on her by gently pushing away in order to set the handsome little fellow down.

He darted a glance at Leah, his face flushed from the sun and his eyes sparkling with the new adventure.

"Martha, I'm so glad to see you!"

Tears flowed freely as Leah once again hugged her childhood friend. Martha returned her hug, wiping at her own tears as they parted.

"I never thought to see you here today. I'm happy you came. Except for Jacob's family, you're the only one from the old church to be here."

Martha nodded. "They came?"

"*Ja*, they responded right away. When I saw Andrew and Rebecca Yoder, plus Jacob's sisters, Malinda, Ruth, and Clara, I was happy as a clam!" She turned to the little boy. "This can't be baby Johnny?"

Martha smiled, her cheeks flushed with pride. "Yep—and he's growing like a weed. But here, I wanted to give you this before the wedding service begins. You'll want to read it right away. I'd best get to the barn—sounds like I hear singing."

Leah took the card, enclosed in a light blue envelope. "That's some of the *jungen* from our church singing. The New Order does that at weddings."

Martha listened for a couple of seconds. "They sound *gut*. I'll see you later. Can't make you late for your own wedding!"

Leah watched as Martha and Johnny made their way down the path to the barn.

Suddenly, Martha turned around. "Go ahead—read that right away!"

She grinned and some of the spark Leah noticed that had been missing from Martha's countenance had reappeared.

Her friend hurried on to the barn, gently tugging Johnny along with her. Martha had lost weight. She looked frail, her mannerisms subdued, as though the whole world rested on her shoulders. Leah felt sad for her friend.

She slipped away from Sarah and Anna, both of whom had been helping her with last minute details and preparations. She wandered into the living room and perched on the side of the sofa. As she turned the envelope over, her heart quickened. *Maem's* handwriting!

Leah opened the envelope with shaking fingers. The face of the card was lovely—filled with blooming lavender and butterflies.

"On your wedding day," Leah read aloud. She opened the card and a check dropped out and floated to the floor. Leah picked it up and turned it over. It was written to her, with her new married name: Leah Yoder.

She drew in her breath. So official—Leah Yoder. Tears gathered as she opened the card.

Under the message printed on the card was a handwritten note from *Maem*.

Dear Leah,

How I wish we could be there with you today. Know that we are thinking of you and praying for you and Jacob. Hold fast to God and He will bless your marriage and your life.

Maem, Daet, Daniel and Sara, Ada, and Benny

Leah's chin quivered. "Oh, *Maem*! I want you here, too." She fought the flood of tears that threatened to overwhelm the happiness she had wanted for her wedding day.

She hurried to the bathroom to compose herself. As she patted the tears dry with a Kleenex, she thought of how different this day would have been if she and Jacob had stayed with their old church. The people she'd grown up with would be here, they'd be at the home place, and her neighbors would be helping—but no. She would not want their marriage starting out with the old sermons and vows made before Bishop Miller.

She took a deep breath and left the room. This day was made for looking ahead, not looking back.

∾🏠∾

As Leah and Jacob walked around the cheerfully decorated barn to greet their guests at each table, she was glad they had made the decision to come to Holmes County.

The sermons had been wonderful—filled with the hope of being a new couple in Christ. The bishop, especially, had reflected on the sacred vows made before *Gott*. His warm smile and kind words had started their marriage on the right foot. Nothing could have been better, save for the presence of her family.

The guests in attendance were not as many as her old church would have included, but here, they were surrounded by people who loved them and wished them well.

She caught the aroma of grilled chicken and her stomach growled. They'd been so busy with everything, they'd only had a bite or two of the meal. The creamy mashed potatoes, succulent grilled chicken, salad, and homemade rolls were of the finest quality. Here and there she caught a glimpse of a few Jell-O desserts still uneaten on the tables, but for the most part, it was obvious that their guests had enjoyed every bite of the scrumptious lunch.

Now Jacob and she could slip away for an hour or so to open a few gifts. A special area had been set aside for the gifts and the table was decorated with pretty flowers and ribbons.

As they walked hand in hand to the gift table, she thought about the devotional Bishop Troyer had given at the close of the lunch.

He'd chosen Corinthians 13—the love chapter— and Leah thought she'd never heard such kind words about the act of loving someone else as he had expressed.

His own marriage had lasted over fifty years. His memories of their first days together, the time it took to get used to living twenty-four hours a day with that "perfect" person and the humor of finding out they were not so perfect after all, filled Leah and Jacob, along with their guests, with a warm glow, as well as with laughter.

"Jacob, I'm so glad we had Bishop Troyer with us today. He's a wonderful man."

Jacob smiled back at her. "Me, too. He's got the gift of making people feel at home and loved."

As they were entering the area for gifts, she heard someone call her name. She turned to see Matthew and Naomi Schrock standing near.

"Matthew and Naomi, I'm glad you found us! We didn't have much time to greet you."

Naomi reached Leah first and gave her a loving hug. "You look so beautiful, Leah. We're very proud of you."

Jacob and Matthew exchanged firm handshakes.

"I tell you, this wedding was simply fantastic, Jacob and Leah!" Matthew's broad smile warmed the young couple. Leah owed this man and his wife so much, she could not put into words all they meant to her.

She gripped Matthew's hand in her own. "We have a lot to thank you and Naomi for, Matthew."

"No, you have the Lord to thank for all these blessings, but I appreciate you sharing that with us. How are you two doing here in Holmes County?"

"We're doing well, and now that we're hitched, I plan to have this young lady here working day and night on the farm." Jacob winked at her.

"How are things going with MAP Ministry, Matthew?" Leah was eager to hear about the ministry and how they were helping others as they had helped her.

Matthew smiled and shook his head. "Well, we're moving into the last phase of getting the apartment houses finished and the bulk food store up and running. That means there's lots to do and some hurdles to jump, but all in all, it's coming along."

"Apartment houses?"

"Yes, we've had a need for housing for years, but as you saw, Leah, sometimes when the young people live together, it may not go as well as we'd like. We're praying for the Lord to lead us on how to equip the youth who leave the Amish with His Word, His plans for their lives, and His power to change them from the inside out."

Jacob peered around Matthew to the crowd beginning to gather near the gift table. "It looks like we're about ready to begin the next phase of this wedding celebration ourselves. Can you send us some information about the new project, Matthew?"

"Sure will, but wait." Matthew fumbled in his suit coat pockets. "I think I have a brochure here in my pocket." He passed the crinkled paper to Jacob. "We're going to head on home, but let me know your address and I'll put it in my phone so I can mail you more info when we have everything ready."

After they finished talking with the Schrocks, Leah and Jacob joined the others at the gift table. They didn't have time to open all of them, but Leah was grateful for the towels, sheets, tableware, and other household items her friends and community gave. Jacob was more than happy with the sets of tools and repair gifts given, too. It was a wonderful start for their new household.

Later that evening, after all the festivities and meals were over, Leah and Jacob headed back to the farm. It was good to be going home together and even better to know they would never part again.

Leah sighed and leaned her head against Jacob's shoulder.

The stars were out, their tiny white lights thick against the dark blue backdrop of the heavens. The trees were shadowed and shaking their leaves in shivery song. Frogs sang, too, and birds chirped their last bit of gossip to their birdie neighbors. The lane was empty of all but Leah and Jacob and Bingo. The *clop clop clop* of his hooves added a peaceful, deep cadence to nature's symphony.

The road stretched ahead into the darkness, but as they pulled up to the farm house, a light was shining in the front window.

"Jacob, how sweet of you!"

He grinned. "It was Sarah's idea. She helped me pick out a candle that's battery-powered. Then we set up that little display there in the window." He glanced at her shyly. "Welcome to your new home."

He kissed her before he led her inside. She stood looking around at the farmhouse in amazement.

Sarah had evidently done some baking, too, for the sweet scent of cinnamon fragranced the air.

She peeked into the kitchen. Yes. There was a pan of cinnamon rolls for her and Jacob's first ever breakfast as man and wife. The coffee pot was placed on the stove and two place settings at the table. She walked to the table and fingered the velvety petals of pink and yellow roses filling an old vase.

Jacob slipped up behind her. "Do you like it?"

The quaver in his voice, the hint of his need for reassurance that all was perfect for his bride, filled Leah's heart with gratitude for his gestures. Tears of joy slid down her cheeks. Her heart ached with love for him.

He turned her to him, held her close and kissed her again. A rustle of paper sounded through the room, and they laughed as he pulled out the brochure the Schrocks had handed Jacob at the wedding.

In the dim light of the kitchen, they looked at the brochure.

We are praying God will lead former Amish to our ministry to be house parents for the girls who will be living in our apartments, as well as someone to manage the bulk food store. Missionaries are also needed. If God is speaking to you about any of these positions, please contact MAP Ministry.

Jacob's gaze met hers. A tiny smile played at his lips. "How odd that this is what we were given today."

Leah drew in a deep breath, her heart racing. "But Jacob, we have our future here—in Holmes County. There's no way—"

Jacob eased his hand into hers and gently tugged her from the kitchen, through the living room to the stairs. He paused, brought her hand to his lips, and kissed her fingers softly.

"Come along, bride. The thoughts for our future can wait for another day."

# CHAPTER TWENTY-ONE

The days following their wedding were busy ones for Leah and Jacob.

She was very happy in her new home, and found herself going from room to room, dreaming how to make it feel like them, pinching herself that, at last, this house was truly hers and Jacobs.

She dreamed of the garden she'd plant in the spring, the changes she'd like to make to the kitchen, the bedrooms, and the outside of the house.

The first thing they bought and hung on the front porch was a swing. Leah enjoyed heading outside at the end of a long day, even when she had to bundle up against the increasing cold and wind, to sit on the swing, gently pushing herself back and forth as she looked over their farm.

Leah was still adjusting to Jacob's work schedule. One of those adjustments was when to eat their main meal together. Since he worked the second shift, worked the farm every morning, then went to the factory at two in the afternoon, it was difficult to squeeze in a planned meal for both of them.

She decided to cook dinner at the noon hour. The time they had together at the table was precious.

The first few evenings after Jacob left for work were tough on Leah. She felt an immediate loneliness as he went out the door to catch his ride. She hadn't had time to get used to the creaks and groans of the house, especially on nights when the wind blew stronger and the cold grew deeper.

Those weather elements created much more sound as Leah finished up her day's work and settled into reading, studying her Bible, or just relaxing in front of the fire.

In those quiet moments, she often jumped at sudden noises or felt her heart rate increase with anxiety when she couldn't immediately identify the source of a creak, a tap, or groan.

Leah laughed about her imaginary trepidations in the light of day and shared them with Jacob at lunch time, but Jacob was uncharacteristically serious the first couple of times she told her stories.

"Are you sure you didn't see anyone outside or around the barn when you heard these noises?"

Leah, taken aback by his question, tried to humor him into accepting the sounds for what she believed they were— normal bumps in the night, caused by the settling of the old house, branches against the windows, or winds whistling through the eaves.

After a few days of Jacob's anxious questioning about whether she'd heard anything the nights he was at work, she decided it was best not to share her silly fears with him—the topic was creating too much apprehension in her sweet Jacob.

Behind her fears, were the cruel jokes Bert Small had played on them in the past. She made up her mind that she was imagining many of the sounds, and the others were just natural noises of the season. Besides, once she learned the patterns of the noises, she could relax as they became part of her evening routine.

She made herself a list of projects to tackle during the hours Jacob worked and she found the time passed quickly and pleasurably as she finished each task.

The season marched on. Autumn had brought torrents of rain and Jacob was ever more concerned that the late wheat crop might suffer.

One day after church, in the middle of a conversation about the cold weather, Jacob suddenly changed the subject.

"Did you happen to speak with Anna Hershberger today?"

Leah scrunched her brows together. "No. I don't think so—well, I take that back. She told me about the apples she was canning. Why?"

Jacob's eyes twinkled. "Her husband, Liam, took me aside to tell me he had asked Jesus into his heart last night."

Leah sat up. "No! Really?"

Jacob chuckled. "Yep. He said he read some of the Scriptures I'd shown him when we were talking a couple of weeks ago. Everything finally fell into place—like a dark curtain lifted off his eyes."

Leah smiled. "I can't believe Anna didn't say anything to me! Did he tell her? Do you think she knows?"

"I'd guess he told her. I can't think why he wouldn't. He also said he and Anna want to start a Bible study for couples. What do you think about that?"

"Jacob! That brings tears to my eyes. We'll have another couple to share our born-again faith with. I'll have to ask Anna about it next time I see her."

She scooted her chair to where she could see out the window. "Is that the van I hear? Goodness! It's two o'clock already."

Jacob jumped up, drew her close and gave her a tight hug. "I can't wait for the day when I'll not have to leave you like this anymore. In the meantime, we'll do what we have to do."

She gave him a quick kiss as he grabbed his dinner pail and thermos and hurried out the door to the work van.

"See you later—have a good shift and be careful with you-know-who."

He waved as he hopped in the van. She watched as the driver headed down the lane and turned onto the road; out of her sight.

She sighed. One day, they'd be able to keep the farm running without Jacob's full-time job. At least, that was the plan.

As she went about her chores that evening, her heart was full. A couple that shared their faith!

Things couldn't get any better. Maybe the Hershbergers would become fast friends for life. She daydreamed about their children growing up together and smiled at the image in her mind.

❧ 🏠 ❧

Leah was in seventh heaven on her way home from visiting Sarah one bright fall day. Jacob had splurged in order to buy Leah a bike.

At first, she'd been leery to ride it anywhere but on the road right in front of the farm, but after she mastered the art of riding, she'd ventured further and further until she'd made it to Sarah's place.

The freedom she felt was enormous. Not having to worry about rigging Bingo and the buggy meant she could visit on the spur of the moment. This was her second trip there and back and she was very pleased with herself.

She was enjoying the sunshine, the fresh crisp autumn air, and the fun of her visit with her friend, when she heard a buggy approaching from behind her. She slowed and steered the bike closer to the berm of the road. As the buggy passed her, Leah recognized her friend from church, Anna.

Anna pulled the buggy to the side of the road and leaned out as Leah pedaled faster to catch up.

"Hi, Leah! A new bike?" Anna's smile could light up the whole of Holmes County. A few wisps of her honey blond hair were dancing in the breeze around her face.

"*Ja*, Jacob bought it for me and I love it. I was just down the road visiting with Sarah."

"That's wonderful! I think I might see about getting one, too, as soon as we can find the time to go shop for one."

"I highly recommend them," Leah laughed.

Anna smiled back. "I wanted to chat with you for a second, if you have time."

143

Leah nodded. "I have time."

"Did Jacob tell you what happened to us? It's a good thing, not something bad," Anna hinted. Her smile grew. "Liam and I gave our hearts to Jesus!"

"*Ja,* he told me about Liam, but now you're telling me about you. I'm so happy for you both!"

"It's a great feeling. We've been reading our Bible every morning, but we'd really love to host a Bible study. What do you think? We're considering Saturday mornings, about eight, if you and Jacob can come."

Leah considered the invitation. "I think that's a great idea. We'd love to come. I'll talk it over with Jacob. Do you plan to start this Saturday?"

"Yes, and I'll serve breakfast so we can all get on with our days after the meeting. What do you think?"

An impatient driver of a miniature scrunched-up looking auto beeped the car's tinny-sounding horn several times before he pulled around them. He shook his head angrily as he puttered past.

Leah glanced at Anna and shrugged. "I guess we're in the way— even for that tiny car."

They laughed. Leah put a foot on the left pedal. "I'd better get going anyway. I'll be sure to tell Jacob about the Bible study tonight after he gets home from work. What would you like us to bring?"

Anna shook her head. "I have plenty of baked goods, and I'll fry some bacon, and sausage patties, too. Plus coffee, of course. How's that sound?"

"Sounds yummy. See you Saturday!"

Leah watched as Anna pulled the buggy carefully back onto the road and headed home.

The sun warmed the back of Leah's shoulders, relaxing her tight muscles from the work day and her long ride to Sarah's house and back toward the farm. For the first time since moving to Holmes County, she truly felt a part of the community. She grinned as she cycled toward home. Yes. Life was good.

As she neared the Coblentz farm, Leah slowed, trying, as she always did when she came to this spot in the road, to see the children or perhaps catch a glimpse of Clara. The warm sun prompted her to stop.

She craned her neck to see around the tall corn drying in the fields. She decided to go down the lane a bit. Since Henry had gotten a suspended sentence for attacking Leah, she'd not seen him or the rest of the family. While she was glad, for Clara's sake, that Henry only served the time before his trial in jail, she worried that his run-in with the justice system hadn't scared him enough to change him.

She eased down the lane, pedaling just enough to keep the bike upright, her eyes moving back and forth in case it was Henry she ran into first. She nearly screamed when one of the children slapped the back of her bike.

"Leah! We've missed you!"

Leah twisted around, put her feet to the ground to keep from toppling, and got off the bike. She eased it to the graveled drive and took hold of little Daniel.

"Daniel, I've missed all of you so much, too!" She knelt to wrap her arms around his slight frame. To her, he appeared even thinner than when she'd last seen him. "Daniel, how is your *maem*?"

He danced loose of her hold and took off flying toward the house calling "Leah's here! Leah's here!"

She shrank back, alarmed that Henry might be nearby. But instead of Henry, Leah was delighted to see Clara hurrying to her, with all the children, including the baby clutched awkwardly by Saloma.

Their reunion was filled with hugs and tears.

"Leah, I've longed for a visit from you! I'd love to ask you in, but Henry will be back any minute and he's not to have any contact with you." She glanced around Leah to the road, checking to see if her husband had gotten close to home.

Leah, laughed as first one, and then another of the Coblentz children pulled her into tight hugs. "I would love to visit but I understand and I wouldn't want Henry to get into any more trouble. Just tell me quickly: Are you and the children okay?"

"Yes, things are settling down now. I'll try to get in touch with you sometime. Okay?" Clara turned her gaze from Leah's and shooed the excited children toward home so Leah could go on her way. She gave her friend a quick hug before she hurried to catch up.

As they scurried away, Saloma twisted around, holding Leah's eyes while adjusting the weight of the baby in her arms. "Bye, Leah! Don't forget me!"

Tears welled as Leah held the frail child's gaze until she'd disappeared behind a stand of tall pines near the house.

Leah picked up the bike, rotated it back to the road and rushed to get away before she met Henry.

*Oh, God—please, please keep them all safe.*

Her heart rate remained elevated until she rode over the next hill where she breathed a sigh of relief. She let the bike's weight defy gravity, coasting down the hill, soaring past driveways and lanes until she slowed to pull into her own driveway. Made it! Another road trip under her belt and not a single accident.

CHAPTER TWENTY-TWO

Saturday arrived, a little gloomier than the past few days, with dampness and chillier temperatures to forewarn them of the coming winter. They bundled up well as Bingo pulled them along the empty road to Anna and Liam's place. When they turned into the lane, Leah was surprised to see a few buggies in the barnyard.

"They're really going to have a great turnout," Leah exclaimed.

Jacob glanced from buggy to buggy. "Yes, it seems that way. I'm not sure who all is here." He faced Leah, his eyes bright. "It's going to be fun, *ja?*"

Leah nodded, her cheeks rosy from the cool air and excitement. "I hope so. It'll be so nice to be able to chat with others about salvation, the way we've experienced it."

Leah waited as Jacob tended to Bingo. They walked together to the house, Leah's smile widening the closer they got to the door.

Anna greeted them before they had a chance to knock. "Glad you made it."

Liam led them to the living room. There were two other couples from church that Leah recognized, but didn't know well. They smiled at each other as she and Jacob took seats along the arc formed by

147

folding chairs. A shy awkwardness stole over Leah. She wished she knew these folks better.

Abe and Verna Borntrager came next, and then turned to introduce the group to an Amish couple who were peeking out from behind the Borntragers.

"This is my cousin, Leroy Borntrager, and his wife Susan."

The man and his wife moved around the circle, shaking hands and murmuring polite hellos before finding a seat together on the settee. The husband of the couple wore scruffy shoes and held his rough hands between his knees, wringing them over and over. His wife had a long face, her cheek bones sharply evident under tense muscles. She kept her eyes downcast, only allowing them to rise every few minutes to scan the group and then flutter downward again.

They looked terribly uncomfortable and Leah's heart went out to them. How well she recalled the first Bible study she had attended back home in Ashfield. There had been mostly English-dressed young people there, but she knew some had once been Amish.

From the clothing style, Leah guessed this couple came from a strict group of Amish—much more conservative than the New Order church she and Jacob now belonged to.

"*Wie gehts?*" Leah asked in Pennsylvania Dutch.

The wife did not make eye contact, but her husband lifted his chin to give a tentative reply. "*Gut.*"

Anna, friendly as ever, bounded over to introduce herself. The Amish man's eyes widened at her enthusiastic greeting. From the look on both the man and woman's faces, they weren't sure what this gathering held for them.

After Anna called them to a hearty breakfast around a table in the long dining room, they assembled back in the living room, where the discussion eventually steered itself to the plan of salvation.

Leah knew then why Abe had asked Leroy and Susan to come. As the talk went on, Leah observed the couple when Scripture was read about being "born again." Their eyes locked together, both of them appearing concerned.

"Would you like to share what MAP did for you when you first became a believer?"

Liam directed his question to Leah, which caught her off guard. She had no idea he knew about her conversion experience while being involved with MAP Ministry.

"Uh—sorry, Liam. I was distracted."

He chuckled. "I was telling the group about ministries that are geared to help those in the Amish communities learn more about Christ and His saving grace. I remembered that Jacob told me you'd had contact with Mission to Amish People and Matthew and Naomi Schrock. Correct?"

She glanced to the low order Amish couple. As she suspected might happen, their eyes widened even further when they heard the Schrocks' names.

She cleared her throat. It had been a long time since she'd shared her testimony. In this group, where she barely knew folks, she was hesitant. Nevertheless, she soldiered on.

"Oh, sure. The Schrocks have a ministry to those who are Amish—sharing literature and such, about growing in the Lord, as well as offering aid to those who have left the Amish. They help with life skills among the English. A transition-type ministry."

Suddenly, Leroy Borntrager stood and pulled his wife up beside him. He turned to his cousin, his voice tense and wobbly as he spoke.

"This is not what we expected to hear, Abe! Everyone knows that the Schrocks are of the Devil. They steal Amish young people and keep them in a sort of spell. They ruin Amish lives and break up Amish families! Why would you ask me and my wife to be a part of something like this?"

The couple pushed through the circle of believers and started for the door. Abe and Liam followed them, their expressions calm and compassionate.

"Leroy, please don't be offended. I only wanted you to meet some who have given their hearts to Jesus—fully and with peace. All here are brothers and sisters in Christ. We care about you and Susan. And, honestly Leroy, the gossip about the Schrocks among the Amish is wrong. We know of them and receive their literature. Nothing could be further from the truth about their motives. They only want to share the freedom of Christ's grace. That's all. Nothing more than that."

Leah stood, hurrying to Susan's side.

"Please don't be frightened. There's nothing going on here or with MAP Ministry that's wrong or sinful. I can tell you from first-hand experience that MAP Ministry is filled with caring Christian people. Their hearts want only to help. The Schrocks have never stolen anyone or kidnapped anyone or done anything like that. I lived, for a time, in their home—in an apartment they have for former Amish, like I was at the time. They were both kind and supportive. And when I went back to my Amish community, I still found they were kind and supportive. They understood all that I was going through because they had gone through it, too."

Susan Borntrager's eyes shimmered with unshed tears. "I'm sure it was okay for you, but we come from a low church and this meeting is not what we are taught is *gut*."

Leroy directed his wife to the door. "We'll be leaving now. Abe, thank you for inviting us, but this is not for us."

After the departure of the couple, a somber mood fell over the remainder of those gathered. Liam led them in a final prayer and they shared a few Bible verses with one another before the event came to an end.

Later that night, as Leah lay under the quilt on their bed, she asked Jacob why her people could be fearful of something as innocent as MAP Ministry. "It, again, is just gossip, Jacob. Even here, in Holmes County—surrounded by folks like our *gut* bishop—gossip and rumors spoil people's lives."

"I know. And if the gossipers would really think about it, it would be very hard to steal people away from their lives and families if they didn't want to be taken."

Leah nodded, her voice softened by exhaustion and the need for sleep. "Yes, but many don't want to know anything else. They like the gossip and want to think *viescht* things about others."

Jacob rolled over, gave her a sweet kiss and sighed. "True. But now it's time for sleep. I'm more tired than I thought I'd be on a Saturday night. Before I know it, it'll be time for my shift again. Love you, wife."

He ended his speech with a fake snore.

Leah laughed. "Love you back, husband. Guess I'll solve the world's problems, with your help, of course, another night."

# CHAPTER TWENTY-THREE

The next Sunday, as she and Jacob hurried to line up before going into church, she noticed a small group of women watching her. She smiled and waved, but instead of the warm welcome she expected, they turned away, their cheeks reddening at her greeting.

She stopped mid-stride, as the significance of the moment grew. She recognized what they were doing. They were letting her know she had done something wrong. But—what?

Jacob broke his step when she stopped. "What's going on?"

She dropped her gaze. "That group over there. I have a feeling they're talking about me."

Jacob laughed. "What? Now what makes you think that?"

"They are! I know it, Jacob. I, of all people, should know when someone is talking about me. Remember?"

Her eyes flashed as she met his gaze. His laughter exaggerated her hurt. His expression fell, and he scrutinized the church members to find the group she was referring to. The women were still huddled in their clique, and once in a while, one of them peeked at Leah and Jacob.

"Not again," he muttered under his breath as he pulled Leah along, guiding her gently to her place in line. Just before he released her arm, he squeezed it. The look he sent her was tender. The hurt he felt for her showed clearly in his eyes.

All during service, she felt eyes on her. She was alternately puzzled and furious. She wished she knew what was going on. She hoped, and simultaneously dreaded, that someone would let her in on what sin she had committed.

And then it hit her. Someone had reported the discussion about MAP Ministry from the Bible study yesterday morning. Someone had thought her involvement with MAP was dangerous.

Her thoughts turned to Anna and Liam. Were they getting the cold shoulder, too?

She leaned across Sarah to tap Anna on the arm just before the last hymn began.

"Are you in trouble?" she mouthed.

Anna's eyebrows furrowed. She shook her head.

Sarah leaned close. "What did you want to ask Anna?"

"I wanted to know if she's in trouble."

Sarah's eyes widened as she whispered "Why?"

"Because of the Bible study. I'm being ignored."

Leah raised a thumb, pointing it to the group of older women, which included Barbara Mast, Elizabeth Miller, and Hannah Yoder, sitting at the back.

Sarah sneaked a peek and then frowned. Her tightened lips and shoulder shrug indicated she was ignorant of their complaints. But she tuned to Anna and whispered to the young host of the Bible study Leah's question. Leah watched as Anna shook her head, met her gaze and shrugged.

Leah nodded as she sat back. So she *was* being singled out once again. Her heart sank.

Obviously the troubled couple who'd been at the meeting had a channel to this church. That channel had wasted no time spreading gossip about Leah. Was it just the MAP Ministry connection that got her in hot water this time? Or had they been able to dig up old tittle-tattle from her past to add to the spicy talk?

She didn't have to wait long to find out which iniquity was being discussed.

After the service, before dinner was fully ready, the bishop asked Jacob and Leah to walk with him in the fragrant apple orchard behind the barn at the host family's property.

There he informed them that one of the ladies had told him about Leah's support of MAP Ministry. She had also included Leah's past history and her wayward days when she'd left the Amish. The bishop made it clear to them, though, with a much appreciated sense of humor in the telling, that he wasn't concerned about her past as much as the gossipmongers were.

His eyes twinkled as he gently reminded her that the Amish were a tad too fond of holding on to past mistakes, especially if it wasn't their own errors in judgment, in spite of the church's mandate to forgive.

"I've met some who, though their mouths said 'forgiven', I could see through their eyes their minds were crying 'Guilty! Guilty! Guilty!'" He chuckled. "I bring this to you only to remind you that when folks are searching for sins in their sister or brother," he nodded to Jacob, "they will certainly find them. I know I'm included in this seeking out of foul things. Oh, yes! A bishop isn't excluded from this kind of scrutiny."

His drollness took the edge off the information. Leah was relieved he kept a sense of humor concerning the gossip he'd received, but she was still embarrassed to be singled out.

She glanced toward Jacob, measuring how he was taking the news of being the topic of discussion among church members. She was comforted to see a wide grin lighting his face.

"Bishop, this *fraa* here, she's going to keep me on my toes."

The bishop threw back his head in hearty laughter. "And you'll never have a dull day because of her, Jacob. What a gift!"

Still chuckling, he turned to Leah. "Don't let this get to you, young lady. A few of our church members are rigid in their thinking. Though they often challenge me, devotion to their faith also shows me a certain strength of character, I suppose. We all have a place in the body of Christ, right?"

He smiled again. "I'm pleased by how much your heart is soft toward *Gott*, Leah. And your youthful enthusiasm makes me happy. The joy of the Lord is never wrong to celebrate, especially when it comes in the form of a ministry that reaches a hand out in charity. But perhaps a little discretion will have to be maintained about who hears these affirmations, eh? And, in the meantime, I hope to diffuse the chatter with some sound teaching on gossip." He winked. "That's always a squelcher of a sermon topic."

Leah felt her cheeks warm. "*Ja.* I'm *gut* with that."

"Are we okay, then, young people?" The bishop's kind eyes sought theirs and when they nodded, he nodded, too.

"*Gut.* Let's go eat."

✺🏠✺

At home, after church service, Leah, Jacob, and Sarah, who had come along with them to spend the afternoon, were chatting about the Bible study.

Sarah tilted her head, her knitted brows questioning. "I don't get why you were the only one that was reported to the bishop, Leah."

"Well, I get why, I just don't get why it still matters what I did when I was young and foolish."

Jacob sat back, a small frown covering his face. "So do you think your time away from the Amish was just you being young and foolish, Leah?"

She started to nod, but then stopped. "You know what? I guess not, because in many ways, I think I grew up a little, too. Finding MAP, making the decision to know Jesus, and even just being my own person, was helpful."

Jacob nodded. "I think so, too. And don't forget, you brought me to Jesus after being out in the world, so to speak."

He splayed his hard-working hands on the table.

155

"Then can we say, from here on out, that you didn't just run away. You weren't just being rebellious or foolish or angry. You didn't give your heart over to Satan. You should *not* be shamed for your actions. Can we make that a rule around here from now on?"

His eyes flashed an uncommon glint of anger, followed quickly by a soft smile as he reached for Leah's hands.

"I'm not going to put up with anyone, from here on out, bringing shame on you, Leah. You're a thoughtful, kind person. A woman after God's own heart. I won't allow undeserved talk to bring your spirit down. Not anymore."

He released her hands, stood, and walked purposefully to the kitchen. "Time for ice cream, ladies!"

Leah and Sarah stared at each other, eyes rounded in astonishment.

"Wow. That was a great speech!" Sarah exclaimed.

Leah's eyes welled with tears as she reached for a paper napkin to wipe them.

"I think you know now why I love him so much. He rarely makes proclamations, but when he does, he means it."

Sarah patted Leah's arm as she stood to get a box of Kleenex. "Here. These were made for tears and are a lot softer than that paper napkin."

She stretched before taking her seat at the table again.

"Leah, I know I've told you about the abuse I suffered, but I've held back telling you about my number one fear. And I think it comes from my childhood— and what happened to me."

Her tender-hearted friend paused to wipe her eyes. "It's very hard to talk about abuse like this. I've not trusted anyone else enough to share my story."

Leah nodded, her eyes riveted to Sarah's gentle face. "I'm honored you trust me. I promise to uphold that trust."

Sarah sniffed. "As a result of all the abuse, both physical and sexual, I'm left with this idea that I'll never be good enough for Heaven."

Sarah choked back a sob, and turned her face away for a moment, gathering her composure before going on. "There's always this voice inside my head telling me I brought on some of that abuse. I liked the attention. Or I enjoyed the—the—well, you know." Her cheeks flushed deep red.

Leah's heart broke to hear her dear friend sharing these sad secrets. "Oh, Sarah—"

Sarah put up a hand. "No—let me *finally* get it all out. I know in my head that I was a child, so I wasn't ever at fault, for any of it. But in my heart, in my soul, just before I go to sleep, all these memories, these doubts about my own innocence, come flooding in. I can hardly rest. I mean, can I be sure that some of those sins aren't part of my doing? If they were, how can I work enough at goodness to overcome those terrible days? My brother told me once that I invited his attentions with my smile."

Leah interrupted Sarah. "No! You can't believe that because it's not true! A predator is a predator. You could not stop him, no matter how hard you tried."

Leah's hands fisted in her lap at the thought of this kind lady taking on guilt that was not hers to own.

Sarah lowered her face, but when she again met Leah's eyes, a twinkle showed in her own eyes. "Leah, oh, my sweet, sweet champion. You'd fight it out with my brother if you could, wouldn't you?"

Leah calmed herself with a deep breath and chuckled. "I abhor bullies so much, my days on earth could possibly end with me foolishly tackling a tyrant three times my size."

The two friends laughed, easing the tension in the room.

After a few seconds of silence, Leah spoke. "You don't have go on with the details, Sarah. Though, if you need to, I'll listen. "

Sarah sniffed again and shook her head. "I think you get the point."

Leah nodded. "I do. I really do. And here's what I know: Jesus cares about what happened to you. The church may have failed you, but He never will. His blood covers any sin you or I will ever commit, even though this abuse isn't *your* sin. However, any feelings you have that you aren't good enough, strong enough, or clean enough to make it to Heaven, are true."

Sarah frowned, a stunned look crossing her features.

Leah hurried to reassure Sarah. "And by that I mean that *none* of us are good enough, strong enough, or clean enough to get to heaven. No matter what our life experiences are." Leah held out her hands. "That's why our Father in Heaven sent His only son to die for us. And that's why asking Jesus into our lives, acknowledging that we'll never be good enough or strong enough or clean enough, is all it takes to receive the gift of grace. Grace means we get the gift without deserving it at all. Our slates, from the moment we accept Jesus into our hearts, are wiped clean. That's good news, Sarah."

Sarah closed her eyes. "I know this with my head, but my heart doesn't always believe it. And, about this grace—how can I know, really *know*, that I'm saved and will go to Heaven? Our church doesn't emphasize that teaching."

Leah was moved to tears at her friend's dejected countenance. She reached for her Bible and opened it.

"This, my friend, is how we're going to fight that battle in your soul. I fight this battle, too. And Jacob does, too, as well as any person who has placed their life in Christ's hands."

She opened the Bible. "*Gott* left us this book to help us know how to carry on. And John 3:16 tells us God wants us to turn to Him—to trust in Jesus. And one more thing—He gave educated believers the knowledge to deal with the damage done by others in their minds, like you by your brother. After we get done climbing this hill about grace, then we'll get ready to climb that one about the abuse with a Bible believing counselor."

Sarah stood and pulled Leah into a hug.

"You keep saying 'we', like you're going to go down this road with me. But you have your own problems to tackle, Leah. You don't need a clingy old woman to worry over, too."

Leah squeezed her friend tightly. "That's where you're absolutely wrong. I said 'we' and I meant 'we'. Got that?"

When Jacob came back in with freshly churned ice cream, he stopped.

"What's going on? Why are you both wiping tears?"

Leah laughed. "Jacob, there's something you need to remember. We women cry happy, sad, and relieved tears. I'm afraid it's going to be part of your life from now on, husband."

He sighed, placed the ice cream on the table, got a bowl and spoon for each of them, and turned on his heels.

"I'll be in the barn. Enjoy the ice cream."

"Now *that's* a good man!" Sarah laughed.

# CHAPTER TWENTY-FOUR

Leah woke to a gloomy, rainy day. Two weeks had gone by quickly as she settled into her new home. She'd washed the curtains, then the windows, and sorted through linens, housewares, and bathroom toiletries to get a feel for what they had on hand and what they still needed.

She took the time at her small *suppah*, since Jacob was away at work, to write out wedding thank-you notes. She'd canned the last of the season's apples into applesauce. All in all, she'd gotten their things, and herself, more organized.

She reflected on the talk she'd had with Sarah about faith, grace, and sin. The result had been that Sarah had turned her life over to Christ.

The thought of it sent shivers down her back—the good kind that comes when folks see changes for the better in their friends. Sarah gained a new confidence in her life. Leah certainly could tell and she was excited to see her friend in church the next morning.

She hurried to the door when a knock came.

Outside stood the postal carrier, her nose cherry red from the bitter wind whipping around the farmhouse front porch. She waved a square package too large to fit in the mailbox at Leah, and handed her letters, as well. "You've got mail, as they say."

"Oh, a package! Come in, please. Warm yourself a bit. I'm Leah Rab—oops—nope! Still can't get used to the last name. I'm Leah Yoder."

She offered a welcoming hand to her visitor.

"Newly married, then? I'm Leonora Keith. I've been on this route about one year now."

The mail carrier stepped inside, stamping the snow off her feet as she offered a wide smile. "This feels great—the heat is wonderfully cozy and warm."

"How about if I fix you a cup of coffee, tea, or hot chocolate to take along with you on the rest of your route?" Leah offered.

Leonora nodded. "That would be super! A cup of coffee'll be a treat on this windy day."

"I have a pot ready on the stove. I won't be a minute."

Leah hurried to the kitchen, calling over her shoulder as she went, "How do you drink it?"

Leonora stood on the rug, jiggling warmth back into her feet as she waited. "Black is great, thank you. I really appreciate the coffee."

Leah found a Styrofoam cup, hunted down its lid, then poured the steaming brew into the cup. She grabbed a couple of brownies, wrapped them in cellophane and headed back to the door.

"Here you go. I threw in some brownies for good measure."

Leonora's smile widened. "Perfect! You sure know how to spoil me. It was really nice to meet you, Leah. Best wishes to you and your new husband, too. I'd better get going—but thank you so much for the hospitality."

"You're very welcome. Hope the rest of your day goes well."

After Leah shut the door, she hurried back to the kitchen with the package and mail.

"Hmm … a package for Jacob. Oh, yes. It's sample seeds."

She shifted her attention to the letter, which bore Martha's name and return address. Eagerly Leah opened it and slid out the letter.

Dear Leah

I know this is last minute, but I have a favor to ask. Do you think you can talk Sarah into accepting me as a roommate very soon? I have a job lined up down there with one of the restaurants and I'm supposed to begin in a week. But first I need a place to live. I managed to save some of my salary from working up here, but I may need another week to earn more, if she requires more. I've enclosed a check, with fingers crossed that all things will work out.

Just think! The two of us near each other again! Let me know as soon as possible if Sarah's place will be available. Johnny will be staying here with my *maem* for a time—until I get on my feet.

Take care until I see you!

Martha

PS—Here's my cell number! (It's a smart phone.)

Leah shook her head as she folded the letter up and put it in her apron pocket. A smart phone. Leave it to Martha to push the boundaries ever further.

She'd call Sarah soon to ask about when she would be ready for Martha to come as a housemate. She frowned when she thought about little Johnny staying with his grandmother. Martha's *maem* had made Leah uncomfortable when she had overlooked the abuse Martha had suffered—even blaming her daughter for it.

"If this is your plan, *Gott*, help things fall into place, for Johnny's sake."

It would be nice, though, for her friend to move close again. Perhaps this would be a road of recovery and restoration for Martha.

Leah finished the chores she'd begun that morning and then feasted on popcorn and apples for *suppah*. She yawned, stretching out sore muscles.

Time to get ready for bed. She glanced at the clock. Ten-thirty. Jacob would be home in about an hour.

She made her way up the stairs and down the hall to their bedroom, where she gathered her gown, robe, and slippers. Across the hall, she ran a hot bath and soaked for a little while. As she was stepping from the tub, a towel clasped around her, she was startled by a thud against the back of the house.

"*Was in die Welt?* What was that?" She stood stock still, straining to hear sounds unfamiliar to the natural creaks of the house.

Nothing.

"You really are turning into a nervous Nelly," she muttered to herself.

Leah moved to the mirror, brushed her teeth, and shuffled back into their bedroom. She stuffed her dirty clothes in the hamper, and scampered down the stairs to the living room.

The cozy room invited her to relax into the rocking chair settled at the side of the sofa. She grabbed a throw from the back of the couch and wrapped herself in its folds. Next to the chair on the corner of a small square table rested the book she'd been reading, so she picked it up and eagerly dove back into the story.

As she gently rocked to and fro in the chair, the lull of the motion soothed her spirit. The tale inside the book took her mind far away from Holmes County.

The sound of the clock ticking away the minutes before Jacob would be home both soothed her and agitated her. She loved and hated this time of night. The minute hand moved slowly every evening he was gone to work, yet she knew each passing minute brought him closer to being back.

Suddenly, she felt as though she was being watched. The back of her neck prickled. Try as she might to get control of her actions, she froze in mid-rock, her muscles refusing her brain's command to behave naturally.

Adrenalin poured through her body, bringing instant heat. She slid her gaze toward the kitchen window, just beyond the living room at the back of the house. Were those eyes at the window?

She jerked forward, all sense of composure drowning under a tidal wave of panic. Dropping the book from her hand, her body trembled, but she was frozen in place as her vision honed in on the framed black square.

Was there truly another human being staring back at her, or was it a reflection of her own wide eyes in the dark glass? What should she do?

As she stared down the shadowy menace just beyond the safety of the farmhouse walls, a rush of indignation filled her being. The idea that someone would *dare* to spy on her through her own window!

She jumped up, the rocker tilting and then crashing back on both curved legs as she marched across the room and into the kitchen. She jerked the curtain fully wide, but nothing was revealed except her own blurry image on the shiny ebony glass.

She huffed on the cool pane and used her sleeve to wipe the window clean. She peered closer, trying to view any movement in the black edges of the yard.

There! Was that someone darting away?

She squinted and tried to adjust her vision, but if it was a person, she could no longer see the voyeur.

She pulled the curtain panels tightly over the window and moved slowly back to sit in the rocking chair. How she wished Jacob was home!

She glanced at the clock. Ten-forty-two. He would clock out of work at eleven.

She exhaled loudly and stooped to pick up the book, its spine stretched and pages splayed carelessly on the wood floor. She shook off the dust and tenderly closed the book. Just as she laid the book atop the side table, a knock sounded on the front door. She jumped straight up.

The caller had to be the prowler that had been spying on her!

She tip-toed cautiously toward the door and edged her way to the side of the front window. Leah pulled the curtain back enough to provide a sneak peek at whoever was standing on the porch, but without a bright moon, she could barely make out the shadow of a man.

Could it be Henry Coblentz? Or Bert Small?

Either man made her heart race if one of them was waiting just beyond the door. Both would know Jacob's work schedule, too.

*Oh, Gott, protect me!*

She dropped the curtain back in place and leaned against the cool wall. Now she was afraid to move. Afraid the person on the other side of the wall would hear her scoot away. Would he try to break in?

A minute crawled forward. She let out her breath, relieved that whoever was out there didn't knock again. Her gaze shifted to the door knob. Thankfully, it remained stationary.

After what seemed like hours, she slowly moved the curtain aside enough to peep outside. Again, it was too dark to see anything clearly, but she sensed, more than observed, that the porch was empty.

She scanned the front yard, focusing her vision on murky obscurities and shifting shadows. Her gaze followed the line of outbuildings toward the barn.

Nothing stood out. She wished with all her heart that a full moon was hanging over her house.

She inhaled, closed her eyes, and then slowly blew out warmed air. Her muscles loosened as her mind calmed the quick staccato of her heart.

Once more she scanned the yard and barn.

Whoever had been on the porch was gone. *Thank you, Gott!*

But, wait! Was that a shadowy form by the edge of the barn—facing the lane?

Her breath quickened as the intruder stepped away from the building. It really *was* a person lurking about her house!

Before she could comprehend anything but alarm, the figure hunched low and scrambled over the black grass toward the road.

Was it Bert or was it Henry?

Her hands shook and knees trembled as her body was drenched once more in fear. *Oh, Jacob! Come home right now!*

She watched the tree line near the road for the emerging figure, but her vision was clouded by panic and she couldn't focus properly. She finally tore herself away from the eerie image and forced herself to pray for wisdom and safety.

Again her eyes darted to the clock. Nearly eleven.

Leah hurried to the kitchen and turned the gas on under her tea pot. She had to calm down. Whoever had been at their house was gone now, or at least not standing on the front porch. She reminded herself that the man had knocked but had done nothing else to try to get in.

A worship song came to mind—one she remembered from the days when she'd left the Amish and attended English church. She sang at the top of her lungs as she waited for the water to boil—inviting *Gott's* peace to quiet her spirit and body.

At last the teapot whistled and she poured the hot liquid into her mug. She dipped the tea bag a few times through the water and added a spoonful of honey.

She carried the tea to the sofa, folded her legs under her and wrapped the soft throw over her shoulders. Humming between sips, she picked up her Bible and tried to engage her mind in His Word.

By the time she heard the work van's tires humming along the road to their driveway, Leah was worn out by the stress she'd felt in the past hour. Hearing Jacob's feet hit the porch from the top step launched her into action.

She ran to the door, pulled it open and flew into his arms.

"Oh, Jacob! I'm so happy to see you!"

He accepted her hug gladly, pulling her close.

Never had she felt more gratitude for her husband's presence than at that moment.

# CHAPTER TWENTY-FIVE

L eah felt Jacob stir in his sleep, causing her to scoot closer to him. His warm presence filled her again with reassurance. Just having him home brought security to her being.

After she'd told him everything that had happened last night, he'd held her tightly, caressing her shoulders and offering comfort for what she'd been through.

They had talked about why either man would try to get Leah to open the door at such a late hour. And lurking around the farm held no other explanation but mischief, even if the intention was just to scare Leah.

"I'm not going to confront Bert at work, but I'm sure going to watch him closer. The thing is that I'm not aware he left early. But I could have missed him going—the line was chaotic," he'd offered.

Leah had shuddered. "That leaves Henry. And I haven't seen or talked to him in weeks. If he's still feeding a grudge against me, he's really a troubled soul."

Their discussion led to no conclusions, but Jacob had brought up the possibility of filing another sheriff's report. He told her he was growing increasingly concerned over these trespassing incidents.

"I pray this will not lead to anything else, Leah. But I do wonder if the sheriff's department should know of the on-going troubles."

They'd gone to bed, mentally exhausted and confused. Leah hadn't really slept at all. Her mind kept going over the problems they'd encountered in the last few weeks. Church, work place, the Bible study, the break in and the threats, and now this latest trespassing. What was going on?

As dawn spilled light over the farmhouse, Leah finally gave up trying to sleep and slipped from the bed. Padding to the kitchen, she yawned and set the coffee pot in place over the burner. Coffee was going to taste extra good this morning.

She fried eggs and thick ham slices, toasted bread, and set out jam, fresh butter, and church spread on the table.

Her gaze was drawn to the back window where she'd first seen someone looking in at her. She moved to the sparkling panes and peered around at the ground beneath the glass. Nothing looked sinister. Everything was a normal and carefree autumn daybreak. A light frost iced the stiff grass and little sparrows flitted back and forth through the chilly air. All was well, mocking the terror of the night before with morning's fresh innocence.

She heard Jacob coming down the stairs and went to stand in the doorway between the kitchen and living room. "Morning, sleepyhead," she teased.

He yawned and stretched as he reached for her. "You, on the other hand, didn't sleep much, I think." He kissed her gently. "Are you okay?"

She nodded, guiding him to sit at the table. "I am. Watching out the window this morning makes everything that was so sinister and threatening last night seem like nothing more than a nightmare. Like it never happened."

She pulled plates from the cupboard and arranged silverware at their places on the table. The scent of brewed coffee and crisped bacon wafted through the air, prompting a growl from her stomach.

"Boy, breakfast smells good!" Jacob pulled his coffee closer, added milk to it and sipped. "Ah—that hits the spot."

Leah dished up the food and settled into her chair across from her husband. "I can't believe how hungry I am this morning. What a feast to my eyes."

Jacob prayed as they held hands and then both tucked into the hearty spread.

"What are your plans for the day, Leah?" he asked between bites of salty bacon.

"First off, I plan to call Sarah and ask her if she's ready for another roomie. I got a letter from Martha saying she has a job offer here in Holmes County and she needs to find a place to live."

Jacob smiled. "Hey, that'll be great for you to have your friend so close again."

Leah nodded. "It will. I'm really hoping Sarah will tell me to let Martha know she's more than ready for her."

"I'm glad she's coming here. What about her boy?"

Leah paused, a frown forming between her eyes. "Martha told me that little Johnny is staying with her *maem*. I'm a bit worried about that, though. Martha's *maem*—well, you know her. She's not been the best mother to Martha and seemed to resent the little guy from the moment he was born."

Jacob dipped his toast in soft egg. "*Ja*, I remember that."

He chewed a minute or two longer, not saying anything else. But Leah knew that look. He was thinking of something. She also knew to wait it out. Eventually, what he was thinking about would be revealed.

Sure enough, as they ate in companionable silence, Jacob finally pushed his plate back, took a sip of coffee, and then met her gaze.

"Why the twinkle in your eyes and grin on your face?" he asked her.

She giggled. "You. I can always tell when you've hatched some sort of plan by the way you look."

He laughed. "Well, you're right. I have."

Leah leaned over the table and gave him a swift kiss. "Tell me."

"I was thinking that when it's time for Martha to move down here, we could hire Ella to drive and go with her to help Martha move. Then we could stay overnight and see my family, too. What do you think?"

Leah jumped up and danced around the table. "I would love that, husband!"

He maneuvered her to his lap. "Then it's a done deal, wife."

Later that day, Leah finished wiping down the tub in the bathroom, when she heard Jacob come back in from the barn.

"Leah, someone's here to see you."

Leah, curious, tossed the cleaning rag in her housekeeping bucket, straightened her hair and *kapp*, and went to see who was with Jacob.

As she walked into the living room, standing just inside the front door was Henry.

She paused. Why was he here? He wasn't allowed to come near her, according to the law.

She folded her arms over her chest. "Henry."

He had removed his hat and the sight of his sallow cheeks brought a lump to Leah's throat. The stress of his experiences over the last year was mapped in his face.

He nodded a greeting, turning troubled eyes to Jacob.

Jacob nodded. "Henry came to the barn to talk with me. He has something he wants to tell you."

The anxious man continued to stand mute, rolling his hat over and over again in his familiar pattern.

"Go ahead," Jacob gently encouraged.

Henry shuffled from one foot to the other. Finally he spoke softly, so softly, Leah had trouble hearing him. Again her heart went out to him, and she moved closer, pointing to the settee, encouraging him to sit.

Henry shambled to the settee and lowered his thin body carefully, perching himself on the edge of the furniture.

After Jacob joined Leah on the sofa, she waited patiently for Henry to begin.

170

"I came to tell you that I'm going to a treatment place for Amish people in northern Indiana. I—I've made a mess of my life and my family's life." He glanced away. "I wanted to tell you that I'm very sorry for what I did to you. The alcohol just took over my mind. I was out of control. And not just to you."

Leah nodded. "I've forgiven you long ago. I mean that. I'm glad you're going to get help with this. Your family deserves to have a happy and sober man in their lives."

He cleared his throat. "*Ja*, they do. I still have to talk it over with Bishop Troyer, but he seems to be a reasonable and kind man. I think he'll agree."

Jacob nodded. "He is, you can count on that, Henry. Godly and fair. What about the court?"

"The court suggested another place, but it wasn't just for Amish people, so I asked if it would be okay to go to the center."

He stood, his visit apparently over. "I'm going to miss Clara and the *kinner*, but I'm looking forward to getting this behind me."

He shuffled to the door, paused, then shot out a shaking hand toward Leah. "Again, I'm really sorry for the way I treated you. I hope you can think of me with kindness one day."

Leah shook his hand. She glanced to Jacob. "Our prayers will continue, Henry. May *Gott* go with you."

Before he left, he stopped, turning to Leah once more. "Do you think it would be too much to ask for you to visit Clara once in a while? I know she'd love that and so would the children."

Leah smiled. "It would be a pleasure to do that, Henry."

Henry turned to Jacob. "I can let you know when I'm going, so you and the missus can freely drive out to the farm for a visit."

Jacob stretched out his hand, giving Henry's hand a firm shake. "I'll be sure to look in on the farm, too, and with the church men's help, we'll keep things going there. You worry about you for now."

Henry dipped his chin. "Much obliged."

They watched as he made his way to the buggy he'd tethered to the barnyard hitching post. Henry untied his horse, climbed onto the ebony seat and squared his shoulders. With a twitch of the reins, he drove to the road, guided the horse to the right and disappeared beyond the pines toward his home.

Leah chewed her lip and sighed. "He looks a little bit stronger already, Jacob. I'm glad he came to apologize." She closed the door. "And his visit also lets us know it wasn't him outside our door last night."

Their gazes met.

Jacob sighed. "I guess I have to admit that it was most likely Bert. I guess he did leave work early."

Leah nodded. "I can't think of any other person who would be out there at ten-thirty, Jacob. Or anyone else who has a vendetta against us."

Jacob shook his head. "I'll have to keep a close eye on him. If anything else happens, we have to report him to the sheriff, for sure." He frowned. "Why in the world is that man so determined to bring trouble down on his own head? We've done nothing to him."

Leah hugged her husband. "Except be Amish."

# CHAPTER TWENTY-SIX

Autumn blazed its glory for a few more days before the killing frosts of winter forced it to its knees. Supple orange and red leaves dulled to crisp, rusty-colored papers, crumbling to dust on the sod beneath shivering trees. Snow showers blew into town, unpacking their bags as they settled in to sift snowy powder over the barren fields around the farm.

Leah never tired of the changing views from her kitchen window. Though the stark swells of the hills were lackluster under their gray mantles of spent vegetation, the mornings when the blue sky and sun dared to battle back forbidding clouds lifted her spirits and gave her a prophetic glimpse at spring.

She shivered, yawning away the fuzzy left-over dreams of sleep. She set the coffee pot on the stove and cranked the heat under its bottom. "Oh, coffee, how I adore thee," she muttered.

A few minutes later, Jacob shuffled into the warm kitchen, lowering his body cautiously onto the kitchen chair at the small table. He wiped a hand over his face, sighing as he accepted her offering of freshly brewed, steaming caffeine she slid across the tabletop to him.

"I can't believe how old I feel this morning."

"All the late nights and overtime hours would make anyone feel old." Leah pointed out the window. "At least the sun is shining today. And I actually think I heard a bird sing out there."

Jacob sniffed the soothing scent of coffee. "One thing I really miss in the winter is the chatter of birds in the morning."

Leah brought warm cinnamon toast and hearty cooked oatmeal topped with cranberries to the table. She settled in a chair facing her husband. "And light. I miss light."

He nodded. "That, too. Winter mornings can be so brutal to the body. That first step out the door—going from a warm house into biting wind ..." He shivered at the memory. "It hurts. Every. Single. Time."

She reached across the smooth oak top to lay her hand on Jacob's strong forearm. "I do appreciate how much you go through to make our life comfortable."

"Aww, Leah, I'm okay. Really. And when I think of the spring, when everything is new and warm, it makes the winter months disappear from my mind." He smiled as he lifted her hand to his lips. "And having a wife that can cook up a storm on cold mornings helps, too."

Jacob had been able to pick up extra morning hours at the factory now that he didn't have to do much on the farm, but the long days took a toll on his body. And Leah didn't want to admit how the hours he spent away from her wore on her nerves.

The truth was that the long gloomy days, which stretched into longer dark nights, were bringing back her fears of being watched.

Every morning, as the clock hands ticked toward nine, her heart grew heavier and her anxiety nearly overwhelmed her, especially during the first hour or two after he left for work.

She sat herself down each day with pen and paper to write out long, complex lists of chores to accomplish while he was away. She pored over cookbooks, planned menus, and had even begun skipping *suppah* so she could bake instead of sitting at the table alone, eating in the hushed kitchen.

But once she'd worn her body out, she was forced to sit in the rocking chair to rest. Then the quiet inside the house invited her mind to invent scenarios that bred apprehension with every creak of the rockers.

She sang as many songs as she could recall, worked crossword puzzles, one after another, and had even tried hiring Ella to take her shopping with friends a time or two. But that was a mistake because then she had to come home to a dark, empty, big farmhouse.

She crossed off the winter days on the calendar that hung by the basement door. Coming out of February had given her a little hope that the days of sunlight would soon grow longer because the darkest part of winter had already passed.

As she penciled in the first day of spring on the March calendar, she sighed. She knew her emotions were out of control, but she was too ashamed of her fears to tell Jacob about them. Besides, he had enough to handle at work. Bert Small had stepped up his intimidation game by taking on the extra overtime, too.

Every chance he got, he mocked Jacob's clothing, his beard, his haircut, and his accent. Leah even tried to send wholesome, fresh lunches with her husband, refraining from packing anything that Bert deemed "Amish" food, to try and keep him from making lunch breaks for Jacob miserable.

If, in the precious time they had together when Jacob was away from the factory, Bert ran into them in town, he never missed an opportunity to let them know what he thought of their Amish life. He was loud, large, and impossible!

Leah didn't see how Jacob could put himself through that torture day in and day out. Her heart suffered for her husband.

They hurried through breakfast and by the time Jacob had showered and dressed, the work van was idling in the barnyard. Jacob gave her a quick kiss good-bye, waved from the porch as she watched at the window and then was off to work. Leah refused to tear her gaze from the frosty pane until the last wisps of white smoke from the van's tailpipe had drifted into the icy air.

She turned away with a sigh. These lonely mornings were the few times she wished they were English so she could turn on a TV to blast the stillness of Jacob's sudden departures.

"But, instead, I'll just talk to myself."

Leah sat down at the kitchen table, once again pulling her paper and pen out from under her Bible to make yet another list. "Let's see—what can I do today?" She tapped the pen against her lips, forcing her brain to engage the way she wanted it to. "Think, Leah. Think!"

As she elbowed the paper into the center of the tabletop, she accidentally brushed against the Bible and sent it crashing to the floor. "Phooey! I hope I didn't tear any pages!" She bent down, retrieved the beloved book and pulled it up and over her "fear list", as she called it.

As she smoothed the pages, her eyes fastened on a verse that immediately spoke to her weary, ragged soul. She read the words aloud.

"For God hath not given us the spirit of fear; but of power, and of love, and of a sound mind."

She glanced to the top of the page. "I know I've read through 2nd Timothy before, so why did I not remember this scripture?"

She read it again. And again. And again.

Leah wrote the scripture on every line of her paper list and then closed her eyes. It had been a long time since she'd simply asked God to speak to her spirit. She'd worked so hard trying to keep busy, she'd feared any kind of quiet time, including her morning prayers and communication with her Heavenly Father.

As she now allowed *Gott* to come nearer to her frantic heart, she welcomed the soothing balm His presence breathed over her. She opened her eyes to eagerly search scriptures about God's peace, comfort, calm, and protection.

"Here's another good one," she whispered. "He shall cover thee with his feathers, and under his wings shalt thou trust: his truth shall be thy shield and buckler."

She scribbled that scripture from Psalms down, too, then repeated it over and over.

After a few more minutes of reading the comforting words of the Bible, she got up and went to the settee.

She drew a blanket over herself and pulled a pillow under head. She felt the warmth of the golden sunlight seep into her shoulders as it streamed into the living room. She snuggled in tighter under the soft throw and rested her hands loosely at her heart.

"*Gott*, thank you for the peace You've brought me today. Help me feel Your protection as the day passes into night. Protect Jacob. Bring insight to Bert. Help me rest in You."

Her breathing slowed. Her pulse calmed. She felt deep warmth and heavy muscles as her body shut down for the respite it craved.

She closed her eyes and slept.

❧ 🏠 ☙

Leah woke to shadows. She rubbed bleary eyes as she sat up. The living room was no longer bathed in sunlight. As she shook away the disoriented feeling that she'd lost years from her life instead of hours, her mind threatened to escalate the odd feeling into panic.

She stood, wrapping the velvety throw around her body as she teetered down the hall toward the bathroom.

"No—I will not allow fear to take away the promises of *Gott!* Not tonight, anyway."

After she'd washed her face and shuffled back to the settee to fold the throw in place, she made her way to the kitchen, pausing to bring light into her dim home with the gas lights hanging overhead.

She yawned. "I don't need to worry about later, either." She frowned. "What is that verse about not worrying?"

She turned on the propane stove and placed a teapot over the burner.

177

"Sufficient unto the day is the evil thereof ... or something like that." She frowned again. "I don't want to think of anything *evil* right now."

After she made herself a sandwich, found an apple, and prepared herself a cup of hot tea, she took her *suppah* into the bedroom on a tray. She crawled into the bed and proceeded to eat a real meal alone for the first time in weeks.

As she ate, she read more scriptures, settling finally on the words of Jesus. His love and compassion impressed her, as it always did, deeply. He promised to be closer to her than a brother, and that vow comforted her heart.

She finished off her dinner and strolled to the kitchen to wash her dishes and clean the countertops.

As she passed the window, she caught movement beyond the dark glass. Her body leaped to defense mode—trembling and shaking, just like before.

"No!" She practically ran to the kitchen sink, dumped her dishes into it, and rushed to the window, her hands reaching for the curtains on either side of the panes.

"*Gott* is my protector, so you, whoever you are, have no business at my house!"

She was shouting louder than she'd ever dared to shout inside a house before. Just before she zipped the curtains across the window, her gaze locked with the trespasser's shocked gaze.

It was Bert Small!

She expected to feel fear rise, but instead, Leah's soul filled with pity. This man was loved by *Gott*, too. He needed Jesus. He needed her prayers.

So she stood behind the curtains and prayed. Out loud. For Bert.

After the ticking of the clock had finally filtered to her brain, she noted ten minutes had passed. Leah sighed deeply and rested her forehead against the cool wall. She lifted her hand and tugged the edge of the curtain away.

Bert was gone.

When she recalled his shocked expression at hearing her unexpected reaction to his leering face at her window, and speculated about what he must have thought hearing her praying loudly on the other side of the wall, she began to laugh.

"He'll *really* think I'm a peculiar person now. And just wait until Jacob Yoder hears what I did. He'll absolutely think he married a crazy woman."

# CHAPTER TWENTY-SEVEN

Jacob was angry when he heard about Bert. He paced back and forth, shaking his head in disbelief.

"I don't get that guy! What *is* his problem with us? All of this, just because we're Amish!"

He stopped, trying hard to get his anger under control. He sat in the rocker, his chin nearly touching his chest as he stroked his beard.

"I know it's aggravating, Jacob, but tonight I actually felt pity towards him."

Leah perched on the edge of the sofa, watching disbelief grow in her husband's eyes as he locked them with hers.

"What! Pity? How? He's making our lives miserable. You have no idea how he's carrying on at work." He put the chair in motion, the rockers speeding faster as his anger grew again.

"I know, Jacob, and that hurts my heart for you. The way he disgraces you at work in front of your co-workers makes my stomach churn."

She sighed and moved to stand in front of him. "But it came to me that *Gott* loves that rascal as much as He loves us." She reached out and gently stopped the rocking. "Isn't that the amazing thing about amazing grace?"

180

He exhaled. "Well, this is when it gets hard to understand *Gott*, I guess." He put up his hands. "I want to ask *Gott* to smite that man and I have to fight myself every day not to keep praying for that."

Leah smiled. She reached out and smoothed her exasperated husband's brow. "You're trying to protect your family and I adore that in you. *Gott* knows it, Jacob, and He understands your desire to safeguard those you love. But only He has the power to work this out to our good and Bert's good, however it's meant to be."

Jacob stood, wrapping his arms about his wife's waist. "I don't think I have a choice, do I? We have to trust Him, don't we?"

"*Ja*, we do. And He'll be faithful."

"Okay. *Gott's* way."

He shook his head again, a smile stealing over his lips. "I guess that means I have to keep praying against my desire to fight the guy."

As they made their way upstairs, Jacob paused, a serious turn to his expression erasing the humor they'd just shared. "I've made up my mind, though, that Bert's going to have to be held accountable. Tomorrow I'm going to the boss and I'm turning him in. And I plan to call the sheriff."

❧ 🏠 ☙

Leah waved to Jacob as the work van took him away. She hurried to wash the dishes and get the house in order. She'd decided to phone Sarah and ask about Martha moving in with her and the sooner she made the call, the sooner they could make plans.

"Sarah? It's Leah. I got a letter from Martha and she's got a job down here in Holmes County already!"

The two friends discussed Martha's move, including the trip home for her and Jacob. Just thinking about being that close to *Maem* and *Daet*, and her siblings, made her heart speed up. Could she possibly sneak in a visit to her folks, too?

They set the date with Martha for the following Thursday. Jacob had the day off and had asked for Friday off, too.

181

At breakfast the next morning, Leah hurried through cooking oatmeal so she could have extra time at the table with Jacob. She was eager to hear if anything had come of her husband reporting Bert to their superior and to the sheriff's office.

The couple said their prayers and dove into the warm cereal.

"So tell me everything, Jacob. You were so worn out last night, I didn't have the heart to grill you for the details about Bert. But now, I'm showing no mercy. Spill it all."

He laughed as he wiped his mouth with the napkin. "You sure don't waste any time, do you?"

She sputtered. "I waited all night, husband! I hardly slept a wink with my mind going ninety miles an hour trying to imagine the conversations."

He grabbed his coffee mug. "Okay, okay."

He took a long, slow sip, wiggling his eyebrows at his wife's impatient expression, before he carefully placed the cup back in the saucer.

"Not to burst your bubble or anything, but nothing happened."

Leah froze mid-dip of her spoon in the oatmeal. "Huh? What do you mean, nothing happened?"

Jacob shrugged. "Nothing happened."

"What!"

"I called the sheriff's office and they wrote down what I said. Then I told the big boss at my first break how Bert had been harassing me, and he wrote down what I said. And that was that."

Jacob slurped oatmeal off his spoon.

Leah heard the clock ticking in the silence that followed. She plunked down her coffee cup.

"I lost hours of sleep for that?"

He shrugged again. "It wasn't my idea for you to lose sleep."

"But—but, you could have told me last night that nothing happened, for Heaven's sake!"

Jacob burst out laughing at Leah's frustrated look.

She finished her oatmeal and drank the rest of her coffee before whisking her dishes to the sink. She swished hot water over everything and then turned to face her grinning husband.

"Jacob Yoder, you scamp! Are you joking with me?"

He got up and reached for Leah.

"No, I'm not." He pulled her close and gave her a good-natured kiss on the tip of her nose. "I'm thinking I won't know anything until both parties have a chance to talk with Bert. I didn't see him as I left work last night so I don't know if he was upset or calm or how he was."

She kissed Jacob back. "Okay. But the minute you know anything, you'd better tell me!"

"Oh, I will, wife, I will."

She pulled away, laughing as she finished running water in the sink for the dishes.

He stretched. "What's on your to-do list today?"

"Anna's coming over with Sarah for a Bible study. And I think she's bringing the new lady we met at church last Sunday—her husband works over at the Hostetler farm. Remember him? I can't think of his name."

Jacob yawned. "Oh, *ja*. From up north—near Middlefield. Uh—Miller, wasn't it? Benny Miller?"

Leah nodded. "I think his wife's name is Katherine or Katy, maybe."

"Are they related to Christian Millers from the church?"

Leah paused. "Hmm, I'm not sure. But they also might bring Lizzie Swartzentruber, if her little boy is feeling better."

"Sounds like a busy day for you. I'd better get outside and see to the animals before time gets away from me. Liam's agreed to look after the place while we're in Ashfield, so I need to set things in order for him."

"I'll get your lunch ready before I start cleaning."

"Great—hope it's something *gut* this time."

Leah snapped the dish towel at his retreating back as he chuckled his way outside.

✥ 🏠 ✥

Late afternoon sun was gleaming across the kitchen floor by the time Leah's friends and the new woman from church made their way from the buggy to her house. She was excited to greet them. Sarah had told her she'd plan the Bible study if Leah baked treats and made the drinks.

Lizzie had her little boy, Mose, by the hand as they entered. He was an endearing little guy who had been kept home from school one extra day to make sure he was over his respiratory infection. His *maem* had brought school work for him to do while they conversed. Once everyone was greeted and settled, Leah passed the refreshments.

Sarah opened their study with prayer and then they got right to the lesson.

"The verse I decided to talk about is this one—about grace," Sarah said. She read from Ephesians 2:8-9 in the English King James Version of the Bible. 'For by grace are ye saved through faith; and that not of yourselves: it is the gift of God: Not of works, lest any man should boast.'"

Sarah closed the scriptures and looked around the small circle. "It's difficult for me to give up the idea that I'm saved by grace alone. I'll be honest with you all that it feels better for me to *do* things. To pat myself on the back and think I'm making my own way into Heaven."

Leah nodded. "I agree. Somehow the idea that nothing I can do will earn my right to Heaven keeps trapping me into doing more and more works."

Anna gave her version of works type thinking. In the silence that followed, the three friends waited for Katy's contribution. Leah studied her face. Katy's cheeks flamed and her lips grew thinner, pressed into a firm line.

184

"Katy? Would you like to add anything to what we've said? You don't have to if you're not comfortable sharing." Sarah encouraged gently. "But we're in a safe place here to speak our minds."

Katy sat straighter, her back rigid and her breath quick. "I'm sure you aren't trying to say that doing good is worthless. Are you?"

Anna shook her head. "Oh, no. Scripture tells us to continue in good works to glorify the Father. But we think that's an outcome from grace—something we do in gratitude and just to do good to our fellowman."

"Okay. Then what's this talk about grace being the only way we get to Heaven?" Katy's dark eyes flashed. "And that nonsense about—about anyone boasting?"

Sarah slowly opened the Bible and read the verse again. "It's just saying that our works aren't what gets us to Heaven, but rather the grace of Christ. His sacrifice on the cross."

Katy shook her head. "Hmmph. Well, scripture to me shouldn't be read in English anyway. Also, there's no man here to explain it to us, least of all a bishop."

Katy sipped her coffee and stopped talking. It was one of the most uncomfortable moments Leah could recall, except for the last Bible study with the low order church couple.

Leah squirmed. Katy sat, saying nothing else while the three other women stumbled on, trying their best to discuss something they now knew wasn't acceptable to Katy.

After a few minutes, Sarah closed the Word and said a prayer. They continued by making small talk until they'd spent another half hour visiting.

Katy joined the conversation about baking once or twice, but she was clearly put off and not enjoying being in their company.

The visit dwindled to a stiff halt and her friends and visitor prepared to leave. As Leah walked her guests to the door, she plastered on a false smile until all had gotten in the buggy and driven away.

She closed the door, her shoulders sagging in relief and dismay. She straightened the living room and carried coffee cups and plates to the kitchen. As she washed the dishes, she thought about the afternoon.

It was twice that she, Jacob, and their friends had been shot down in their thinking. Twice that other church folk had admonished them about their interpretation of scripture.

Were she and Jacob wrong? Had they been deceived?

She glanced to the clock—nearly *suppah* time. She shook off the gloomy depression that had settled over her and decided to work through the evening gathering her and Jacob's clothing that needed to be packed in preparation for their overnight trip.

It was only a day away now and Leah was excited, as well as apprehensive, about going home.

"Father, all I can do for my family and for our church family is to leave them in Your capable hands. My mind is way too puny to handle my own spiritual life, much less others, as well."

She scurried around, keeping herself too busy to bother thinking about anything else.

But down deep inside, doubt was growing. Fear was growing. And confusion was like a sprouting seedling, ready to bloom, threatening to fill her spirit with its chaotic entwining roots.

*Was* this the simple life?

# CHAPTER TWENTY-EIGHT

L eah squirmed restlessly in her seat as the van Ella was driving drew closer and closer to Ashfield. Soon they would be riding on the rolling roads along the hills of her home area.

Early spring was showing off in the delicate buds on tree limbs and soft greens on the fields. She smiled as roadside eateries that were familiar to her came flashing past the car windows.

The pull off onto the main road to Ashfield popped up and Leah sat forward, eager to catch a glimpse of recognizable homes and businesses.

Finally, they eased into the parking lot of The Olivesburg General Store. Immediately, Leah opened the door and stretched as Jacob and Ella also got out of the van.

Ella came around the car and patted Leah on the back. "Feel good to be home?"

Leah nodded, suddenly struggling to hold back tears. She glanced down the roadway, past the edge of the building, toward her parent's farm.

They were less than two miles away. Her heart longed to go home. She wanted so much to see her family. Even knowing they were unhappy with her decisions, her soul longed for them and for peace in their relationship.

Jacob edged closer and hugged her. "It's good to be back. I only wish we could hurry down this road to your home place, Leah." He kissed the top of her head.

She nodded, trying to wipe tears without drawing attention to herself.

Ella dipped her chin. "It's okay. I know how you feel." She took out a tissue and wiped her own eyes and then nodded toward the store. "I'm going in for a cool soda. Anyone else want one? Then we can call Martha, and let her know we're here so she can tell us where to meet her. After we know that, I can drop you two off at Jacob's house."

Leah took a deep breath, feeling the air expand inside her body, willing her muscles and nerves to relax. "I think I'll come in with you. I'm thirsty and need the restroom."

"Well, I'm coming in, too, then," Jacob laughed.

As they entered, he pointed to a shelf filled with unusual candies. "Look at that! Chocolate covered insects! Things have changed, for sure, since we were here last."

"Eww," Ella shuddered.

The place had indeed changed, but to Leah, it still felt like a friendly, relaxed oasis.

She smelled pizza baking and heard wonderful music playing in the background. As they wandered through the aisles, they glimpsed an area where tables were lined up and folks were enjoying a live bluegrass band.

Leah stopped and shook her head. Memories flooded into her mind and heart.

This was where she'd waited after she'd left home. This was the place Naomi had first picked her up from. It had been the beginning of a long learning curve for her, and she was feeling nostalgic being here.

After using the restroom and paying for their soft drinks, Leah used Ella's cell phone to call Martha.

"We're here, Martha."

Martha was thrilled and anxious to get moved. Unlike some young people who left the Amish secretly, Martha had fully worked out a plan with her *maem* to move this time.

Martha's family agreed to keep little Johnny until she was settled and had a job in Holmes County. And then she would come back for him. Her happy voice coming through the phone made Leah smile.

"Jacob and I are going to his folks' place tonight, but if you want us to come on over so we can get your stuff loaded first, we can do that, too."

"Yes—come over now. I talked *Maem* into giving us *suppah*. Then we can load my stuff. That way, we'll be able to leave earlier in the morning."

Leah hesitated. Mixing with Martha's family didn't seem like a good idea, but she didn't want to stir up trouble where there didn't seem to be any, so she agreed. Maybe Martha's *maem* had mellowed.

After Leah hung up, she explained the plan to Ella and Jacob. He frowned.

"Eat *suppah* at Martha's place? Anna's going to allow us to come there?" He shook his head. "I can't see her being happy to cook for us."

Ella coughed. "I don't mean to interfere, but I can't see that happening, either. Her *maem* and step-*daet* aren't known for being hospitable."

Leah paused, unsure what to do next. "Well, I can't very well tell her we're not coming now. She said her *maem* cooked *suppah* for us—like, already did it."

Ella walked back to the van. "I'm fine with taking you two there, waiting while you load and then coming to get you later, but I have another visit planned with friends in between, so *suppah's* not in the cards for me at Martha's place."

Jacob snorted. "I wish we were going with you, Ella."

Leah rolled her eyes at Jacob. "Now, let's be fair—it could be a nice *suppah.*"

This time Ella snorted as she got in the driver's seat. "Miracles happen, I suppose."

Leah crawled into the front passenger seat, turning back to face Jacob in the backseat. She shrugged in a sudden moment of indecision and regret. "Do you think I should I call Martha back and tell her we'll come tomorrow instead?"

Jacob shook his head as Leah rushed to apologize to him.

"It's fine, Leah. No problems. We'll be okay and we won't be there too long, anyway. Besides, we have the excuse that my parents are expecting us if things get *schlecht* and we want to get out of there."

Too soon, it felt to Leah, they were pulling into Martha's driveway. Leah was taken back to that day when Martha's brother had behaved in such an ugly way to her when she had been visiting with Martha.

But she took another deep breath, whispered a quick prayer and got out of the van.

Martha was out the door of the house and running to greet her before Leah finished smoothing her apron and straightening her *kapp.*

"Leah!" Martha squealed as she grabbed her friend in a tight hold. She stepped away and shook hands with Jacob. "Looks like married life suits you both," she laughed.

"*Ja,* it does, for sure." Jacob took off his hat and wiped his brow.

"*Maem's* got *suppah* ready, so why don't we go on in and eat." She leaned into the open car window. "You're welcome to come in, too. "

Ella smiled, but shook her head. "No, thanks. If you want to load now I can wait, but I have plans with friends for *suppah.* I can come back in about, oh, a couple of hours, if you'll be ready to load up then."

Martha didn't hesitate. "Great! See you in a couple of hours."

Ella waved as she backed the van out onto the road. Before she knew it, Leah was walking with Martha toward Anna Mast's house. Jacob trailed behind, but when she glanced his way, he gave her a teasing smile.

The house felt dark and tight when they went inside. Anna Mast came out of the kitchen, wiping her hands on her apron, and shook hands with Leah, and Jacob.

Leah glanced around, but did not see Martha's step-*daet*.

"*Wie gehts?*" Anna twisted her apron, not making eye contact.

"*Gut. Gut.*" Jacob was all smiles as he replied.

Leah was glad for Jacob's friendly manner because she found herself tongue-tied. Martha's *maem* wasn't going to make this easy for any of them.

Anna backed away and pointed to the kitchen table visible through the doorway. "C'mon in and eat. It's ready."

As they entered the steamy kitchen, Leah was surprised to see a table filled with *kinder* and *jungen*. Anna led them past the jam-packed table to a crowded corner near the back door.

Leah felt her face flame. Of course. They had to eat separately. The small table was crammed against the wall and fitted with two place settings.

Martha ducked her chin and hurried to the main table where Leah caught sight of little Johnny. He was sobbing, his thin arms reaching for his *maem*. As one of the boys tried to give Johnny something to chew on, the toddler threw out a hand, knocking the boy's arm away.

Jacob quietly drew out a chair and motioned for Leah to sit. Leah lowered herself onto the seat, her muscles instantly stiff and rigid. Jacob sat down across from her, reached for her hands, and prayed quietly for the meal they were about to eat—just as he always did at home.

She felt, rather than saw, several pairs of eyes on them as he prayed. When he was finished, he squeezed her hands and lifted his head. He made eye contact with Anna Mast. She drew herself up, ramrod straight, and hurried to the stove.

The food platters were passed along the main table. As they emptied, Anna stacked the platters on the counter behind the table.

Finally, she nodded to Martha, who immediately stood and retrieved smaller bowls of food for Leah and Jacob.

The meal proceeded quietly. Not many spoke, but Leah knew they all strained to catch a glimpse of Leah and Jacob at *der sindfol Disch.*

The thought of her and her husband sequestered at a "naughty" table caused Leah to almost giggle out loud. Before she lost control of her laughter, she swiftly took a bite of chicken and swallowed. Jacob let out a tiny snuffle, causing her to glance his way. His eyes were moist. Was he crying?

She was surprised to think his feelings could be so easily hurt, but when she felt his leg jiggling under the table, she looked closer.

No. He was trying, with all his might apparently, to stifle a laugh.

Leah drew in a deep breath, holding it until she felt control of herself return. Laughter was never closer to the surface for her as at that moment. If she dared meet his gaze, she would surely burst out giggling.

The torturous dinner finally came to an end. Martha gathered Johnny into her arms and motioned for her friends to follow her outside.

No one spoke until they neared a tumbled down shed. Martha turned to them then, her eyes nearly disappearing into the folds of her cheeks as she laughed.

"I'm so sorry," she sputtered. "I was hoping to convince *maem* to not go through that silly shunning thing, but just before you got out of the car, she did it anyway!"

Leah couldn't help but join in with her friend's amusement.

Jacob grinned, his hands rolling his hat over and over again. "I thought Leah was going to cause a scene. She nearly choked on her chicken because she got the giggles."

Leah smacked him. "Me? His eyes were filling with tears and his leg was jiggling ninety miles an hour under the table as he tried to hold back his chuckles."

As the laughter waned, the three friends wore easier expressions.

"I'm glad you aren't offended, Leah." Martha reached out and pulled her friend into a hug.

"Well, I have to admit, my heart sank a little bit when I saw where you were leading us."

Martha shook her head. "I know. It's happened to me often enough. But, really! Why shun you both when you're still Amish?"

Jacob pointed to his wife. "She made us leave under a cloud of suspicion and shame, that's why."

Leah giggled, turning loving eyes to her husband. His humor was one of his best gifts to her.

Soon Ella returned and Jacob, Leah, and Martha, with little Johnny firmly attached to his *maem*'s arms, loaded Martha's meager possessions into the van.

It was time to head to Jacob's home, but they would be back for Martha early the next morning.

Leah couldn't bear to think about the parting of Martha from her little boy. Already, she dreaded that moment.

As they pulled out of the Mast driveway, Leah sighed. She hated the very thought of Johnny having to stay behind in that dark house without his *maem* by his side.

## CHAPTER TWENTY-NINE

A s soon as Ella guided the van into the Yoder driveway, Jacob's *maem* was at the door of her house, flinging it wide and stepping out onto the porch. Her smile was ear to ear as she waved at them.

"Wow—look at your mom, Jacob. She sure isn't shunning you guys." Ella grinned at the difference between the Yoder and Mast welcomes.

"*Maem*—good to see you!" Jacob was immediately wrapped in his mother's arms, and after they embraced, Leah was next.

"Ella, I'm happy to meet you. *Wie bischt?*"

"I'm *gut*, thank you. But I need to go so I can get some rest for the drive back to Holmes County in the morning. Nice to meet you, too."

"Wait just a sec—"

Jacob's *maem*, Rebecca, dashed into the house. A minute later she was back holding out a covered paper plate filled with warm chocolate chip cookies.

"Please, take these along with you. I'm sure you'll be able to find friends to help you eat them."

Ella sniffed the cookies. "Oh, great! Thank you—that's so nice of you." She nodded to her friends. "See you two in the morning."

Jacob and Leah followed his *maem* inside as she led them to the kitchen. Soft lamplight filled the cozy room, accented by the sweet scent of baked cookies.

"Have a seat while I get some milk. Let's enjoy these goodies while they're hot."

What a difference showing love makes to a home, Leah thought. Though she knew her parents loved her, the demonstration of love she felt inside this house made a world of difference. The warmth was welcome and friendly.

She pulled a couple of vanilla-laced delights from the pile on the plate in front of them and bit into the chocolaty treat. "Mmm—these are delicious, *Maem* Yoder. I'll need to get your recipe."

Jacob stacked a small tower of the goodies in front of him. "Yes—make sure Leah gets *this* recipe. Hey, where are my sisters?"

Rebecca Yoder pulled out a chair and joined the couple, enjoying a cookie of her own. "I have to say, I think butter tastes better, but shortening keeps the cookie from spreading too thin as it bakes." She turned to Jacob. "They're staying with friends so they can all go shopping tomorrow."

Jacob rolled his eyes. "I'd hate to be in that gaggle of girls." He laughed as he gestured to Leah. "Talk about a gaggle of females—*that* would be torture!" Jacob popped the last bite of a cookie in his mouth and chewed. "Is *Daet* coming in soon, or should I go give him a hand yet?".

"No, he's nearly done with chores. Only has the milk to strain."

Leah yawned. "I'm guessing it's been a long day for him. Long day for me, too.

"*Ja*, it gets long, but he's got a helper coming in a week or so when the planting gets going."

Rebecca hopped up. "I almost forgot! I have two pies for you to take home with you. I baked too many for the Leeway restaurant this week and I sure don't want them to go to waste. Let me get them ready now before I forget in the morning."

She bustled about the kitchen, placing the pies on the counter and covering them with cling wrap.

As Leah watched, her gaze strayed to the kitchen window which showed the road to her own home, winding away into the evening mist. It wasn't until she felt Jacob's hand curl around her own that she realized he'd been watching her.

"You want to go see them before we leave in the morning?" he asked gently.

She shook her head, dropping her eyes to the flowered oilcloth table covering. "I'd like to, but—well, I don't want to cause more trouble with them from the bishop."

Rebecca came back to the table, placing her hand on Leah's shoulder as she sat. "I'm sorry, Leah, that it's been so hard for you to see your family. I can tell you that your *Maem* seems sad—and sorry that she's had to keep you at a distance."

Her blue eyes shone with tears. She pushed her graying hair back under the *kapp*, and turned to Jacob.

"Son, I think you know it would be unbearable for me, as a mother, to obey if the church insisted I'd have to shun you. Your *daet* and I have talked about this before. I think—and this isn't something I say lightly—that we would have to leave if it came to that."

Leah was stunned into silence. Jacob's parents would truly consider leaving their Amish church rather than shun their children?

Her heart swelled to think of the sacrifice that would mean for them. Before she could make a comment, they heard Jacob's whistling father making his way to the house from the barn.

Jacob cleared his throat. "I think you know I'd do everything in my power to keep that from happening. But there is something I think you and *Daet* should know about how Leah and I feel concerning, um, being born again."

Rebecca put up her hand. "Let's talk about this once your *daet* gets in, washed up, and ready for his coffee."

Leah observed that Jacob's father wore the same wide smile and gentle expression her husband did. His joyful attitude had always come across to Leah as naturally cheerful and compassionate. She had quickly grown to love her wonderful in-laws. She was grateful she was in the family now.

"Well, well, well! Here they are! My favorite couple!" Andrew Yoder took off his hat, wiped his brow with a handkerchief and headed to the sink to wash his hands. He turned to them as he lathered with the fragrant soap. "I hope you get to stay for a day or two?"

Jacob grinned. "I wish we could, too, *Daet*, but I have to get back to work. We're leaving in the morning as soon as Ella and Martha are ready."

Andrew joined his family at the table, grabbing a few cookies to eat with his coffee. "I'm relieved to see Martha's moving forward with her life, but I have to say I'm worried about her leaving the little one with her *maem*."

Jacob's mother scooted the cream and sugar across the table to her husband, nodding as he spoke. "Yes, me, too. Little Johnny needs his mother, and—well, I don't want to speak unkindly of Martha's *maem*, but she has had too much on her plate the last few years."

Leah shook her head. "There's so much that feels wrong about that household and I agree. I wish Martha would take Johnny along, too. What we saw tonight—"Leah stopped, fearing she was straying into gossip rather than concern.

"No need to stop talking, Leah." Jacob wiped cookie crumbs away. "This family knows there's trouble at the Mast place. We're all praying for answers and a better life for both Martha and Johnny."

Leah sighed. "I know I'm going to do everything I can to help her get settled as soon as possible so Johnny can live with her."

Once the chat was drawing to a close, Rebecca spoke up. "Andrew, these two have shared that they'd like to talk about being born again."

Jacob's *daet* cleared his throat, pulled another sip of coffee from his mug and then looked to Jacob.

"I just want to let you both know how we feel about the verses concerning being born again in scripture." Jacob toyed with the cookie crumbs on his napkin, clearly struggling for a way to go on.

Andrew put up his hands to stop Jacob. "No need to go on, son. Your *maem* and I both understand. You might say, we *fully* understand how you feel, if you catch my drift." He winked.

Leah looked to both her in-laws faces as it dawned on her what they were trying to convey. "You mean—"

Rebecca Yoder clasped her daughter-in-law's hand. "*Ja*, we do mean that we also believe in being born again. We've spent time studying those scriptures since receiving some literature that comes in the mail. It truly gives us peace."

The four of them spent a few more minutes discussing the scriptures and how it settles many questions about their faith before finally saying goodnight to one another.

Leah's heart was full as she and Jacob snuggled under the quilts that night. How wonderful to know Jacob's parents were joined with them in the same faith promises! *Gott* had provided them with perfect family support. She slept in deep contentment until morning.

The day dawned bright and sunny with a hint of frost lingering in the air when they woke. The brisk, clear weather gave Leah an extra spurt of energy to help pack Martha's things and get going for home.

After goodbyes to Jacob's parents, mixed with promises to come back and visit longer, Leah and Jacob climbed into Ella's packed-to-the-rim van and headed for Martha's house.

As Leah had expected, the goodbyes between Martha and her son were wrenching. Johnny shrieked when Martha tried to hand him over to her mother, kicking wildly as he strained to get back into Martha's arms.

She winced when Anna Mast finally pulled his little arms away from her daughter, smacking his tiny hands as he tried to reach for his *maem*. Sadly, Martha seemed oblivious to his sorrow to part from her.

Leah's heart was bleeding inside for the boy, and she simply could not comprehend how her friend could blithely walk to the van, place herself inside, and close the door. Not once looking back. The scene settled in Leah's spirit, causing her to sit quietly as the van sped onward to Holmes County.

Along the way, her friend talked nonstop about her new life, the promise of beginning again, and how she was going to prove herself this time around. She sat crosswise in the front seat so she could meet Leah's eyes in the backseat.

It bothered Leah how Martha chattered away, speaking very little of her son. Finally, she felt she had to speak up.

"I'm all for you beginning again, Martha. I'm praying this will be a great new start for you, in fact." Leah paused, considering how to speak of her unease concerning Johnny. "But what are your plans for Johnny? I do wonder whether your *maem* will be able to handle the responsibility for him—at least, not for a lengthy amount of time."

Martha laughed. "Oh, believe me, there's no way on earth *Maem* will let me forget about him for long." She frowned. "Not that I want to—I love him. It's just life, since he was born, has been a roller coaster. I do think I need some 'me time' for a while."

Leah glanced to Jacob, catching a frown creasing his brow. She swallowed and turned back to her friend. "I understand, but I think your son's health and well-being should come first—as much as possible during a move like this, that is."

Martha nodded, but her demeanor showed she had already moved on from the discussion about Johnny, her face turned toward the window and the passing scenery.

Leah's lips formed a tight line as she thought of the innocent small boy caught between adult decisions. There had to be a way to give support to Martha while encouraging her to plan for her baby's arrival back in her life quickly.

A thought came to her: Martha living with Sarah would be a plus. There'd be no way she'd be able to keep putting off bringing her son home, once Sarah got the gist of the story. Leah rested against her seat, a tiny smile lifting her countenance.

Jacob scooted closer. "You look like the cat that caught the canary. So what are you thinking?"

She nodded, suppressing a giggle. "One word: Sarah."

Jacob grinned. "Yep. True."

The rest of the trip home she chatted about everyday things, leaving the details of Johnny and Martha to Sarah. And to God.

# CHAPTER THIRTY

The drive home seemed to go on longer than it usually did. By the time Ella turned the wheels to the road leading to the farm, Leah was exhausted. Helping to off-load Martha's things at Sarah's place, staying for a short visit, and then chatting with Sarah to give her a quick heads up about Martha's situation, had lengthened their time on the road to three hours.

Leah stretched. "I'll be glad to get home and get into a warm bath."

Ella yawned. "You and me both. It's been a short drive, but a long trip, if you know what I mean."

"I do," Jacob laughed, "and I'm with both of you."

Ella sighed. "It's the emotional baggage. Going back to where trouble was, seeing the control once again, and feeling that yoke pull down on your shoulders—I know how that is. It's wearing on the body—"

Ella stopped, her mouth falling open at the shocking view of a sea of fire trucks, police, and rescue vehicles surrounding Jacob and Leah's farm.

"My word! What's happened?"

Leah sat bolt upright, her spine crawling with a tingle that left her shaking. "Jacob! Oh, no—is it a fire?"

Jacob grabbed the back door handle of the van and tried to open it. When he met resistance, he smacked the window. "I need to get out! *Now!*"

Ella twisted around. "Jacob—you have to wait until I put the van in park! Wait—just a second until I pull over!"

Once Ella got the auto stopped and out of gear, Jacob jerked the door open and jumped out. "Stay here, Leah—don't get out until I come back to tell you what's happened!"

Leah put her hands to her face, her heart thumping as though it would explode as she looked through her fingers at Jacob running through a horribly frantic scene. She fought nausea as sick fear uncurled in her stomach. Was it Bert Small? Had he finally gotten his revenge?

She craned her neck to see past the line of emergency vehicles, and watched, stricken, as fire fighters ran to and fro, tugging heavy hoses behind them. The house and barn were out of view from where they parked on the edge of the road, but as she rolled down her window, the frenzied shouts of the men and the acrid smell of smoke filled her senses.

Her eyes widened. Turning to Ella, she grabbed at her friend's hands. "It's burning! I can smell it!"

Ella squeezed back hard. "We don't know what's really happening, Leah. Don't jump to conclusions yet—it could be a field fire."

Leah wiped tears she didn't even know she was crying from her face.

"I have to see what's happening!" Leah hopped from the van and took off running, dodging fire fighters, equipment, and vehicles. She didn't get far before Jacob spotted her.

"Leah! Over here!"

She ran to him, one part of her needing to see the source of the heavy smoke and one part needing to be wrapped in her husband's arms.

"Oh, Jacob! Is it the house? Is it gone?"

He hugged her to him, rubbing her shoulders and back as he gently shushed her. "No. It's not the house. It's the barn and part of the crop."

She shook her head. "No! You worked so hard! No! Who did this to us?"

As she drew away from him, she took her first look at their farm. Heavy wisps of smoke floated past the house, but it was intact; no fire there.

When her gaze moved toward the driveway, barn, and the fields, her knees buckled at what she saw.

The barn was smoldering. Through a flood of water, she spied a last flicker of red flames winking beyond the charred doors at the front. She groaned as she viewed the buggy near the doors. It was smoldering, too, sodden under a blanket of cold water.

The field to the left of the barn was a black charcoal looking mess—nothing but burnt sticks and saturated ashes.

A man dressed in fire gear, a chief's button pinned to his coat, approached them. "This here your place?"

Jacob nodded, unable to speak at first.

"You're Jacob Yoder, then?"

Leah watched her husband swallow, his Adam's apple jerking up and down in the effort. "Yes. What—I mean—how—did this happen?"

The chief shook his head. "That's what we want to know. Were you gone?"

"Yes, my wife and I were just returning from a trip to Ashfield County. We stayed there overnight last night."

"Okay." The man shook his head again and looked at the ground. "This is a shock, I'm sure. What a thing to come home to, eh?"

Jacob nodded, tightening his grip on Leah and she knew he was trying hard not to show his emotions. Leah wanted to sob out loud, but held back the sobs and tears, realizing Jacob needed her to be strong, too.

The captain waved to the field and barn area.

"We think it got started in the field. A strong wind then blew it toward the barn. With no one here, there was nothing or nobody to raise an early alarm. Took hold on the left side there," he pointed to the totally burned side of the barn nearest the charred field, "and caught the hay, stacked against the wall inside, on fire. After that, *whoosh!*"

He stared at his booted feet. "Good thing one of your neighbors saw the smoke. It had spread through half the barn by the time we got here. We tried to save the buggy. One of your neighbors managed to get the horse out before we came. He's there in the paddock."

"Oh, thank goodness! Poor Bingo! He's okay, isn't he?" Leah pulled out of Jacob's arms and started across the yard.

The chief stopped her. "Miss! Don't go through there. It's still very hot. Your horse is fine. He's a little shook up, but he's munching his oats now."

Her next thought was for the two milk cows. They had not named them and had jokingly called them Cow 1 and Cow 2.

Jacob caught her eye and nodded to the barn. "The cows?" he directed his question to the fire chief.

The chief didn't meet their eyes. "I'm sorry. We didn't get to them in time."

Leah groaned, her heart turning over in her chest. The poor, poor animals!

The two cows had always greeted them with a serene, unperturbed expression when they came to the barn. She and Jacob took turns milking the animals each day. They'd felt blessed to have them. It hurt her to know the panic and pain the poor cows must have felt as the flames devoured the barn.

Jacob shifted from one foot to the other. Leah brought her gaze to his, and at once, knew she couldn't hold back the sobs any longer.

His face was filled with despair. His brows formed a deep V between his moist brown eyes, and the skin around his mouth was white.

"Jacob! Oh, Jacob! What are we going to do?" she cried.

He reached for her and pulled her tight. The chief backed away and left them to their grieving.

Hours passed as they stood shivering together, watching the firemen roll up their hoses, put away the equipment and slowly leave the farm.

Neighbors came by and offered consolations and promised help when it was time to rebuild.

Red Cross workers offered coffee and doughnuts to them and to the men who cleaned up the fire debris.

Leah and Jacob had taken to the front porch, sitting close together on the porch swing under a warm quilt as they watched the aftermath of the fire unfold.

Leah had tucked her face into Jacob's chest, only lifting her head when she heard footsteps approaching as everyone took their leave and came to offer support on their way to their homes.

Finally no one was left but the fire chief and Sheriff Thomas. Both men made their way to the porch.

As Leah focused on them, she could see another flame firing on the horizon. The sun was fighting the coming night with a fierce blaze of its own, reluctant to move past the vanishing point and to its bed. It spread its wavering glow across the unresisting hills and soft fields, igniting them with colors of red, orange, and yellow.

How odd, she thought, that fire can be so diverse. Destroying *and* building, with opposite hands.

The sound of shuffling boots moving through the new grass and along the wood of the porch brought Leah's attention back to her own front yard. She rested her tired gaze on the two men who approached them. They, also, looked worn to the bone, both with their work and their news.

The sheriff nodded to Leah as he addressed Jacob. "Son, I'm sorry you had to come home to this. In light of the troubles you all have had out here, we're going to be investigating this fire."

The fire chief joined in when the sheriff stopped talking. "It's early in the investigation, of course, but one thing we're pretty sure of is the fire in the field was set. Maybe the person who lit it didn't mean for it to get out of control, but that doesn't stop whoever ignited it from being held responsible for the damage done here."

Jacob nodded and stood. "I'm sorry to hear that, but I have to be honest and say I'm not surprised."

Sheriff Thomas tilted his head, squinting his eyes as he fingered his report. "You thinking about that man who's been harassing you?"

"I hate to admit it, but yes. I don't want to accuse someone, though, with no proof."

Leah grimaced, her mind screaming that Bert deserved the accusation.

The fire chief, Todd Stonebridge, put up a hand. "No need to worry over that. We'll be taking care of the official fire report end of the event. You both have enough to deal with already. You can expect to hear from the Fire Marshall tomorrow. His team will lead the investigation to rule arson in or out. After that, the sheriff here will be in touch to let you know what's going on." He put out his hand to Jacob. "I'm very sorry for your losses."

Jacob shook his hand. "Thank you for your service to us today. Your men and you were a God-send."

The chief nodded and headed toward his car.

Sheriff Thomas shook his head. "This is a downright shame, Mr. and Mrs. Yoder. I'm real sorry you're going through all this. But if someone did this on purpose, I assure you we'll do all we can to find him and have him face justice."

Jacob shook his hand. Both of them watched in silence as the lawman made his way to his car.

Leah shivered, the cool night air tickling her neck and the darkness setting off radar in her body that all was not well.

She stole a look toward the black hulk of the barn and got a whiff of lingering odors of burnt wood on the breeze. Her gaze seemed to hone in on the obscurities that shifted and transformed from ordinary harmless shapes into threatening shadows as the faint moonlight flickered in and out of shrubs and trees.

Jacob's gentle voice startled her. "Leah, let's go inside now. Okay?"

He took her by the hand and led her through the door into their living room. Earlier, kind neighbors had lifted the windows a couple of inches allowing trapped smoke to be freshened with clean air, but the lightweight curtains lifting and falling with the breeze against the windows and sills brought fear to the surface for Leah.

The sounds reminded her of the night she sat, frozen in fear, as the house noises teased her mind with possibilities of danger. And now, danger had reappeared like a stalking hunter.

She hurried to each window, slamming them all shut against whatever wickedness may be lurking outside. Her legs suddenly gave way and she collapsed onto the sofa. She leaned her head against the cushions as tears once again squeezed past her closed lids. Soft whimpers broke free of her resolve not to cry anymore, filling the air with her distress and fatigue.

Jacob sat beside her, wrapping her in the soft quilt and holding her against his chest. They didn't speak. She cried and he rocked her in tight hugs until her body gave way to fitful sleep.

# CHAPTER THIRTY-ONE

A finger of sharp white light pierced Leah's closed eyelids when she struggled to sit up.

She found she was still on the sofa and Jacob was with her. He was fully stretched out, long legs spanning the space between his body and feet, which were resting against the floor.

One arm was protectively around her shoulders and she marveled that he was able to sleep at all. Sometime in the night, she had curled into a ball under his arm. As she unwound her body, she winced at the sudden points of pain that snaked along her taut muscles with each movement.

The living room looked so normal in the morning sun that it was hard to believe anything at all had happened to the farm.

She eased off the sofa and padded to the window that overlooked the farm yard. The damage the fire had wrought caused her heart to speed up. The shock of seeing it all again triggered profound anxiety.

Behind her, Jacob stirred. She waited for him to sit up, his face reflecting the same strain and ache in his stiff muscles she had experienced.

"It seems we both fell asleep in an odd position," she said. "Good morning, love."

Her voice sounded raspy. She headed to the kitchen for a drink and to put the coffee pot on.

The cool water from a pitcher in the fridge slid down her parched throat like honey. She poured a tall glass for Jacob and glanced at the clock on her way back to the living room. Seven-thirty.

A sigh escaped her lips as she thought of all that lay ahead today.

Jacob gave her a weak smile as he stifled a groan when he straightened his legs. "Morning, Leah. I feel like an old man." He took the glass and drank the cold water in one gulp. "That hit the spot. Thank you."

He stood, reaching his arms up and arching his back to ease his muscles into shape. "It's a new day." He scratched his head. "Guess we're going to have to face the disaster, whether we want to or not."

"Yes. I'm tired just thinking of it."

As the coffee brewed, its unique scent drew them into the kitchen. Leah pulled open the fridge and sorted for eggs, bacon, and butter. Placing them on the counter, she reached for a fresh loaf of oat bread and looked to Jacob. "Church spread or jam?"

"What kind of jam?"

"Um, looks like blueberry?"

"Jam, please."

He gingerly lowered his body onto a chair at the table and grabbed at Leah's hand as she moved to the stove. "A morning kiss first?"

She complied, smiling as he winked when she pulled away. "Some things can't be stolen from us, Jacob. Can they?"

"You are right about that, wife. You sure are right about that."

They ate breakfast in silence, Leah feeling content to be near her husband, both unharmed and still alive. The thought uncoiled from the depths of her being that things could have been so terribly different. She struggled suddenly to swallow her toast.

If they'd been home, Jacob would have certainly tried to fight the fire, putting himself in direct danger attempting to rescue the horse and the cows—trying urgently to save the barn. Risking his life.

209

The horrible possibilities knifed through her heart and mind. She could be having her first day without him this morning, instead of sitting here with him in their peaceful kitchen.

She gagged down the bite of toast, quickly swallowing a sip of coffee. As her gaze met Jacob's, she felt her eyes widen.

Immediately, Jacob responded to her alarmed expression.

"What! Leah, what is it? Are you okay?" He pushed back his chair and rushed to her. "Are you choked?"

As he pulled her back into his arms, she sputtered at the dark heavy thought of how fragile life was for her and for all those she loved. Tears trickled down her cheeks. She gasped for air and control. "Jacob, how frail we all are! Why did God make us so ... *breakable?*" She could barely stand as her terrified mind railed at the unfairness of life.

"Leah, hush now. Shhh—don't cry so." He stroked her hair gently as he tugged her closer. "You're still in shock. It's hit you once again about the fire and how terrible it all is. But there are blessings, too. I'm okay and you're fine, too. Between the two of us, we'll be able to start over. We have the house, our friends and family, and *Gott.* What else do we need?"

She pulled away, reaching for a tissue from the box on the counter.

"I know—I know." Her breath came in hiccups as she fought to stifle her fears. But why? That's what I want to know? Why did Bert do this to us? How can he hate us so much?"

Jacob led her to the table and helped her sit.

"We don't know that it was Bert who did this. But if it was him, he'll be found out. The sheriff seems set on doing that—making sure he finds out who did this and bringing getting justice to the person."

Leah shook her head. "We only want to live our lives in peace. It's so confusing to think someone can destroy our farm out of pure meanness!"

Jacob nodded. "It does. But if it is Bert, he's got a lot of hurt inside to do this for no good reason." He looked at her. "How we handle this, Leah, is the only part of this whole thing that's our concern. The law is the sheriff's concern, the origin of the fire is the Fire Marshall's concern, and Bert's actions are his concerns, if he set the fire."

Leah sniffed. She stood and went to the stove, pulling out a pan for the eggs and bacon. "I know you're right, Jacob, but *Gott's* going to have to help me leave it to them and to Him. All I want to do this morning is whip the tar out of Bert Small!"

She cracked an egg sharply against the edge of the pan and instantly regretted the anger she used as goopy egg innards covered her stove and her hands. "Oh, no! Look at this! That's what I get for being so angry."

Jacob chuckled, and hearing his laughter lifted her spirits. He was right. They could do this, and with *Gott's* help, they would thrive.

The morning wore on endlessly, it seemed, but between the two of them, they steadily managed to get some of the buggy debris sorted out and were starting on the barn after lunch when a line of buggies approached from the road.

Leah paused, shielding her eyes with her hand as she watched the buggies turn into the lane.

"Jacob, I think it's church folk. *Ja*, I can see Liams', Abes', and Jakes'."

She waited as the buggies lined up in front of the barn and then greeted her friends eagerly. It was so good to see them.

"Anna! It's kind of you to come. What's in the casserole dish?"

"Leah, Liam and me brought rice and chicken to have for dinner, and Verna's made rolls and beet salad. Lizzie baked a couple of pies and brought her ice cream churn."

"Ice cream, pies, casserole, rolls, and salad? Sounds good enough to eat!" Leah laughed.

The instant relief that flooded her as she watched her church family hop from their buggies, greet one another, and cheerily set to work, settled in Leah's heart. The burden was now shared and she felt thankful all the way to her bones for their caring friendships.

211

The women made their way inside the house as Liam, Abe, and Jake met up with Jacob at the barn. The men's low, friendly voices lifted Leah's heart for her husband.

Jacob would have help. She'd have her good friends to cheer her as they faced the first of many difficult days ahead. It was amazing how a few kind hands, outstretched in support, could immediately brighten their day.

They worked hard. Leah and the women helped move piles of debris to a corner of the barnyard while the men carefully knocked down charred walls and beams in the barn.

After a break for a much needed dinner, a couple of the neighbor men, along with a friendly English family from down the road they had not met before, came along and offered a hand, too.

By evening, much of the debris had been gathered, while only a few burned spots in the barn were still in place. Another few days of demolition and cleaning should take care of most of the mess.

As they gathered in the living room before going to their homes, the talk turned to when they would be able to rebuild the barn.

Jacob shook his head, pulling his dark beard as he spoke. "I'm going to have to rely on Amish Aid, I suppose. I hate to do it, but we don't have the finances to repair it all, otherwise."

Liam nodded. "It's there for this kind of thing, Jacob. Do you think they'll find whoever started the fire?"

Liam's fair face was smudged with soot and his red hair and beard were speckled with black ashes. In fact, all of their friends, women and men both, sported speckles of soot and ash on their faces, hands, and clothing, as well as in their hair. Leah stifled a giggle at their disheveled appearances, including her own.

"I don't know yet if it even was arson but the sheriff and fire marshal are handling all that."

Leah stood, heading to the kitchen. After this blessed day with these wonderful friends, she didn't want to talk about *why* they were all here.

Instead, she pulled out glasses and poured refreshing drinks of ice-cold mint tea. Anna came to the kitchen, placed a hand on her arm, and without a word, began taking the drinks out to the others. Grateful for her friend's thoughtful help, Leah gathered her thoughts and put on a smile before following her out.

Finally, the tiring, emotion-filled day came to an end. As she and Jacob waved the last couple down the lane, she let out a deep sigh.

"What would we do without our friends, Jacob?" she asked softly.

"We'd still be clearing that barn, for one thing."

"Yes, we would."

She linked arms with him as they walked slowly back to the house. The night air was sharp with chill as sparkling stars winked on and off above their heads.

She breathed in a deep drought of the fresh air, seeing only a little wisp of her breath as she let it out.

Soon, the nights would be warmer and the daylight would reach bedtime.

Soon, the fields would be fully planted and summer would be here once more.

Soon, this day, and these weeks to come, would only be memories.

She felt the Lord's goodness, even in the midst of their troubles. "I think this fire may become a blessing in disguise, husband."

Jacob pulled the hat off his head with his free hand, and slapped it against his dusty trousers. "You think?"

"Well, for one thing, we're getting to know our church family much better than before."

Jacob chuckled. "In that case, be prepared to get to know the preacher and deacons and their wives a little better, too."

Leah stopped. "Why do you say that?"

"Because Liam told me they're *all* coming over tomorrow."

"Hmph. That should be ... fun."

Jacob tipped back his head and laughed out loud. His delightful voice echoed around the barnyard and Leah snuggled closer to him, giggling at the irony of all those folks who weren't that fond of her, showing up to help them when they needed it most.

"It's a funny old world, isn't it, Jacob?"

"It is, for sure." He stole a kiss as they climbed the porch steps. "And we'll need some proper sleep—not on the sofa sitting upright all night—to handle the day tomorrow, *ja?*"

"Oh, yes. For sure."

# CHAPTER THIRTY-TWO

Leah swept the front porch clean of dried mud and decaying leaves which had been tracked in on her and Jacob's shoes every day since they had worked to clean up the barn debris.

It had taken them, with help from the church families and friends, including Martha, Sarah, and even Clara and the children, more time than they had originally planned to clear out the barn and prepare it for repairs.

Thankfully, not all the walls were damaged. And only two needed to be replaced, along with the roof and inside stalls.

She stopped and gazed out over the fields. The vibrant beauty of spring was changing their farm's colors. Since the fire, it seemed the season had galloped in, raring to go, heavy with dew, sun, and food for the birds and animals that lived around them.

The charred field had been turned under with new topsoil added. Time would restore the soil and one day, nothing would be left to remind them of the fire.

Her gaze turned to the barn—still mostly useless, but they had repaired a stall for Bingo, and soon, it would be reborn to purpose and shelter more animals.

Tomorrow morning was going to bring about a burst of activity. Their friends and church family had taken today off work so they could get their own homes in order before returning tomorrow for the final barn repairs. If things went according to plan, by this time next week, the farm building would be fully restored.

Leah and Jacob had spent yesterday finishing up the cleaning and getting everything set and ready to go for tomorrow morning. Today, Jacob hired Ella to take him into town so he could purchase more nails, screws, and other needed supplies. She was expecting him back soon, so when she heard the crunch of tires on the gravel lane, she turned to meet him.

The car that slowly made its way toward her house wasn't Ella's van. She squinted, trying to see through the glass to the visitors inside. Puzzled and wary, she faced the callers.

Though Bert Small had not been arrested, the sheriff had told them he'd been questioned about the fire. The case was still open while the investigation carried on.

A paranoid thought leapt to her mind. Did this unfamiliar car have anything to do with Bert? She shuddered, praying there was no evil intent in this visit.

As the sedan pulled even with the house, Leah was delighted to find Martha opening the back door. And as she got out and waved to Leah, a little head popped out from the backseat. Little Johnny! Leah ran to the car and hugged her friend. "Martha, you have Johnny with you! How wonderful!"

From inside the car, Sarah smiled at Leah. "Here we are! I convinced Martha it was past time to go get him. And these great folks came from Ashfield to pick us up, take us back there to get this little guy, and then bring us home again."

Sarah pointed to the driver, a friendly man wearing a huge smile. "This is Wayne Brown." She waved to a petite lovely lady in the front seat. "And this is his wife, Christina."

Leah offered a shy grin to the couple. "Nice to meet you. Please come in for a little visit while we get reacquainted with Johnny. I'm so happy you helped Martha get her little boy. It's wonderful to know that you went out of your way to do this for her."

Leah led the cheerful group up the porch steps and into the house. She was relieved that so many women had helped her keep the house clean over the last few days, and was thankful to be able to receive guests without worry over an unkempt home. She invited them all to take a seat.

Sarah settled onto the sofa next to Leah. "Christina and Wayne do volunteer work for MAP Ministry. Ella was too busy to go as far as Ashfield today, yet we hated to put off the trip to bring Johnny home. Martha remembered that MAP sometimes sent drivers to help Amish folk, so she called, and here we all are."

Johnny scrambled into his mother's lap and Leah was comforted to see Martha pull him close and kiss the top of his little head. Her eyes were shining to have her child near. Things appeared to be getting off to a good start between mother and son.

"Your home is lovely, Leah," Christina Brown looked around the neat, welcoming living room.

"Thank you. We had a fire a few days ago, which put quite a bit of pressure on us to work in the field and barn, so I'm afraid I haven't had a chance to bake over the last few days. The women of the church, along with Martha and Sarah, have been helping me keep things together. But I can offer some mint tea, if anyone would care for a glass."

Sarah reached over and patted Leah's hand. "I was so *gworiched* when I first got word about the fire and am thanking God He was watching over you two."

"Me, too!" Martha hugged her son closer. "That was a close call."

"Wow—that's a difficult thing to overcome." Christina's concern warmed Leah's heart. So many good people in this world brought light to many dark places.

Wayne gestured toward the farmyard outside the windows. "What happened, if I may ask?"

"The Fire Marshall hasn't told us exactly, but he and his team suspect arson."

"Arson!" Wayne's brows rose as he shook his head in surprise. "What? My word. I wonder why someone would do such a thing?"

Leah stood, ready to head to the kitchen for the tea, but paused to explain. "There is a suspect, a man my husband works with. But there's no proof yet that he was involved. Still, he is being investigated."

She hurried to the kitchen to prepare the drinks. She turned to see Sarah right behind her, willing to help set the glasses out and load them on a tray as Leah poured the icy tea.

Sarah leaned closer and whispered to Leah. "I have something to talk over with you and the ladies from Bible study. Something that's been bothering me since this fire. Will you be able to host the Bible study this week? Is that manageable—after the barn is repaired, that is."

Leah nodded. "I think I'll be fine hosting this week. I'll look forward to getting at least one part of my week back to normal, in fact." She broke off, realizing her face was suddenly as hot as a flame. "My! I'm feeling really warm, suddenly."

She fanned her face with a paper napkin. "Must be the scurrying I've been doing. Thank you for helping me, Sarah." She nodded toward the Bible resting on the kitchen table. "I sure need a Bible study this week."

She bustled to the pantry and pulled out a container of cookies she remembered one of the ladies from church had brought. "These will hit the spot."

Sarah sighed as she picked up the tray. "I'm glad we can meet. This fire has me going round and round about my relationship with Jesus. I'm wondering if I'm truly ready to meet Him, if my time to leave this old world should come sooner than I expected."

Leah stopped, facing her. "Sarah, I'm sorry this whole thing has got you worried." She gave her friend a quick hug. "But I think we all should be asking that of ourselves, to be honest. It'll make a great topic for the study."

They brought the drinks and cookies to their guests, passing around the tea and sweets.

Leah hadn't forgotten Johnny. She placed a small cup of milk and a plump oatmeal raisin cookie on the short side table for him.

The little boy shyly knelt at the table as he surveyed the treat, giggling.

Martha ruffled his silky blonde hair, leaving his tow-head in a fluffy jumble. The serene expression Leah caught on her face further convinced her that Martha was, indeed, taking to motherhood in a positive way this time around.

The chat turned to MAP Ministry as Leah asked the Browns how things were going with the new market and young women's apartments that the ministry had opened.

Christina's face brightened. "The market's doing well, though the first year was tough, as any new business can attest to. But we think it's headed for success."

Wayne nodded. "And the apartments are nearly filled with former Amish young ladies, too."

"That's good news. Jacob and I pray for Matthew and Naomi Schrock daily. They were so helpful and supportive of me when I left my Amish community before Jacob and I moved to Holmes County. I hope the store and the apartments are blessed by the Lord. The Schrocks have made many sacrifices for the ministry."

Christina carefully placed her glass of tea on the desk near the sofa. She gestured toward Martha. "I don't want to rush things here, but I think Martha has some news to share with you."

Martha met Leah's gaze, but hesitated.

Leah was puzzled. "C'mon and tell. Don't leave us hanging."

Christina gestured to Martha. "It's great news." She encouraged Martha with a little nod and smile.

"It's the main reason we popped in on you, in fact," Wayne laughed.

Martha hugged her son close as he scrambled into her lap. His mouth was ringed with a milk mustache and his bright eyes shone as she wiped cookie crumbs from his shirt. She raised her eyes to meet Leah's expectant gaze. "Well, you know me and how I've struggled with the Amish faith, and how I've rebelled against anything having to do with *Gott.*"

Leah nodded, aware of a growing spirit of anticipation in the room. Her voice softened as she thought of all Martha had been through. "Yes, I know. You haven't had an easy path, though, my friend."

Martha waved away her troubles. "Much of it was my fault, for sure." She paused, her eyes focusing on her boy. "Anyway, while I was talking with the Browns on the way up to Ashfield, they asked me what I thought of Jesus." Her words caught in her throat, and Leah could see tears glistening behind her friend's lashes. She was surprised to see the tears—Martha had always tried to hide her feelings under a tough exterior.

The young woman swallowed and started again. "To get to the point, I'm trying to say I gave my heart to Jesus on the way back here today. I don't know why that was so hard to say." Martha laughed as Leah stood and ran to her.

"Martha! That's the best news I could ever hear!" Tears rose in Leah's own eyes as she hugged her friend. "Your adventure is just beginning, girl!"

Leah caught sight of Sarah, also wiping away tears and even Christina was moved by the moment.

Leah chuckled. "Look at little Johnny here. He's wondering why all we women are crying and laughing at the same time."

Wayne spoke up. "Johnny, you'll be wondering that for the rest of your life." His bemused smile broke the tension and everyone laughed.

Leah clapped her hands together. "Martha, I thought of something. You're just in time to join our Bible study this Thursday!

It'll be right here at my house in the afternoon. Bring Johnny—there'll be other children for him to play with."

Martha offered a shy grin, something Leah was also shocked to see. "I will try to come, if I don't have to work. I'm supposed to start on Wednesday evening."

Leah settled back into her spot on the sofa. "I'm just so happy for you, friend."

"Is the Bible study open to visitors?"

Leah turned to Christina. "Sure is—we'd be glad to have you join with us, Christina."

"I'll look forward to it then."

The rest of the visit felt like a very good dream to Leah. Her best friend—truly beginning anew with Christ—was the sweetest of surprises. Though she knew life wouldn't be all roses for Martha as a single mother, Leah trusted *Gott* would lead Martha in adventures she would never think could happen.

As the guests prepared to leave, the clouds parted and a brilliant shaft of sun lit up the farm, bathing even the burned out hulk of the barn in a golden radiance.

Leah's heart stood still. She tucked away the sounds of the happy visitors, Johnny's sweet giggles, the shine of peace on Martha's face, and the shimmering promise of the farm into her heart.

Later that evening, after the *suppah* dishes had been washed, Leah and Jacob settled on the sofa.

Jacob ticked off a list on his fingers. "Well, I have all the supplies I think we'll need. You have the food menu planned with the ladies, and the Lord's providing a perfect day for the barn repairs in the morning." Jacob tapped Leah's hand with his own. "I'd say we're as ready as we'll ever be for tomorrow's frolic."

"And I'd say you're right, husband."

"The only thing missing is a good night's sleep, wife. What do you say about heading to bed?"

Leah put her finger to her lips. "Hmm. Only if we're allowed to chat a little bit before we go up about Martha."

Jacob smiled. He gently smoothed his wife's hair under her *kapp*. "I see you're still thrilled to your toes over her happy news."

Leah nodded, her eyes shining with excitement. "It'll be a whole new way of living for her. Just think: Martha will be relying on *Gott* to guide her for the first time in her life. I can't wait to see how He leads her."

"And the best part is little Johnny will have a better life, too. Only a loving heavenly Father could work all that out in the end."

"Yes. Only *Gott*." Leah blinked back joyful tears.

Jacob stood, holding out his hand to Leah. "I say it's time for bed. Was that enough chatter to soothe your heart until morning?"

Leah laughed. "*Ja*, I think so. If it isn't, I'll be sure to wake you up to tell you."

# CHAPTER THIRTY-THREE

L eah smoothed her apron and tucked the last bit of flyaway hairs under her *kapp* before hurrying to the bedroom window. She peered down on the barnyard and spied Jacob setting out the last of the supplies before turning to welcome the first load of Amish men pulling into the lane. This was finally the day their farm would receive its first patch of healing work and she was both relieved and excited.

She hurried down to greet the women who were helping her feed the group of men who would put their barn back together again. Many were church members and some were friends and acquaintances.

As Leah stepped off the porch, she caught sight of Bishop John Troyer being helped from a buggy. His nephew, Deacon Andy Troyer, was his buggy driver.

Leah walked to the barnyard, greeting families and instructing women where to put their food contributions. She and Jacob had set up tables on the porch for the food and had borrowed the church benches for seating while folks ate or rested.

She reached Bishop Troyer's side. "*Gut morgen*, Bishop Troyer."

The elderly man turned to see who was speaking to him. His long white beard caught the morning rays as they shivered along the strands of gossamer hair, disappearing into shadows when he moved. His lined face held a pleasant expression, which Leah knew was typical of this kind man.

"Ah, Leah! How are you this morning? Ready for the hoopla?"

"I am, Bishop. And we're grateful for the community's help in getting the barn rebuilt."

"How's Bingo? Recovered completely?"

"Leah nodded. "He is, though he sometimes eyes the barn with suspicion when we take him to his stall. It's repaired, but of course, the rest of the barn is in need of a lot of help."

"How about the arsonist?"

"No official word yet, but the sheriff let Jacob know they were nearer to an arrest. Jacob's been back to work for four days and hasn't seen the man who had been harassing him."

The bishop leaned closer and whispered a quick prayer for safety and for resolution.

Deacon Andy slipped up behind and tenderly took his uncle by the arm. He waited for the "amen" before he nodded to Leah and then led the bishop to a group of comfortable chairs that had been placed in a circle under a newly leafing tree. The dappled shade it provided was just enough to shelter the older folks from the beating sun, but allowed enough light to keep them warm.

The bishop was greeted affectionately by most who crossed his path, but Leah took note of the sour expressions the Melvin Masts, Christian Millers, and Peter Yoders wore. Their grim appearances were a constant reminder of the last few weeks as they butted heads with Bishop Troyer over his indulgence to those who read English Bibles.

Barbara Mast, Elizabeth Miller, and Hannah Yoder approached her with a variety of casserole dishes and pie tins in hand.

"I don't suppose you've hired a fridge trailer for the day, Leah?" Barbara held out her chicken *bot boi* casserole, gesturing to it as she spoke. "This really should be refrigerated since we won't be eating it until lunchtime. And Elizabeth and Hannah have cream pies, too."

She ended her inquiry with a "tsk," assuming she was correct in Leah's inability to foretell the needs of the food committee.

Leah smiled her friendliest smile and pointed to the white trailer parked just beyond the porch under a shade giving oak.

"Good of you ladies to contribute to the frolic. We appreciate your offerings very much. Of course, if you'd like, I can take your casserole and pies to the fridge for you."

"No, no—we can manage." Barbara waved away her offer with a languid movement of her wrist. Off the three sailed toward the refrigerated unit, without a thank you or a "*gut morgen.*"

She was definitely not one of their favorite people. Leah guessed if it weren't for the need to be seen giving aid to Jacob and Leah, the three would have preferred to stay home.

She shrugged and went to greet her friends.

Before the men got to work, Bishop Troyer said a prayer for the frolic. After the prayer ended, the men began organizing their labor force.

The next few hours were nothing but a frenzied rush of keeping up with drinks for the men and leading the women in clean up, food preparation, restocking the mint tea and water containers, plus keeping the children safe and free of dangerous shenanigans.

Before she knew it, the men were taking lunch in shifts. The constant chatter and laughter filled her heart with love for these people. She was happy to see Martha, Johnny, and Sarah arrive to the frolic after lunch, too. They had wisely hired a driver since they knew the lane and fields would be crowded with buggies and horses.

Martha offered her contribution of food, several dishes of pasta salad, and even little Johnny held out a platter of cookies.

"Thank you, Johnny. You sure are *Maem's* helper today, aren't you?"

He giggled and ran off as several youngsters converged on him in a chattering horde. Martha called to his disappearing back "Don't you dare go off too far, Johnny! *Maem* is watching you!"

She smiled at Leah. "That boy has already made a ton of friends. You'd think he'd be too shy, but somehow, the other *kinder* take to him right away and he just joins right in."

"I'm so glad to see him smiling and laughing, Martha. And you, too—you look much happier."

"Good, because I am much happier." She grinned in evidence and pulled Leah along with her. "Walk with me to the fridge, Leah. I want to tell you something."

"Okay, but where'd Sarah get to?"

Martha searched the crowd and then pointed. "Looks like the three sourpusses have cornered her."

Leah shaded her eyes as she scanned where Martha indicated. Yes. There was Sarah. But if she knew her ex-house mate at all, she figured the three sour—er—women were the ones getting cornered by Sarah.

Sure enough, she watched as Elizabeth shook her head, frowned and walked away. Her cronies also scooted past Sarah as quickly as they could, too.

Leah followed Martha to the trailer. "What's going on? What do you want to tell me?"

She helped Martha open the heavy door and stowed her bowls of pasta inside.

"I heard a rumor while I was waiting to get my uniform at the Amish Way Restaurant yesterday." She wiped her hands on her apron to dry the moisture the cold salad had created as she carried them. "That man Jacob knows, the one who set the fire?"

"*May* have set the fire, Martha. *May.*"

Martha put up her hand. "Well, *may* have set, then. I heard two men talking and they think he's left town."

"Left town?"

"*Ja.* Trying to run from the law."

Leah grimaced. "So that's why Jacob hasn't seen him at work."

"I think it's good that he's gone. Now you won't have to worry anymore." She stopped and craned her neck, searching for her son among the jostling, yelling, playing children. "Speaking of worry, I better go find that stinker."

"Okay. I've got to get back to the house, too, to check in on the ladies heating up lunch foods."

Leah strode across the yard and onto the porch, her mind preoccupied by the news Martha had shared. To be honest, she knew it was really just gossip that Bert Small may have gone into hiding to avoid the law. She was surprised to find she wasn't pleased about the notion because if he was guilty, she'd rather know where he was.

Before her thoughts went too far down that rabbit hole, she was called on to help carry out a platter of hot chicken sandwiches.

The day sped toward late afternoon before the men were nearly finished restoring the barn. Leah marveled at what the guys could accomplish once they put their minds and labor together.

She took a break from kitchen duty to wander close to the area where Jacob was straddling a new beam. Though she was immensely proud of him, she was anxious watching him so far off the ground— and with just one hand gripping the wood.

She shaded her eyes with her hand. Just as she turned to go back to the house, a sudden rush of excited voices rose up like a wave and rolled over the yard.

She looked for the source and caught a glimpse of a frantic group of women and men gathering around the older folks sitting under the shade tree.

As she ran toward the trouble, she heard the name Bishop Troyer being passed from person to person.

Leah pressed through the throng until she was within a few feet of the Bishop. Deacon Andy was kneeling by his uncle's chair, chafing the elderly man's hands, but Leah could see that something was dreadfully wrong with their kind bishop. His head lolled toward his chest and his eyes were closed. His legs splayed as though the muscles could no longer hold together. His shoulders were slumped forward, with arms that dangled, showing no life.

"Oh, no!" Leah stifled a groan and immediately began whispering prayers.

Andy Troyer faced the crowd, asking someone to find a phone to call 911.

Jacob appeared at her side and then ran to the driver who had brought Martha, Johnny, and Sarah. By the grace of God, the driver had decided to stay and sample the delicious food offered to her as she watched the progress on the barn. The startled English lady pulled out her cell phone and punched the buttons for help.

Several minutes later, after the EMTs had pulled out of Leah and Jacob's driveway and were headed to the local hospital in Millersburg, Leah sobbed as she watched the solemn passage.

Deacon Andy had climbed into the back of the emergency vehicle, holding his uncle's hand. There was no longer a need for haste. The Bishop had gone home to his reward in Heaven with nothing more than a soft sigh to announce his journey.

She was in shock, as were most of the church family. How could they pass this devastating event along to the bishop's elderly wife? A few of the women had gone along with the deacon to be at her side when she received their sad news.

Leah searched for Jacob. Oh, how she needed his arms around her.

The men had quietly gathered tools, materials, and equipment and stowed them neatly in the nearly finished barn. The women gathered their dishes, wiped up spills, and cleaned tables and benches, while the boys waited to carry the scrubbed seats back to the bench wagon.

Slowly, men donned hats, wrangled the horses and hitched them to buggies, and mothers corralled their children for the somber trip to their homes.

As Leah said goodbye to her friends, she caught a glimpse of the three women who had harshly judged the bishop. They were whispering. Plotting something, Leah surmised.

And then it hit her. Melvin Mast would be one of the names written on a piece of paper for the *Ausbund*. The choosing of the new bishop would come soon. She was sure he would be among the men who were asked to serve. If his name was left in the hymn book, he would become their new bishop. And further, as men who held important positions in the church already, Christian Miller and Peter Yoder most likely would also be asked to serve. The three men would await the pulling out of the short paper that would give one of them the title of bishop.

Leah shivered at the thought. Any one of those men would be bad for the church. She hurried to the house, her eyes scanning the sorrowful church members she passed along the way. She had to find Jacob.

Martha and Sarah were gathering their belongings and Johnny was clinging to his *maem's* apron strings as Leah approached the porch. They pulled Leah into a group hug.

"The bishop was a good, good man, Leah. His reward in Heaven will be great." Sarah met her eyes. "We could do nothing to stop what happened today. Don't dwell on it—*Gott's* ways are not our ways."

Martha swept Johnny into her arms, gave Leah an unhappy wave, and headed to the car. The English driver helped her put Johnny in his car seat and both women got in. They waited for Sarah.

Sarah grabbed Leah's hands. "I mean it. Don't dwell. It *is* God's will to choose the Bishop's time and place to go home."

Leah nodded, already fighting the urge to ask God why.

Sarah turned and hurried to the car.

After the farm was emptied of all who had helped, the tidiness of the barnyard depressed Leah. Just like that, she snapped her fingers, everyone was gone. Only the barn showed evidence of what had been achieved. Somehow, the loss of their kind bishop made this place feel lonely.

Jacob shuffled out of the barn, his hat in his hand. He stopped when he saw Leah waiting for him on the swing, then wiped his brow and his eyes, and slowly made his way to her side. His body caused the swing to jump as he allowed his legs to crumple under him as he sat. He wrapped Leah in his solid embrace. And once again, they sat together, watching the sun unfurl its vivid inferno over the trembling helpless hills.

"Life and death, Leah. Every morning and every evening. The sun has rolled it out in front of us through hundreds and hundreds of years. Yet we're still shocked by the sudden disappearance of light from the horizon. The depth of the darkness and the black void of the shadows astonishes us every time. Life and light go so quickly. So quickly."

Leah sniffed, wiping her tears with a sodden paper napkin she'd found on the ground. "I'm weary, Jacob. I can't think anymore."

She stood, her body wavering over trembling knees. "I just want to sleep, and sleep, and sleep."

He lifted his sore body off the swing and took her in his arms.

"That's what we're going to do, wife. Sleep and sleep and sleep."

# CHAPTER THIRTY-FOUR

Two days after the bishop's death, his funeral was held at his home. His wife, children and family filled many of the front benches in the old Troyer barn. Watching his children, Leah could see their deep sadness, and wondered how it felt to be left with no *daet* at all.

Even though her own *daet* was distanced from her, she still knew he was there. It was something she couldn't quite fathom—the knowledge that the generation ahead of her was disappearing as her own generation stood at the precipice of eternity.

Following the service, dinner was served. A solemn atmosphere permeated the customary afternoon church lunch. The bishop's sudden death had shaken everyone. Very little laughter and chatter were heard, making the unfamiliar silence at the tables difficult to bear.

As Leah and Jacob headed to their buggy after the meal, Sarah rushed to stop her. "Leah, can we speak a minute?"

"Sure." Leah stopped in her place and waited for Sarah's approach.

Jacob nodded a greeting to Sarah and then turned to Leah. "I'll go get the buggy and Bingo. Be right back."

Sarah took a quick breath. "Whew! I need more exercise. That little jaunt to catch up to you left me breathless."

She swallowed and put a hand up as she took another deeper breath.

"There. Much better. I was wondering if you're still planning to host the ladies Bible study? And, well, I'm hoping we can do it tomorrow? I know we were planning to have it today, Thursday, and of course that had to be cancelled. But do you think we could get the ladies together tomorrow, instead of waiting until next Thursday?"

Leah nodded. "I don't see why not. If some can't make it, we can still have it."

Sarah gave her friend a quick hug. "Thank you. I've been struggling with something, and the bishop's death has made things even worse for me. Tomorrow, we can dig into the Word. I know it will help me cope."

"Are you okay? I mean, you could come home with us and we can chat now, if that would help."

Sarah waved away the invitation. "No—I can wait for tomorrow. No problem. It's something I'd feel funny sharing around men."

Leah raised her brows. "Is it a problem with relationships? You know, with men?"

Sarah chuckled quietly. "Oh, no! Not at all. It certainly isn't *that* kind of relationship issue."

"Okay. And if you happen to see Anna, Lizzie, and Verna, can you pass along the invitation for tomorrow to them, too? Let's say, about three o'clock. That way Jacob will be at work and most will have had time for house chores."

Sarah nodded. "What about Katy? She was there last time."

Leah considered the way Katy and her husband had been showing loyalty with the Mast, Miller, and Yoder couples, and wondered if she would be willing to come to their Bible study now? Even at the last study, Katy had balked at the discussion concerning salvation by grace alone. Would she want to spend time with them?

She shrugged. "I guess so. It's up to her if she wants to come."

Jacob pulled up with the rig, so Leah said her goodbyes and climbed aboard. "See you tomorrow."

Bingo's hooves struck the pavement in his slow rhythmic manner, but Jacob didn't hurry him on. They moseyed home at a leisurely pace.

"You know, Jacob, I was thinking about how it must feel for the bishop's children to be without a *daet* now. Do they feel like orphans, in a way?"

Jacob nodded. "I would imagine they do. It's been a hard week for all of us. Nothing brings to our minds our own deaths more than the sudden passing of someone we care about."

"You're right about that. But you know what? Since I gave my heart to Jesus, I have more peace about it. I might still be a little scared—it's such an unknown world we'll be going to, but I do think the old fears are eased. My soul is ready, even if my body is not."

"New mercies to face life. Every morning."

"Covered in fresh mercy, Jacob. Think of that."

✎🏠✐

Two Sundays later, they were sitting in church, and before them was the petition to add names of the men who were considered worthy to become the next bishop. Being bishop was for life and was an awesome responsibility; one that often brought tears from the family of the man chosen by lot from the hymnal.

Leah scribbled the names of two men she knew were mature enough spiritually and emotionally to handle the task. Then all the names were gathered from the members. The deacons and ministers rose and went to another room with the list.

They came back a while later with a stack of hymnals. As each man's name was read from the list tallied, he stood, walked slowly to the front and chose a hymnal. After each man chose, the stack of hymnals was reshuffled. A slip of paper with a verse on it had been placed in one of the hymnals. As each man opened his *Ausbund*, a

233

sigh of relief escaped his lips when he didn't find the piece of paper. The others waited in great trepidation. Leah knew no one really wanted to be the bishop. Even wives wept if their husband found a slip of paper.

Finally, they were down to the last two men. One of them would be bishop. The choice would be between the current preacher, Jonas Stutzman, and Melvin Mast.

Leah bowed her head, pleading with *Gott* that the preacher had a slip of paper in his hymnal. Even though he was a mild mannered man and would have a difficult time standing up to some of the more forceful members of the church, he would still be a better bishop with the people than Melvin.

But the Amish church believed the lot would fall to the man *Gott* thought was better for the task. Leah wasn't convinced this method of choosing the church leader was the best way, but she was Amish and she would comply.

Preacher Jonas timidly opened his hymnal. He flipped through the pages, and even shook the book by its cover, but no slip fell to the floor.

Slowly, he turned to look at Melvin Mast. Melvin's face was shading toward beet red, but he remained stoic.

Leah glanced to his wife. Instead of seeming concerned, she was looking straight ahead at her husband with a strange little smile turning up the corners of her mouth.

Melvin opened his hymnal. The pages fell back, revealing the white slip of paper. Its illumination glimmered against the black letters spilled over the background.

The congregation held its breath, waiting to see the reaction from their new bishop. Like his wife, Melvin held himself still. Only his lips revealed the inward pride of his heart by that same strange smile.

Expecting an eruption of sorrow from the Mast family, the church members didn't know how to handle the extraordinary lack of emotion on display. Instead, slowly, the brothers in Christ finally stood and made their way to Melvin. Each shook his hand, murmuring scripture or platitudes, while the same thing happened with the women.

It was not what was expected. This left the meeting hanging open, with a foreign numbness of no closure. The gathering broke up awkwardly after Melvin read the scripture on the piece of paper and said a prayer from the prayer book.

He would have six months to memorize sermons, but would be expected to give the opening sermon in just a couple of weeks. By the way he stood tall and straight, Leah doubted he'd suffer from the overwhelming feelings others had struggled with after being chosen to become bishop. He looked in control and confident.

Leah was filled with foreboding. On the way home, she asked Jacob how he felt about the turn of events.

Jacob cleared his throat. "I'm trying hard to find the positives in the choice, Leah. I really can't say anything else right now."

Once they got home, Jacob did chores while she cooked a late *suppah*. After they'd eaten, Jacob had talked about everything but the new bishop. He'd kissed her goodnight and had gone straight to bed.

Leah realized it had taken him a while to get back into the groove of his work schedule after being off for a few days following the fire. He'd come home each night, already weary, wolf down his *suppah*, and hit the farm chores.

And while Leah understood his physical need for sleep, she was more than a little curious about what he thought of Melvin Mast as their new bishop and was irritated that he'd cut off any discussion concerning church. Still, there would be time to talk tomorrow. She hoped.

Leah cleaned up the kitchen, turned off the gas lights and headed to bed herself. As she crawled under the covers, trying not to jostle the bed and wake Jacob, she examined his features. Long dark lashes outlined his lids and fanned themselves against his cheek bones. He often looked like a little boy when he slept. Leah could never resist sweeping her hand lightly over his soft ebony hair.

She rested her weary head against her pillow and settled in for sleep. But sleep was a long time coming. Somehow, she knew things were going to change for them at church and not for the better. Questions popped up in her mind like bubbles, one after the other, only to burst and drift away before she had time to think clearly about them.

After fighting her body and her mind, she stole out of bed and knelt at the window.

Moonlight illumined the tops of trees and hills, its muted glow gently shimmering over the earth. The hard winter was over and the cheerful moon was a welcome guest in her bedroom, but the night air was still chilly so she tip-toed back to bed, sliding under the quilts and sheets to curl up against her husband's warm back. There would be plenty of time to think about this day in the morning.

# CHAPTER THIRTY-FIVE

L eah brought gooey brownies and piping hot coffee to the table where the ladies were gathered, Bibles in hand and notepaper ready. She glanced at each one, saying a silent prayer that they would be blessed by the gathering. It had been a tough winter and early spring. Their hearts were sore and drained.

"Ooo, brownies!" Lizzie exclaimed. "And I didn't have to bake them with a screaming baby on my hip."

Everyone chuckled, knowing exactly what she meant. Leah could fully understand the relief of having a break from child care and she wasn't even a mother yet. She'd spent many a day in her younger years caring for siblings.

Sarah reached for coffee and a sweet treat, too. "I think having a brownie baked for us is always a treat. Thank you, Leah."

Leah handed out napkins and small plates. "You're so welcome. I'm glad we're able to be together. This week, especially. Lizzie, is Jake watching your little Mose today?"

Lizzie nodded, wiping brownie bits from her mouth with the napkin. "Yes. He worked the sawmill this morning, but was done just in time to help out with the baby."

237

Leah turned to Katy. "How about you, Katy. I'm glad you could find someone to help with the children at the last minute."

Katy sipped her coffee, refusing a brownie. "Um, *ja*. My mother-in-law is visiting so she stayed with the *kinder*."

"Great! It's good for us to be able to get together."

"Actually, I'm kind of shocked you wanted to do this so soon after the old bishop's passing and all." Katy lowered her cup and met Leah's eyes with a frown.

The chatter from the other women stopped, each watching Katy with careful expressions. Leah swallowed her bite of brownie, not sure how to respond.

Verna spread her hands out on the table in front of her. "Katy, if you felt this was an inappropriate gathering, you didn't have to come. We'd have understood."

Leah's gaze swung back to Katy. Was this woman going to enjoy their discussion or was she going to cause trouble? She wasn't sure and didn't know how to politely ask her to leave if Katy did cause a ruckus. *Lord, guide us, please.*

Katy placed her coffee cup on the saucer. "No, no. It's okay, I guess. Maybe some scripture reading will help some of us focus on the church and our duties to it."

Sarah caught Leah's eye and slightly shook her head.

Time to read scripture as Katy had suggested. Leah plunged ahead.

"I was thinking that reading about Heaven would be appropriate today. Does anyone have a favorite passage that can focus us on our home there?"

Lizzie opened her Bible, a version that also had the English translation on the side. "I read this verse before the bishop's funeral, and it really gave me peace. It's found in John 14, verses two to four. And it says 'My Father's house has many mansions—'"

Katy cut her off. "Are you reading that in English or translating as you go?"

Lizzie looked up, her brows drawn and her head tilted. "What do you mean?"

"I'm just saying that it should be read in the Luther version. We *are* Amish, after all."

Lizzie turned to Leah, her expression one of helpless confusion.

Leah cleared her throat. "It's fine with me if we refer back and forth between English and Luther Bibles, Lizzie. I'm sure Katy will understand that, sometimes, we can grasp the meanings a bit better when it's in English."

Katy scowled, but nodded to Lizzie, as if giving her permission for continued reading.

Lizzie licked her lips. "Well, I don't want to be a hindrance, but I was saying that it comforts me to know Jesus has assured us He has prepared a place for us in Heaven. I guess that's all I wanted to say." She bent her head, breaking eye contact with everyone around the table.

Katy placed a finger on her own Bible, pointing to the passage in question.

"It *actually* says *'In meines Vaters Haus sind viel Wohnungen. Wenns nich so ware, so wollt' so ich zu euch sagen; ich gehe hin euch die Statte zu bereiten.'*" She glanced around the table, her steady scrutiny challenging anyone to dispute what she'd just read in Luther German. Then, assured of the other women's attention, she went on.

"To help those who need to hear it in *English*, that translates to 'In my Father's house are many mansions. If it were not so I would have told you; I go to prepare a place for you.'" She straightened her spine. "It does *not* say we are assured of that place in Heaven. Jesus is preparing it, but he is *not* assuring us we will be good enough to get there."

She closed her Bible and picked up her coffee cup, confident in her proclamation.

Verna let out a tiny grunt. "Hmm. If we read further down, we see that Jesus said *He* is the way to Heaven. Not our goodness, but our faith in *Him*. It seems to me He is reassuring us that when we believe in Him, we most certainly are assured of our place in Heaven."

Katy sighed. "I see this is going to be a sore point for some, so I'll take the high road and refrain from commenting any further." She sipped her coffee, placing her Bible aside to emphasize any further participation.

An uneasy silence grew until Sarah spoke up.

"The reason I asked Leah to have this Bible study is because I've been struggling with the notion that I'm not good enough to go to Heaven. And since the bishop's sudden death, the question haunts me all the more."

She turned to Katy. "I know you have no fear of death, seeing that you believe yourself worthy of Heaven by all the good works you do, but I know myself. Inside, I know my own sins. I lie sometimes. I fib. I do. I also have selfish thoughts."

She pointed to the plate of brownies in the middle of the table. "For instance, I selfishly wanted that bigger piece of brownie and secretly hoped none of you would choose it. And then I felt guilty about wanting it, so I told myself to sacrifice that desire. And that thought was immediately followed by pride that I'd been so good."

She held out her hands. "But, see? That pride at being good is also wrong. And when I lie awake at night, I realize there's nothing I can do to stop myself being this way. It's in my nature to slip and not do good. So then I fear death. I fear facing God."

Katy used her fingers to imitate zipping her lips closed. Her stubborn refusal to discuss the issue unintentionally demonstrated to the group exactly what Sarah had been talking about. Pride.

Leah struggled to hold back the smile fighting its way to her lips. Instead, she leaned forward, opening her Bible to John 3:16. "I understand what you're saying, Sarah."

She reached her hand to her friend and grasped Sarah's hand gently. "If we're honest with ourselves, we'll have to admit that we *all* struggle with the sins that can't be seen. Pride. Selfishness. Envy. Jealousy. These are things that can't be covered up with clothing, life styles, or outward actions."

She sat back, fingering her Bible. "I'll be honest. I left the Amish once because of these sins. I didn't know how my being Amish cured these soul-driven sins in me."

Sarah nodded, her eyes moist. She drew a tissue from her apron pocket. "That's the gist of it for me, I suppose."

A quiet *tsk* from the right side of the table swung Leah's attention to Katy, who was making a statement without using words. Her demeanor showed her disagreement with the discussion.

Leah shifted in her seat, not sure how to handle Katy's attitude, but wanting to share what might help Sarah. She continued on, ignoring Katy as best she could.

"I think what gave me true peace about this is acknowledging I'll never be able to control these soul sins, though I do try, and realizing this is why Christ was sent."

She pointed to her Bible. "Like it says here in John 3:16—God loved us so much, He sent His only Son to take on our sins." She smiled. "I like to say that the church is proof Christ was needed, and the proof that He came. We can do good to others, that's something our Lord calls us to do—to be salt and light— to add flavor to this world. We're also to bring relief from darkness. We become His hands and feet. In that, our good works show whom we have believed in and whom we follow. But in the end, our faith in Him to take on our sins, to mediate for us with the Father, is what we must trust. I remind myself that it's not *me* fighting for my soul, it's Jesus who has already won the court case against me."

Sarah rose, walked slowly around the table and threw her arms around Leah's shoulders. "I don't want to be like my ninety-year-old grandfather, who cried out on his deathbed that he feared judgment. He didn't know if he would wake in Heaven. He said he'd done all that he could do to be worthy, and still he didn't know if he'd done enough."

A sob broke her voice. "What you've shared with us has helped me, Leah. Thank you."

Katy stood, gathering her Bible, pencil, and paper pad. "Well, this has been an interesting afternoon, but I have to get back home. Thanks for the brownies and coffee, Leah."

She stalked to the door, her back stiff and cheeks flushed. She turned her eyes to Sarah. "I'll see you in church, I hope?"

Sarah nodded, but Leah could see her stifling a giggle as she wiped her tears.

Once Katy left, the atmosphere became easier. The women chatted about home, their families, and their church.

As she spoke about the meeting later with Jacob, she reflected on how freedom seemed to enter the room when self-righteousness walked out.

"It's not that I want to cast Katy as a villain, Jacob, it's that I see so much pious pride and rigidity in her behavior. Truthfully, I can see that in myself. Often."

She shifted in her kitchen chair. "Like whenever I'm in town, and I see tourists clamoring for Amish goods or Amish food or anything Amish, I feel my heart swell. I suddenly get to thinking that by being Amish I have it right. By wearing these clothes, I self-identify with the Amish, who I *know* are being put on a pedestal by tourists and other Christians. I feel like it's the world telling us Amish that *we* have it right. That the Amish are doing God's work."

Jacob sat at the kitchen table, his hands clasped between his knees. He was listening to her, really listening, and when he was like this, Leah wanted to hug him tightly. It felt so nice to be listened to by her husband.

"Leah, that's how I feel sometimes, too. But that kind of thinking, that being Amish automatically makes me a shining beacon for God, feels like a heavy burden at the same time."

He stood, ruffling his hair as he walked to her. Leah reached for him.

"I know, oh, how I understand that, Jacob. We're nowhere and nothing without Christ. Yet, the world seems to think we have all the answers just because of how we live and dress."

He snuggled her closer. "If they only knew how often we fail in our human endeavors! How much we're like everyone else."

Later that night, before they went to sleep, Jacob opened scripture and read one last verse.

"From second Timothy, chapter one, verse twelve: 'For the which cause I also suffer these things: nevertheless I am not ashamed: for I know whom I have believed, and am persuaded that he is able to keep that which I have committed unto him against that day'."

He closed the scriptures and placed the Bible on his nightstand. Reaching his arms up to tuck behind his head, he sighed. "That's what we have to hold to, Leah. It's not us. Or our puny power. In everything happening around us—my work, the farm, the church—Jesus is able to keep us. And only He."

Leah kissed Jacob, nestled closer to him and closed her eyes.

"Goodnight, husband."

"Goodnight, wife."

# CHAPTER THIRTY-SIX

Within days of the Bible study, a knock came at their door after *suppah* was over. Jacob glanced at Leah. He was drying the dishes as Leah washed them.

"Are you expecting company?"

"No, not me. Are you?"

Jacob shook his head. "I'm not, either. Best go answer then, eh?"

He grinned at her as he walked through the hall on his way to the front door.

Leah was curious about who would be visiting, too, so she hurried to rinse the last cup and followed Jacob into the living room.

He was just opening the door when she stepped behind him. She peeked around Jacob's shoulders to see Melvin Mast, Katy's husband Benny, and Preacher Jonas standing on their porch.

Leah's stomach turned over. Her past history told her this was not a casual visit.

Jacob, surprise in his voice, invited the men inside. He indicated the chairs and sofa. "Please have a seat. This is an unexpected visit. Hope everything's okay with the church, Bishop Mast."

Melvin Mast grunted as he lowered his body to the rocking chair. "Not going to stay long as I know it's a work night for you, Jacob."

Jacob took a seat on the footstool that was pushed under the window while Preacher Jonas quickly sat on one end of the sofa and Benny took the other end.

Leah remained standing, but backed herself toward the doorway between the living room and hallway.

Jacob glanced to her. "Can Leah get any of you men a cup of coffee?"

Benny and Preacher Jonas swiveled to face Bishop Mast. He shook his head. "No need. We won't be long, as I said."

He cleared his throat.

"We came because Benny's Katy told him there were strange beliefs being taught by your wife at her Bible study."

*Here we go again.* Leah's heart raced. She looked at Jacob. He looked back. But instead of the concern she thought she'd see on his face, he was wearing an amused smile.

He immediately stood and walked to the door, opened it and smiled back at the visitors. "I hate that you've all bothered yourselves to come out this way after your good *suppahs* and all, but there's really nothing we need to talk about. I hope you have a safe journey back to your homes." He glanced out the window. "Looks like it's getting dark pretty quickly. Best not be too late on the roads. We'll see you on Sunday."

Melvin Mast's face turned as red as a tomato in August, but he also stood, without another word, and marched out the door.

Jacob nodded to Preacher Jonas, the amused smile still showing, as the embarrassed man hurried to catch up with the bishop.

Only Benny stopped at the door. He twirled his hat as he blew out a loud breath.

"I guess there's just no way to keep a rebellious woman in check, is there, Jacob? She left once and came back. But why come back when she doesn't want to be Amish anyway?" He pointed his finger at Jacob. "Think about that, young man. Think of the life you're going to have with a woman like *that!*"

He stormed off, shaking the porch floor boards under his heavy tread.

Tears sprang to Leah's eyes at Benny's harsh warning to Jacob. She leaned against the doorframe, her knees weak.

Jacob closed the door softly. Walking quietly to where she stood, he enveloped her in his arms. He held her for several minutes, not saying anything.

Finally he led her to the sofa and pulled her onto his lap. He covered her with the soft afghan, still not saying a word.

Leah, trying hard to stop the sniffles and hiccups threatening to grow into sobs, waited. She'd never seen him like this before, although the last few days he'd been less talkative than usual. He wasn't angry; he just seemed to be thinking.

After a few more minutes, Jacob shifted her to the sofa so he could reach into his pocket. He pulled out a leaflet—some kind of brochure that was battered from many foldings and unfoldings. He held it out to Leah.

She took it with trembling fingers and read the bold headline at the top of one of the pages: MAP MINISTRY

Leah shook her head, puzzled. "Is this the brochure Matthew Schrock gave us on our wedding day?"

Jacob nodded. "It is. And I held onto it because I felt something in my soul when I took it."

"You did?"

"I did. I can't explain it, but this whole time I've felt the Lord calling me to do more."

Leah caressed his face, her heart beating quicker with each word. "Tell me."

"I know you've wanted to talk about the new bishop and all that means to the church, Leah, and I haven't put you off, not exactly. It's just, well, I've been praying for direction."

He lifted his arms, waving them around him as he turned. "This farm, this house—it's all been a beautiful dream. It's been the Amish dream, for sure. You, farming, keeping the hat and vest, the beard, the buggy, Bingo—it's all part of who I was supposed to be."

Leah nodded, her eyes never wavering from him as he spoke. This Jacob was talking like a man. His own man. A grown man. And she was fascinated by it.

"But Leah, I think—no—I *know*, that *Gott* has something else planned for me. For us." His deep brown eyes sparkled. "I've known for a while now that everything I'm doing here is for my Amish heritage and has next to nothing to do with why God put me on this earth."

Leah nodded again, her eyes rounded as she listened. "Go on."

"I'm not unhappy, but I'm not doing His will for my life. I feel, well, kind of empty inside. I love being with you, I love working the earth and taking care of the animals, but the whole time I'm doing it, I feel like I'm living in someone else's life. Like I'm looking to the future for our *real* life to begin."

Leah swallowed. Her throat was parched and her lips were dry. "Like you know God has another plan rolled up in His pocket and He's just waiting for you to ask Him to show it to you?"

Jacob jumped up, lifting his hands above his head. "Yes! Yes, that's it! Do you feel that, too?"

She jumped off the sofa and ran to him. "I do! I was trying to ignore the feelings. Trying not to question. Trying not to embarrass you or make trouble or fail as an Amish woman again."

Jacob settled himself long enough to kiss her.

"Leah, you have no idea how relieved I am to hear this! I've wanted to talk about it, but you were trying so hard to fit in, and I thought maybe it would be unfair to subject you to what happens if we would leave. The second time for you. I know how some would think and talk about you."

Leah had to sit down. Suddenly, her head was spinning. "Oh, wow. Jacob, I could not be happier, but I want to be sure we're on the same page. Are you saying you want to leave?"

Jacob sat down, too, his eyes growing calmer. He grabbed both her hands in his. "It is what I'm saying, Leah. I feel different now. I know my Amish heritage will always be important to me, but I need more of Jesus, first and foremost."

She tilted her head, wondering if he knew what leaving could mean. "Are you sure? It's not easy. We'll likely be shunned for joining the church and going back on our vow to it."

He took a deep breath, holding it before slowly releasing the air from his lungs. "No need to deny that, but I know this is where the Lord is leading us. I sense Him drawing me and showing me He has another plan."

She pointed to the MAP brochure. "What do you think about this? What about MAP ministry?"

He took the brochure and opened it. He ran his finger along a line.

"It says they train missionaries to the Amish, Leah. It's where I feel the Lord is leading me now."

Leah's eyes widened. "Missionary work? To our own people?"

Jacob laughed. "Yeah, I know. Who'd listen to *us*, right?"

Leah laughed, too. "There are few Amish who'd listen to us; that I know. But who better to help those who have left and are searching for that hole in their souls to be filled?"

His face had softened. He was hearing another Voice. She could read that he was.

"Well, I'm in it for the long haul, Jacob. Wherever this adventure with God takes us, I'm there with you."

Jacob eased to his feet and pulled her up with him. "Two things: We need prayer and we need to seek Godly counsel. I'll contact Matthew Schrock in the morning and also ask the fellows I trust here to pray with us." He paused. "I don't think I'll share all the details with them, but I know when they pray, they'll be asking God to help."

"Jacob, about what happened tonight, I want you to know, there was nothing said at the Bible study that was strange or off key."

He closed his eyes and held her tighter. "You don't have to tell me that. I already know. In fact, their visit was something I had prayed about. I'd asked God to use your Bible study to open my eyes to His plan."

"What?" Leah was flummoxed.

He chuckled. "I even asked Him to give me a sign. I asked the Lord that if what I was feeling was real, that it was time to leave, time to move on, time to stop questioning His Word and how it's always been interpreted to me, the bishop would confront us soon."

"You mean you weren't happy with the bishop being Melvin Mast?" Leah leaned back to get a better view of her husband's face.

Jacob shook his head. "I didn't want my personal feelings about Melvin to get in the way, though I didn't think he was the right man, but when I saw the odd smile Melvin wore when he discovered that piece of paper in his hymnal, my spirit sank. It seemed to be proof that the church was simply following a tradition that didn't rely on God's wisdom."

"I was shocked at his reaction, too, and his wife reacted the same way. Jacob, I understand why you were unsure about how it would all work out and I wish you'd talked to me. But now that we've made the decision to leave, I'm relieved. I feel like I can breathe again."

"It won't be easy." He kissed her nose.

"Oh, how I know that."

He kissed her cheeks. "And we have the farm to sell."

"Yes. Yes. I understand that."

He smiled. "And lots of packing to do ..."

"Yes, that's true."

He walked to the doorway. "So right now I think we should definitely celebrate with homemade ice cream."

She giggled. "With homemade chocolate sauce, as well!"

# CHAPTER THIRTY-SEVEN

The days following their decision to leave the Amish church were filled with more decisions.

They went together to let the bishop, deacon, and preacher know what their plans were and, as predicted, it did not go well. But Leah marveled at how kind, yet firm, Jacob was in his discussion with the men.

He wanted to end the meeting in prayer, but Melvin Mast was in no mood to pray. This grieved Leah's heart since she recognized what a lack of prayerful leadership would mean for the church body. There would be issues and problems that could only be decided through prayerful consideration, yet, he did not want to pray with them over this serious decision.

They left the meeting with sadness, but there was also a gleam of joyful expectation in knowing their lives would now be led by the Holy Spirit alone.

The farm was put on the real estate market. There were shocked looks and whispers behind hands from neighbors and folks in the community, but Leah was almost oblivious to the gossip. She spent her free time packing away boxes of their material goods. What was needed, and what was not.

One sunny afternoon, while Jacob was at work, she had donned a headscarf and was cleaning the winter grime from the porch windows. As she heard an approaching buggy, she stopped to watch who was going past. Unexpectedly, the buggy and horse turned from the road into their drive.

She shaded her eyes, trying to see inside the dark vehicle, but she could only make out a lot of bobbing heads—some taller and some shorter. It didn't take long for Leah to recognize the little voice calling out to her.

"Leah! *Ist mich*, Saloma!"

Leah spied a little hand waving furiously from the buggy. It was Saloma—and all the *kinner* with Clara.

She was overjoyed to see them!

It had been several weeks since she'd last seen them in town. Leah had walked to their place a few times in the spring after Henry went away, but only twice had she been able to see them all. Most days, whether Clara was too embarrassed to greet her or some other reason unknown to her, Leah's knock on the door went unheeded.

Once she caught a glimpse of Daniel hiding in the corn field as she left the Coblentz house, but no amount of coaxing had made him come out of hiding. She'd been puzzled by this lack of friendliness on the part of all the children and Clara, but she put it down to the troubles Henry had brought to his family. Since Leah'd been the target of much of his harassment, perhaps Clara had instructed the children to hold off visiting with her.

She dried her hands and hurried to the barnyard to greet the family.

"*Wie bischt*, Clara?"

Leah helped Clara tie up the horse and get the children out of the buggy. Baby Ada was babbling and had grown so much since Leah last saw her, she barely recognized her.

"Leah, I have two puppies at home, now," sweet Saloma grabbed her hands, trying hard to tell Leah everything is a single sentence.

"And I learned to read some big words, too! And look—my two front teeth have come out!"

Leah smiled at the little girl's gap-toothed grin. "So they have! You must be growing up."

Daniel was his usual happy self, running around them in circles, until his *maem* caught him by the wrist and told him to settle down.

"Oh, Clara, he's okay. Just as excited to see me as I am to see him." She knelt down to be eye-level with Daniel. "And guess what? I happen to have cookies in the house—your favorite chocolate chip ones, too."

Daniel glanced to his mother, one eyebrow raised in question.

Clara laughed. "Okay, I suppose a cookie won't hurt you."

Leah walked with Clara as the children made their way toward the house. Their chattering voices were a blessing to her heart. Before they reached the porch, Clara pulled Leah back. She stopped, adjusting baby Ada into a tighter hold.

"I wanted to come by once I heard you and Jacob will be moving soon. We'll be moving, too."

"Clara—will you?"

"*Ja*, Henry has finished his treatment and he wants us to move to Indiana. We'll be closer to the house where he had his treatments, in case, you know, he has to go back in for some reason."

She cast her eyes downward and shuffled her feet in the gravel.

Leah touched her shoulder. "I think that'll be a good idea. Do you think he's better?"

Clara nodded, but dropped the subject as Reuben approached.

"*Maem*, is it okay if Saloma and me go see the horse?" He pointed to where Bingo was munching away at some grass near the edge of the paddock.

Clara followed where he pointed. "I guess it's okay, if Leah says you can go. But don't wander off—we need to get back home soon."

Leah was swept up by Daniel and a much taller William, clamoring for cookies. She shooed them into the house ahead of her and Clara.

"My, Clara, William looks like he's grown double in size since I saw him last. He's nearly as tall as Daniel!"

Clara laughed. "I know. I think Daniel's shocked that his little brother can now hold his own against him when they tussle."

Leah bustled about pouring milk into glasses and getting napkins for cookies. By the time she'd gotten the two little guys settled, Reuben and Saloma were back from seeing Bingo.

"Just in time for cookies, you two. And here's some cold milk to wash the cookies down with."

Finally, Leah was able to settle with Clara on the sofa while the children ate their treats in the kitchen at the table. Baby Ada was content to carry her sippy cup about as she explored the windows and doors and cupboards in the living room.

Clara looked around. "You have a nice place here, Leah. Will you miss it much when you move?"

Leah nodded. "Considering this is our very first house together, I will miss it. But I'm also very excited to see what the next chapter in our lives will be."

"Are you moving far?"

"No, not really. We plan to go back to Ashfield, the county we both came from. We want to train with MAP Ministry to become missionaries to the Am—"

Leah hesitated. It would be her first time telling another Amish person that she and Jacob planned to become missionaries to their own people. It was like being a Baptist and saying you want to be a missionary to the Baptists. Awkward.

Clara was waiting for her to finish her sentence, so Leah smiled and went on. "Um, we plan to become missionaries to the Amish and to those who leave the Amish."

Clara nodded politely, but Leah could see the confusion in her eyes.

"How about you and Henry? Do you have a house in mind when you move west?"

"We do, but it depends on how much we can get from our place before we can actually purchase the property. In the meantime, the owners are going to let us rent from them."

Their chat was interrupted by a kerfuffle coming from the kitchen. Clara jumped up. "Oh, dear! What have they done?"

She hurried into the kitchen and Leah could hear her sort out the battle, ordering the children to put their glasses in the sink, wipe their mouths, throw away their napkins, and march themselves back into the living room.

As Leah listened, she smiled. Clara was sounding stronger and sure of herself. Like the mother of any household of children would. That was a good sign.

Her friend resettled herself on the sofa and turned back to Leah. "Where was I? Oh, yes. The place we plan to buy is pretty large. It has five bedrooms with a barn and a lot of acreage. Henry's been working in a machine shop nearby, so he's sent me some money to live on and saved some money for the new place. He's doing well. He's ... better in his mind."

"That is so nice to hear, Clara. You must be relieved to be able to be back with him again."

Clara chewed a nail, hesitant to reply.

"Is everything really okay," Leah prompted.

Clara let out a deep sigh. She shifted her feet under her skirt, but finally replied. "I think it *will* be. It's been hard for him to give up the, you know, the alcohol, but he's a much better person without it."

"I'm sure he is. Once you get settled in, I hope you can send me a note with your new address."

"Surely! That is, if you're not gone before we are."

Leah studied her packing results. "Well, we plan to be out of here no later than the end of July. And maybe sooner if the house sells quickly."

"We plan to go in three weeks, when Henry gets back to help me pack and get the *kinner* ready."

"Are you hiring a van?"

"*Ja*—we are."

Ada bumped her mouth while running from William which set off a cacophony of wails and protests from the pair. The visit was short-lived as Clara gathered the children for the ride home.

"I'd like to visit longer, but this one needs her nap right after lunch and she missed it today. If I'm to have any peace, I'll need to get her to sleep for a little while yet this afternoon."

Clara smiled at her sweet daughter and Leah was glad to see how genuine that smile was.

"Of course. Let me help gather everybody together. I'm so happy you dropped by before you moved, Clara."

Leah herded the older children toward the buggy. Once they were all stowed away for the drive home and all necks had been hugged, and all goodbyes had been said, Leah was exhausted. To think Clara did this day after day, all by herself!

Leah shook her head as she waved goodbye. Her prayer was for this family to heal completely and for Henry to find a way to keep his role as father in good form. *No more alcohol, Lord. Please.*

For the first time in a long while, Leah allowed herself to stretch out on the bed upstairs, slip off her shoes and take a nap.

It felt so good to lie down in the middle of the day. She had the window open and she could hear birds chirping from the oak tree outside near the porch.

The passing cars hummed on their tires as they carried their English cargo on errands or shopping or just to sightsee. And once in a while, horse's hooves announced another Amish family heading to some place other than home.

The breeze blew across her face, cooling her cheeks as it filled the room. Before long, Leah's eyes shuttered closed and she slept.

"Leah ..."

Her dream of holding a newborn calf drifted away and she slowly came awake.

Jacob was leaning over her, his warm brown eyes shifting back and forth across her face, a worried frown between his brows.

"Hi, wife." He kissed her softly. "I sure was startled to find you here sleeping."

Leah struggled to sit up. "Oh, Jacob! Whah time izzit?" Her words slurred as she fought to shake the fuzzy dream from her mind.

Jacob chuckled. "You must have worn yourself out today. It's after eleven, my usual time to finish my shift. How long have you been sleeping?"

Leah came wide awake. "What? I just wanted to catch a short nap after Clara and the children's visit. It can't be eleven already! I came up here about four o'clock or so."

Jacob laughed at his wife's startled expression. "Feels a little like Rip Van Winkle, eh?"

He moved about the room, first turning the gas light on and rummaging through his drawers for his PJs.

Leah put her feet on the floor and tried to straighten her *kapp*, only to recall that she'd worn her scarf while cleaning and then forgot to take it off before her nap. It had skewed itself into a wad on the side of her head while she slept.

"I must be a sight!"

She heard Jacob stifling a chuckle as he listened to her from the bathroom. "Did you even have *suppah?*" he called.

"No, I sure didn't and my stomach is making all kinds of noises to prove it."

She stumbled down the hallway and stuck her head in the door of the bathroom. "I'm going down to cook scrambled eggs. Do you want some, too?"

He nodded. "That sounds really good for a midnight snack, wife."

"Okie-dokie, husband. They'll be done in about ten minutes and fifteen seconds so don't let them get cold."

"I gotcha."

Leah made her way to the kitchen, still fighting a fuzzy-headed notion that she had a new calf in the barn.

"That would be a miracle since we've had no cows since the fire," she mumbled.

She got out the eggs and cracked them into a bowl, swished them with a fork, and poured them into the sizzling pan. She cut two thick slices of bread and slathered them with honey and blueberry jam, then she made some tea and set the table.

The eggs smelled so good in their butter baths, she nearly had to wipe the drool from her mouth.

"I need to get a grip. But I must say, having a midnight feast with Jacob is a fun thing to do."

By the time Jacob came down, she had the eggs ready at his place on the table and the tea poured and sweetened with honey.

"Wow—this looks so good, Leah. Thank you, wife!"

He said a quick prayer and they tucked into the food.

"You said Clara came by today," he spoke around the bread filling his mouth.

"Yes, she brought all the children along. They all looked great! But she told me they're moving in about three weeks to Indiana."

Jacob scraped the last of his eggs onto his fork. "Really? Why Indiana?"

As Leah filled him in on the details of their move, he listened and made appropriate replies, but Leah sensed he was holding something back.

After chewing her last bite of bread and egg, she put down her fork. "Okay. Let's have it. What are you keeping from me?"

He shrugged, but a smile stretched across his face and a twinkle appeared in his eyes.

"C'mon now! What's going on?" She leaned across the table and grabbed for his hands.

He laughed as they wrestled for a minute or two.

"Okay. I give in. Yes, I have some news. Two bits of news."

"Is it about the farm? Did we sell it?"

Excitement grew as Leah contemplated the freedom they would feel once the farm was sold.

Jacob shook his head. "No, but thinking about that, we do have a nibble, so we need to pray for that to happen if it's in God's plan."

"Who?"

"I don't know yet but the agent did say someone called and was interested. That's not my news, though."

Leah stood and ran around the table to plop into his lap. "Tell meeee," she whined.

"I was trying to! Okay. Well, the first news is that Matthew called today and they've accepted us into their missionary training program and he thinks there's a house available nearby."

Leah jumped up. "Woohoo! That's awesome!"

He stood and headed down the hallway to the living room, Leah at his heels.

"That's two pieces of good news we needed to hear!"

He settled on the sofa and patted the seat beside him. "That's one piece of news. The second piece isn't as exciting and really, it's kind of sad."

She scooted in next to him, her heart catching as his face grew serious. "What's the sad news, Jacob?"

"They found Bert Small and he's been arrested for arson."

Leah's heart slowed. It wasn't sad news for *them*, but it sure was for Bert and his family. "Oh, wow. I'm glad and sad at the same time."

"Yeah. Not such a good day for Bert."

"I wonder if he's going to admit what he's done?"

Jacob drew in a breath. "I went to see him on my lunch break."

Leah stopped playing with a pillow. "What? Why?"

Jacob shrugged. "I felt like I should. He was pitiable in that cell, Leah. He really looked lost."

"Oh, Jacob. Don't you go feeling too sorry for him. He had many opportunities to stop what he was doing."

"I know. And he did act like he was sorry."

Leah's eyes widened. "Did he?"

Jacob nodded. "He told me things had gotten out of hand. And he knew he was facing jail time. I even saw a tear roll down his cheek. He let me know his hatred wasn't just toward me. He had a hard time as a child because his *daet* wasn't loving or kind. Instead, his father pointed out all the good things Amish young men could do. The Amish man that was hired to help his dad on the farm was always the best at everything, according to Bert's *daet*, and the hired man could do no wrong in his father's eyes. Bert was beaten, while the Amish man was praised." Jacob shrugged. "I was an easy target, I guess, for Bert's pain."

Leah sighed. "Oh, don't tell me anymore. You're making me feel sorry for him myself." She balled the pillow up. "I have a feeling *Gott's* trying to make me pray for him."

Jacob laughed out loud. He got up and went to turn down the lights in the living room.

"Praying for Bert Small is a given, wife. I think we'll be doing that for a very long time."

As they headed to the stairs, Leah stopped her husband. "I have news, too. Something I've been holding back."

Jacob scrunched his eyes at her. "Holding out? On me?"

"Yes. And when this little one makes his appearance, I hope we have a baby crib to put him in."

Jacob's eyes grew round and his face paled. "A *bobli!*"

She nodded. "My news was the best yet, husband."

Jacob pulled Leah close, a tender light growing in his warm brown eyes. "You win, wife. Hands down."

# ACKNOWLEDGEMENTS

Thank you to Joe and Esther Keim for their continued inspiration for this series. Their dedication to the Mission to Amish People ministry is beyond amazing. May the Lord continue to richly bless their steadfast faithfulness.

Thank you to my good friend and mentor, Verna Mitchell. She has always been in my corner. Her love, friendship and support are blessings I highly treasure. The Lord truly gave me a lovely mentor in Verna.

Thank you to Barb Thompson and Chris Vallowe. As my steadfast beta readers, I'm amazed and blessed that they willingly gave of their time to help polish this story. I'm beyond grateful for their support and love.

Thank you to my readers who have patiently waited while this second book was in process. It was a long wait! I'm blessed beyond measure to have their encouragement.

Thank you to my husband, Arlen, and son, Joseph. How many times did I interrupt what they were doing to ask for their help, to listen to my ideas, or to hear my frustrations? Many times. They were both patient with me. Their guidance led to this book's printing. The loving support of Eli, Rachel, and the sweet, sweet grandboys are rich, unexpected gifts only God could give. My Father has truly blessed me with a wonderful, loving family.

Finally, my heart can't contain the blessings of my God and Creator. He never fails to whisper His inspiration to my soul. Always.

GLOSSARY
*Ausbund:* Amish hymnal
*bisli glay:* little bit small
*bobli:* baby
*bot boi:* pot pie
*buvli or buve:* little boy, boy
*daddihaus:* Grandfather's house (or grandparent's house)
*Daet:* father, dad
*danke:* thank you
*der sindfol Disch:* the sinful table
*Dochder:* daughter
*Doktah:* doctor
*ferhudled:* confused
*fraa:* wife
*fronzel:* lint
*gut:* good
*gut morgen:* good morning
*gworiched:* worried
*hoch gmay:* higher, less traditional and restrictive church
*hochzich:* wedding
*hochzeit Lied:* wedding hymn or song
*Ist mich:* It's me
*Ja:* Yes
*jungen:* youth, young people
*kind, kinder, kinna:* child, children
*Maem:* mother, mom
*mawt:* servant, maid, mother's helper after birth for about 2-4 weeks
*schlecht:* bad
*schtobb:* stop
*schvetzing:* talking, gossiping
*smachs gut:* tastes good
*unterricht:* the ministry team reads the article of faith to the baptism candidates, which is done Friday or Saturday before joining the church

*Vater Gott:* Father God
*viescht:* bad
*Was in die welt?:* What in the world?
*Wie bischt?:* How are you?

53505728R00146

Made in the
USA
Lexington, KY